The Devil in the Dock

RICHARD JAMES

For Toby.

CONTENTS

SPRING, 1892

"We are each our own devil, and we make this world our hell."

Oscar Wilde

Prologue

It had been eleven months since he'd killed his wife. At first her words were faint, indistinct. She stood in silhouette at the window, the low morning light at her back. If he squinted, as one who looks into the sun, he could just make out the contours of her face. Slowly, she solidified before him. At first her hair revealed itself, tumbling over her shoulders as it had on their first meeting. Looking down to the floor, Bowman could see she was wearing her favourite yellow dress, which he felt flattered her skin favourably. She stood, hands on hips, with a quizzical expression on her face. Her eyes were alive with a playful insinuation. She held her chin in just the way Bowman remembered it. He was beyond any doubt that his wife stood before him.

He lay, delirious, upon the threadbare chaise longue in the parlour, Nero's portrait gazing imperiously down from the wall behind him. Dust motes danced in the air. Somewhere, a lazy fly banged against a window. Having eschewed the marital bed as was now his custom, he had finally fallen asleep in the early hours of the morning. He had passed a few fitful hours in what could only just be described as sleep, to be woken by the first touch of the sun upon his face. His neck and shoulders were stiff. Shifting himself upon his unforgiving cushions, he had turned his face to the window. It had come as no surprise at all to see her standing there.

"Anna".

Her name was a balm. The sound of it soothed him. He felt the beginnings of a smile play about his lips. She was moving towards him now, her hand outstretched. A dip of her head gave him to understand that he should stand. Swinging his legs from the chaise longue, Bowman stood but a few feet in front of her. Now her face was clear. Her eyes danced as she pulled him towards her. Bowman could smell her perfume, feel the warmth of her body against him.

"Anna."

And now they were dancing. The parlour had dissolved around them to be replaced by a grand ballroom decked with bunting and

1

flowers. A banner hung from a makeshift stage where a band of musicians struck up a waltz. They were whirling about the room, almost reckless. Bowman recognised the space, knew the moment. This was their first dance.

"Father approves," Anna purred as Bowman led her about the floor. She was a graceful dancer and forgiving, too. Bowman struggled to master his leaden feet and, more than once, had to effect emergency manoeuvres to avoid the other couples.

Bowman looked about him, seeking the gentleman in question. There he sat, at a table near the band. His wife busied herself beside him as he looked out across the dance floor. The only movement was an absent-minded drumming of his fingers on the table in time to the music. His face was granite.

"Of what?"

"Of you," she laughed.

"Are you sure?" Bowman asked. "He's inscrutable."

"Only to those who do not understand him." Anna shook her head. Her hair had been curled for the evening, and her ringlets danced about her shoulders. "He finds you charming. As do I."

Bowman felt himself flush, the button at his collar pinching at his neck. Daringly, he allowed himself a smile. "And I find you captivating, Miss Mortimer."

Anna laughed in spite of Bowman's earnest gaze, or perhaps because of it. His moustache twitched in agitation.

"I do not think I would mind at all if you should call me Anna."

At this, they seemed to lift in to the air. Bowman caught his breath as they waltzed up and around the room. The air became their dance floor as the hall became a blur. Somewhere, improbably, he could hear marriage vows.

"Do you remember how you felt on our wedding day?" she was asking.

Bowman swallowed hard to contain his emotions. Tears pricked at his eyes as he recalled. "Of course," he whispered.

Her voice was clear as a bell. "Tell me."

One word came to his mind. "Afraid."

He looked around his parlour, as if to anchor himself in reality. All signs of the ballroom had gone. There lay the book he had been reading, there his glass.

"Silly," she purred, smoothing his frown with a finger. "Are you still afraid?"

Bowman opened his mouth to respond but before he could even form a word, he was somewhere else again.

The water lapped at the bank to his right. The low sun gave the grass a coat of gold and the trees were heavy with blossom. They were in Hampstead Heath. Beside him was the viaduct pond, like a mirror to the sky, the water still and implacable. The viaduct itself stood like a beast, basking in the sun. It had stood for over forty years, intended to be an entrance to an ornate villa. Bowman admired the industry that had produced such a redundant piece of work, for the villa was never built. A thwarted vision, thought Bowman. A squeeze of his hand reminded him of her presence and he turned to her, blinking in the sun.

"I have been thinking," he began. "In the whole of London, I should like to live here."

"Hampstead?"

"Let me see what I can find. I can think of no finer place for us to make our home."

They stopped beneath an ancient oak and kissed, and Bowman was full of the future. In truth, he had already found a set of rooms not twenty minutes away.

"Are you sure your father won't miss me?" he teased.

"He yearns to be free of you!" she laughed. She pulled him to her. "And I yearn to have you to myself."

As they kissed, they whirled and rose amongst the trees. The Heath spread out before them like a blanket, its kinks and wefts the paths and beds. As Bowman looked down and to his left, he could see the house he had visited not two days previously. It would be perfect, he knew.

And it was. Now they were in the parlour, Anna dressing for the day in coat and bonnet.

"Must you go?" she was imploring. "I had hoped you might accompany me to the refuge."

"I am called for, Anna."

"By whom?"

"Williams has need of men to put an end to a case. He has this past fortnight been close to bringing an end to a case of slavery. A troupe of hawkers in Whitechapel has been abducting children, sending them north to the industrial cities for fodder. Well-to-do children sometimes, not just urchins."

"Ah," Anna breathed, smoothing Bowman's habitual frown with a gloved finger. "So now the toffs are angry and the case must be solved." There was a look of gentle reproach in her eyes but Bowman forgave her easily, as he forgave her all things. He knew he was being teased.

"It is good work, Anna. Children will be saved."

Anna dipped her head. "Then, who am I to stand in your way, Detective Inspector George Bowman?" She pronounced his name slowly, deliberately and quietly. In the spaces between each word, she rose up on her toes to plant the softest of kisses on his lips.

"Well, I shall be in Whitechapel too." Bowman could hear the hooves. She was moving to the door now. "Perhaps, when you have saved the world from blight, you might pass by the Women's Refuge to walk me home?"

Now came the rattle of the carriage. Some moments ago, Bowman had loosed the shot. It had cut through the canopy and found a home in the driver's chest. He sat slumped at the reins, the brougham thundering over the cobbles, teetering dangerously at the corner with Hanbury Street. Anna turned to look, a flash of confusion clouding her face. The horses were upon her.

"No, sir!" Sergeant Graves held him tight about the shoulders, "It's too late!"

Bowman knew the distance between them was too great, that he could not save his wife. All at once, she was beneath the hooves and then beneath the wheels and then the carriage was gone. Bowman lifted a gloved hand to his cheek. Her blood was on his face.

A sharp breath caught in his throat and woke him. Rising from the chaise longue, Bowman made his way to the mantle. There, beside her picture was a printed calendar. Tracing the days with his fingers, he could not imagine how he'd survived so long without her.

I

Hunted

Harry Pope was easy quarry. No matter how fast he ran, he knew the hound would catch him. Even amongst the slums and gin palaces of Drury Lane, there was one thing it could always follow. His scent. He stared wildly about him as he turned off White Hart Yard. Pope was a physically able man, some six feet tall with a long stride. His strength and speed had equipped him well in the boxing ring but he feared they would not save him now. Spittle flew from his mouth as he struggled to breathe. He must have run some three miles from Shad Thames, tracing the river along Clink Street and Bankside to cross at Waterloo Bridge. It was there that he had heard the dog. By the time he had spanned all nine of the bridge's arches, Pope knew it was upon him.

He veered right onto The Strand, darting through Angel Court in a desperate attempt to gain advantage. His legs felt as if they were on fire, his lungs fit to burst. All around him was chaos. The hustle of the day had begun in earnest. Pope tripped over prostitutes and vagrants as he fled down Drury Lane, kicking up dirt and excrement from the gutter with his heels. The crowds pressed against him so that Pope could barely see his way. Traders and hawkers mingled with the hoi polloi. Looking over his shoulder as he ran, he felt a glancing blow to his chest. Casting a glance down he saw he had floored an old, toothless woman who had rolled into the road. She swore after him as he ran, raising a fist at his retreating back. His only hope, Pope reasoned, was to find help. Running recklessly to the middle of the road, he waved down a hansom cab as it rattled out of Russell Court. The horse came to a halt with a bad tempered whinny, rising on its hind legs to show its disapproval. Pope ran to the cab and leaned in to address its passengers, an elderly lady and a rather upright-looking man in a top hat.

"Help," he gasped. "Please help me."

The man leaned over to shoo him away, holding a protective arm across his companion. Pope looked savage. His thick, black hair was plastered to his face with sweat, his cheeks burning a ferocious red, his eyes staring with a manic intent.

"Joseph, what does he want?"

"Nothing, Mother," the man replied. "And nothing is what he'll get."

Reports of robberies under just such circumstances had placed the man on his guard, and he planted a fist squarely on Pope's jaw. Instinctively twisting his head to lessen the force of the blow, Pope fought the urge to respond with a left upper cut.

"Be off with you," shouted the driver from his perch. The whip snapped just inches from Pope's face. The horse gave another whinny of impatience.

"Please, I need – " Pope's plea was in vain. The cab clattered away as he fell to his knees in exhaustion. Following the hansom with his bloodshot eyes, he could see the man offering comfort to his mother as it rounded the corner onto Blackmoor Street, scattering a mob of urchins in its path.

Feeling a presence at his shoulder, Pope turned to see a young woman with a parasol and a large bag holding out her hand.

"You all right, dearie?" she cooed. "In a spot of bother?"

Pope shrugged her off. He could hear the hound. His only hope was to head for the crowds outside The Theatre Royal. Slipping in the dirt, Pope mustered all his strength for a final burst of speed. Gritting his teeth against the pain in his legs, he rounded the corner into Russell Street and then he saw them. Their distinctive helmets and smart blue coats marked them out amongst the throng of theatregoers, shoppers and prostitutes. Peelers. The three police constables were in attendance at a jeweller's store, one with a notebook in hand, the other two standing absentmindedly at the door. Pope slowed his pace. The one thing he couldn't do was alert them to his predicament. Ducking under the portico on Catherine Street, Pope hid himself from their view behind the pillars, slowly skirting his way round the theatre's entrance. A pantheon of great actors gazed down from tattered posters on the walls. A banner proclaiming the appearance of Dan Leno, 'The Great Irish Comic Vocalist and Clog Champion', hung limp from a window, its loose end trailing in the dirt below. Passing into Brydges Street, Pope pleaded desperately with passers by. A gruff man in an ostentatious hat and coat attempted to palm him off with a ha'penny from his pocket. A baker's boy offered nothing more than a mouthful of curses for his pains. Pope stumbled on, his breathing erratic. He cut a desperate figure as he loped painfully into an alley behind The Theatre Royal. Vinegar Yard was famous as a home to dissolutes. The tenements that rose around it offered lodgings to actors and other vagabonds who could part with a penny. As Pope stumbled along its length he passed a couple pressed against the wall sweating in their exertions. In the throes of a drunken lust, they barely noticed Pope as he limped past. Holding onto the wall for balance, he staggered to a stop and fell to his knees again, defeated. He opened his mouth to cry for help but no sound came. His throat was dry, his chest heaving. As he fell to his back, gasping for breath, he succumbed to his delirium.

He could hear the claws skidding at the ground as the dog tore into Vinegar Yard. The sight of a large hound careening into the yard, its eyes blazing with a primal appetite, was enough to rouse the couple from their lustful stupor. Sporting a look that was almost comical, they tucked themselves away and staggered from the alley to the wide street beyond. Pope barely had the energy to focus on his grisly assailant. It fell upon him, snarling and frothing in its frenzy. Its teeth ripped at his soft flesh, its claws shredding his clothes. It tore at him until he was just a heap of bloodied rags, its yelps and cries echoing off the high walls around them.

A whistle pierced the air. The dog stopped at the signal, ears pricked in recognition, and ran panting to the alley's end, blood foaming at its jaws. There it stopped, cowering at the feet of a hooded figure, its hand held out by way of a command.

"Good boy," the figure growled. "You good boy."

Taking a last look up Vinegar Yard to see that Pope was still, the silhouette bent to scratch the dog by the ears. "Let's go back by the butchers. You've earned yourself a chop or two."

At the sound of another whistle, the dog turned from the alley and walked back into Catherine Street. As the denizens of Drury Lane went about their business both lawful and unlawful, the hooded figure melted into the crowd, its canine companion trotting obediently at its side.

Bowman was trying hard to resist clearing his throat. The commissioner's office sat at the very top of Scotland Yard. It was mostly given over to shelves of books and piles of paper heaped haphazardly on desks and bureaux around the room. Bowman knew that, even though this new Scotland Yard building had only been completed for some eighteen months, there were already concerns that space was running out. The previous commissioner, James Monro, had expressed concerns in his annual report detailing the issues as he saw them. The Metropolitan Police Force, in short, was over-stretched. From the sum total of over fourteen thousand officers, many were engaged in station duties or on secondment to various government departments. Still more were employed at sites of national sensitivity such as docks or military stations. Yet others still were on leave or absent for reasons of health. And all this, Monro had complained, while crime in the metropolis was on the rise. Recent episodes of social unrest had been a drain on police resources. The commissioner was afraid it had been at the cost of solving crime. Little wonder, thought Bowman as he gazed around the room, there was so much paperwork to be seen.

It had been a period of turmoil for the Force. Three commissioners had come and gone within the space of two years. The present incumbent of the office stood before the inspector now, a distinguished looking military man with the unfortunate distinction of having only one arm. In lieu of it, his sleeve was pinned to the breast of his frock coat in the manner of a badge of office. A haze of white hair framed his gentle features, a luxuriant moustache bristling at his upper lip.

"We must present a professional face to the world, Inspector Bowman," Sir Edward Bradford was opining from behind his desk. "It is only by the conducting of our duty from a position of respect that we can be truly effective." His voice had a gentle timbre, in keeping with his generally benevolent nature.

"Yes, sir," Bowman swallowed.

"We need stability," the commissioner continued. "Now more than ever." Turning to the window to gaze out over the London skyline, he smoothed his hair with his hand. "Our very livelihoods depend upon the existence of crime."

Bowman nodded, sagely. It had always struck him as a supreme irony that the very building in which they now sat had been faced with granite quarried by prisoners in the wilds of Dartmoor.

"But I for one," the commissioner was musing, "would be

willing to forgo that livelihood in exchange for safe streets." Bowman was wondering just where the conversation was leading. It was rare enough for an officer to be called into a private meeting with the commissioner. He doubted it was solely to discuss the present state of the Force.

The commissioner was clearing his throat. He seemed to be marking time. "But, for now, we must be entirely beyond reproach." He turned back into the room to face Bowman, squarely. "In short, inspector, I need men I can trust."

Stung by the insinuation, Bowman opened his mouth to respond. He was interrupted by a knock at the door. "Come!" barked the commissioner, plainly relieved at the interruption.

Bowman blinked into the light as the commissioner moved away from the window to greet the visitor. "Ah," he was purring, 'thank you for coming."

"Good morning, Sir Edward."

The voice caught Bowman unawares. It was enough to dry his mouth. He felt his palms sweat. In a moment he had placed it. It was a voice he associated with isolation and despair. With treatment.

"Inspector Bowman," the commissioner was saying, "you of course remember Superintendent Athol Wilkes of Colney Hatch?"

Feeling his face flush and his heart racing in his chest, Bowman turned. The superintendent stood with a hand outstretched, a kindly but professional look upon his face. "George, it's a pleasure to see you again." He spoke deliberately and gently, clearly aware of the effect his sudden appearance would have.

Bowman swallowed hard and stood to return the gesture. His head swam as two worlds collided. Somewhere just beyond the here and now he could smell the carbolic corridors of the lunatic asylum.

The superintendent placed a Gladstone bag on the desk and took his place in the empty chair next to Bowman. The inspector was in thrall to the man's face, a face he had hoped never to see again. He was an exceedingly thin man, the bones of his skull clearly visible through his face. The superintendent was dressed formally in high wing-collared shirt, frock coat and pinstriped trousers. He rested a top hat on the desk next to his bag.

The commissioner pulled his own chair from the desk and sat

opposite the men, knotting his brows in agitation. He was clearly finding this difficult.

"Superintendent Wilkes is here to complete your evaluation and decide if you are fit to continue in your employment at Scotland Yard."

The superintendent rose from his seat and snapped open the clasp on his bag. Reaching inside, he withdrew a sheaf of papers. He turned to face his erstwhile patient. "Inspector Bowman, you will know that it is some twelve weeks since your discharge from Colney Hatch. It falls to me to make an evaluation as to your state of health and present a full report to the commissioner regarding your fitness to continue in your work."

Bowman could not speak.

"Do you understand?" The superintendent was leaning towards him, his eyes searching Bowman's for signs of comprehension.

Bowman's moustache twitching nervously at his lip. "I understand," he rasped.

With a sudden vigour, Wilkes sprang towards him. Bowman felt his bony hands on his face as he first pulled down his jaw to peer into his mouth, then opened his eyelids between a finger and thumb to examine his eyes, first one, then the other. Bowman gripped the arms of his chair, the superintendent's actions reminding him of a time when he had felt like nothing more than a specimen on a slab.

"I understand this must be very difficult for you, George," Athol Wilkes was saying as he scratched a note in a volume of papers. Bowman resented the use of his first name. "But I have some questions to ask of you."

Was the inspector to be tested for signs of insanity? He was willing to make a wager that too few men in this very building would pass such a test. Bowman was careful not to let his feelings show.

"Are you now, or have you been at any time in the last twelve weeks, habitually in the throes of melancholy?" asked the superintendent.

"I have not."

"Could you speak up a little, Inspector Bowman?" The commissioner was resting an elbow on the desk, rapt with attention.

Bowman coughed. His collar felt tight. "I have not," he heard himself say. "I am not."

The superintendent scratched at his paper.

"Are you of sound appetite?"

"I am."

Another note was made. Bowman felt the room was growing smaller, the wood-panelled walls closing in around him. The air seemed thick and heavy.

"Are you visited by dreams?"

"No," Bowman lied.

With a final note, Wilkes placed his paper and pencil to one side. He looked Bowman in the eye. "How do you feel?" he asked, simply.

Bowman was stumped by the question and how best to answer it. He swallowed hard, shifting his weight awkwardly in the seat of his chair. The commissioner leaned in to hear, his benevolent stare encouraging Bowman to respond.

"I feel," he began, struggling to find a form of words the superintendent would be happy to hear. "I feel better." He smoothed his moustache between his finger and thumb, wishing he were anywhere else in the world but in that room.

The superintendent sat back with a non-committal expression. Resting his hands in his lap, he nodded to the commissioner that his interview was done.

Sir Edward cleared his throat and rose to his feet once more. He moved back to the window. Bowman realised this was his favoured position from which to conduct a difficult conversation.

"Inspector Bowman," he began, his hand playing restlessly behind his back. "You were given leave to return to your duties as a detective inspector by the superintendent some twelve weeks ago." Bowman shot a look at Wilkes who regarded him with a benign smile. "It is my place to reach an informed opinion as to whether you are fit for those duties," the commissioner continued. He turned into the room, deep in thought. "Tell me about Lambeth Bridge."

"Lambeth Bridge, sir?" Bowman blinked. He had thought the matter long forgotten.

"Sergeant Graves has given us a detailed report of the events that took place there and I, of course, have read your report. They differ slightly, inspector."

"In what respect, sir?"

"In the respect that Graves mentions you were not fully in control of your faculties during much of what passed there."

Bowman nodded. "It's quite simple, sir," he began, falteringly. "With the assistance of Sergeant Graves I apprehended Doctor Henderson, resulting in his conviction for the death of his daughter."

"I understand you underwent some form of melancholic episode."

Bowman's face flushed. He was aware of the superintendent's gaze.

"I - " he stuttered. "I was momentarily overcome. But recovered sufficient to discharge my duty."

"And Smithfield Market?" The commissioner regarded the inspector with a steely gaze.

"Smithfield Market?" Bowman chewed his lip. What on Earth had he done wrong at Smithfield Market?

"Inspector Hicks described what might be termed a manic episode. He said you were belligerent, and changeable."

Hicks. Bowman might have known. He recalled an altercation with the bluff inspector during his investigations at Smithfield Market. "Inspector Hicks wished to reopen the market with undue haste, sir."

"He says you were hostile."

"A murder had been committed, sir. My only thought was to preserve the scene."

"And the Hackney workhouse? Sergeant Graves says you were particularly disputatious."

The superintendent raised his eyebrows. Bowman had a look of defeat about him.

"Inspector Hicks had withheld vital evidence." The inspector felt he was fighting a losing battle. "It was crucial to the success of the case." It stung that Hicks had turned informer, but hurt all the more that Graves had been so free with his opinions.

"You must understand, inspector, that these men were pressed to give their views." Bowman guessed that Hicks had not required much pressing. "You are not to hold their testimony against them if you remain in post."

The words caught Bowman off guard. "Sir, I can assure you I am quite recovered."

The commissioner affected a conciliatory tone. "Not many men could go through what you went through, inspector, and emerge unscathed. There is a growing body of evidence to suggest that a man may be changed by a disquieting event. I must deliberate on your attestations here today, and will endeavour to reach a conclusion that will be to the benefit both of yourself and those whom you serve."

It seemed to Bowman that those whom he served would only benefit from his remaining on duty. If the police were so thinly stretched, losing a detective would hardly help.

Bowman opened his mouth to speak but was met with a sharp "Thank you, inspector, that will be all."

Bowman smoothed his coat about him as he stood. The superintendent stood in his way to the door.

"How lovely to see you again, George." Wilkes stood with an outstretched hand. As Bowman lifted his own hand to return the gesture, he saw with some alarm that the tremor had returned. Gripping the superintendent's hand tightly to dispel the involuntary movement, he met the man's eyes to see what lay there. It was clear he had noticed.

"Thank you," mumbled Bowman redundantly. Giving a curt nod to the commissioner, Bowman left the room, closing the door quietly behind him.

The mood in the room seemed to lighten at once. The superintendent puffed out his cheeks in an expression of relief.

"Well?" asked the commissioner once he was sure Bowman was out of hearing.

The superintendent shook his head and rubbed his chin. An expression of concern clouded his sharp features as he turned to the commissioner to deliver his verdict. "I'd keep him out of harm's way if I were you."

II

The Parting Of The Ways

"They say he lost it to a tiger." Sergeant Anthony Graves was in as fine form as ever he was when drinking at The Silver Cross. Bowman looked around him from his favourite chair by the fireplace. Even on this April evening there was sufficient chill in the air to warrant a fire. As the door flew open to admit new patrons, the flames would gutter and dance as a fierce wind whipped through the saloon. Harris the landlord was busy about his duties; jollying his customers along with a free drink at the bar or cuffing the cellar boy about the ear for his conduct. All around them, a raucous display was in progress as a slim young woman with an enormous voice scaled the heights of a music hall ditty that Bowman didn't much care for. The inspector had been about to down the last of his porter and be on his way when Graves had spoken up above the din.

"A tiger?" spluttered Bowman, struggling to make himself heard above the final chorus of The Honeysuckle And The Bee.

"He was a cavalryman in Rajputana, India. Went out hunting in Sixty Three, lost his arm to a tiger." Graves' eyes were alive with his story, his youthful face beaming with the adventure of it all. "They say," he continued, slurping from his beer, "that he was sewn up at the roadside."

"Was he invalided home?" Bowman couldn't help but be intrigued.

"Not a bit of it," Graves' voice rose above the final bars of the song. "He got back on his horse and rode away, the reins between his teeth." He raised his tankard to his lips. "Common knowledge," he said matter-of-factly, downing the last of his ale. As if in response to his tale, the small public house erupted with applause. Comically, Graves almost sprung to his feet for a bow. Bowman was suddenly aware of the time he had lost whilst at Colney Hatch. Sir Edward Bradford had been in post since Eighteen Ninety. Bowman had known him barely a year before the incident in Hanbury Street which had seen him incarcerated. In the time he had been away, it was clear that Bradford had endeared himself to the men in his command.

"He's got some bright ideas, that man." Graves wiped the foam from his lip with the back of his hand. "He's of the belief that a man's fingerprints might be used to implicate him in a crime."

Bowman nodded sagely. He had heard that Bradford had seen the taking of fingerprints in India for the purpose of identification. "How might they be collected and stored?" he asked.

"Cut their hands off?" Graves twinkled at his own joke. "P'raps the tiger gave him the idea." Looking up suddenly from the table, Graves could see there was a press of customers at the bar following the end of the evening's entertainments. "Better be quick, sir. Will you have another?"

Bowman shook his head. He really should be on his way. He regarded Graves thoughtfully as he made his way through the throng to the bar. The young sergeant had promised to keep the salient facts of the affair on Lambeth Bridge out of his report to the commissioner. Bowman was surprised he had it in him to be so duplicitous. Perhaps he didn't know him at all.

His tankard full to the brim again, Graves returned to the table. Careful not to spill a drop, he took his seat with a grin.

"Harris says the piano's waiting if I fancy a tickle."

Bowman threw a look to the landlord at the bar. As Harris busied himself at his pumps, he gave Bowman a wink. The inspector could tell he was in his element, never happier than when The Silver Cross was busy. The building had been in use as a tavern for two hundred years, Harris was fond of telling his clientele. With his lined, leathery skin and long, lank hair, Bowman wouldn't have been at all surprised to learn that Harris had worked the bar for all that time.

"And he said there'd be a free drink in it for me, too."

Bowman was about to make his excuses and leave when there came a bustle of activity at the door. It swung wide on its hinges to admit Detective Inspector Ignatius Hicks; a force of nature no less in strength than the tempest that blew in behind him. The fire burned all the brighter in the grate, as if in defiance.

"Ah, Bowman!" he roared, holding his hands wide in greeting. Hicks made for a fearsome sight at the door, his great beard hanging down to his chest. He was dressed in a coat and scarf that only seemed to accentuate his size, and a battered top hat was balanced precariously on his head. His habitual pipe, without which he was never seen, was held before him as a conductor would hold a baton. "I have news from the Yard," he announced, his words accompanied by a salacious grin.

Bowman suddenly regretted not making his way home earlier. "I was just on my way, Inspector Hicks," he said, gathering his coat from a hook by the chimneybreast. "You may have my chair if you wish." Bowman retrieved his hat from the mantle, bashing it into shape as he made his way to the door. Hicks stood his ground.

"We are to make our way to Drury Lane," he proclaimed.

Graves looked up from his beer. As much as he was enjoying the contents of his jar, his heart quickened at the prospect of a case.

"What shall we find at Drury Lane?" Bowman asked, resigned to a night's work.

"Sergeant Graves and I are to investigate the discovery of a body at Vinegar Yard. The commissioner has other plans for you," he jabbed the inspector in the ribs with the end of his pipe. "You, Inspector Bowman, are to report back to the Yard and, first thing in the morning, to board a cab to Shad Thames."

"Did you ever see Macready's Macbeth?"

As Sergeant Graves walked with Inspector Hicks down Bow Street, his rotund companion was in expansive mood.

"Is this a dagger which I see before me?" Hicks was declaiming to any who would listen. The glances from passers by only served to encourage him in his performance. Graves had no experience in play going, but he knew enough to suspect that Hicks was far too young to have seen Macready's Macbeth. "And I saw the great Dan Leno give his Railway Guard at The Theatre Royal." For a moment, Graves was tempted to believe him, until he saw a tattered poster for the very same entertainment peeling from a wall beside them.

Drury Lane was a wide thoroughfare, though not wide enough for the throng that moved along its length. Vagrants and beggars sat at the kerbside or scuffled amongst themselves in dingy alleyways. Ruffians, already drunk at this early hour, disgorged themselves from the gin palaces to berate the lamplighters about their work. Stallholders and barrow keepers shouted their wares to the rooftops. The lower floors of the buildings around them were given over to shop fronts; jewellers, milliners, bakers and butchers all jostling for position with shadier establishments whose occupants were less likely to be guessed at. Those two perennial companions, vice and disease, had made themselves at home on Drury Lane.

The two detectives barged their way through the crowd on their progress to Vinegar Yard. More than once, Hicks had to be cajoled away from an oyster cart or costermonger. If there was an end to Hicks' appetite, mused Graves, it had not yet been found.

"Why is Inspector Bowman sent to Shad Thames?" Graves asked, narrowly avoiding an urchin with a pie and a floppy felt hat.

"He is to report to Bermondsey," Hicks said with some authority. "They are concerned at the rise in theft from their docks and need men."

"He has been sent on a security detail?"

"Ours is not to reason why." Hicks gave an almighty shrug that saw his hat shift dangerously on his head. Kicking his way through the filth in the street, he made his way across to Vinegar Yard, the conversation apparently over. Following in his wake, Graves was left to muse how Bowman's presence would be sorely missed.

A constable stood guard at the alley. His presence had drawn a large, curious crowd to Vinegar Yard. A rope had been placed across the alley mouth to keep them at bay, but still they vied for position, each trying to pry over their neighbour's shoulder. The constable's jittery demeanour gave the impression of one uncomfortable with his lot. As the two men approached, shouldering their way through the crowd, it was clear to see why. A crying woman clung to him for comfort, tugging at his sleeve for support.

"Constable Prendergast," the young man announced, standing stiffly to something approaching attention.

"Prendergast, what the bejabbers is going on here?" Hicks demanded, planting his hands firmly on his wide hips.

"This is Kitty Baldwin, sir, stage door keeper at The Theatre Royal here. It was she what found the - " He hesitated, not wishing to cause the poor girl even greater distress. "The body, sir." A sob issued from somewhere within the folds of Prendergast's sleeve. Graves lifted the rope to let them pass.

"It's a rum place to end your days," offered Hicks, unhelpfully.

He attempted to peel Kitty from the constable's arm. His chosen tactic was to be horribly ingratiating. "Calm yourself, madam," he leered to the young lady, placing a fat hand on her shoulder. "At what time did you discover the body?"

"Just before curtain up," she sobbed. "I opened the door to let in the artistes when I caught a sight of it. At first I thought it nothing more than rubbish thrown by the butchers, but then I saw the clothes, ripped and torn to shreds. Horrible, it was." She was dressed in a faded cotton dress and a shawl that had plainly seen better days. Graves felt a wave of sorrow for the poor girl.

"Could you lead us to it?" he ventured, carefully. With a nod and a tug at Prendergast's sleeve, she made it plain she would only do so with the young constable's company. "All right, Prendergast," said Graves, fixing the rope behind them. "Let's take a walk, shall we?"

They picked their way carefully through the alley, stepping aside to avoid the nameless detritus at their feet. Vinegar Yard really was the most squalid of places. Heaps of filth were piled at either side. Discarded food mixed with the ordure on the ground such that the most terrible stink rose to greet them. Rats scurried at their feet as they passed.

Eventually they stopped in the darkest, dankest part of the alley, Kitty clinging to her constable with even greater determination. Unable to let go, she nodded her sad head in the direction of a tangled pile of skin, bones and clothing.

As Graves sat on his haunches to examine the body, Hicks took the opportunity to strike up a conversation. "I too am a man of the theatre, you know," he pronounced to anyone who would care to listen. "Seen 'em all, I have. Could fancy m'self treading the boards." He gave Kitty a nudge. "What d'you think?" She nodded weakly, unsure how to respond.

"It got him good and proper whatever it was." Reaching for a length of wood from a discarded pile to his side, Graves held a hand over his mouth and nose as he prodded the corpse. Flies buzzed angrily at the disturbance. Already, maggots were emerging from the poor man's wounds.

"Could've been rats," Hicks contributed, unhelpfully. Graves rolled his eyes. "I have heard tell of extraordinary creatures lurking in the filth," continued Hicks, holding his hands dramatically before him. "Perhaps it was the Golem himself!" He threw Kitty a ghastly wink, clamping his pipe between his teeth.

"No Golem, Hicks," sighed Sergeant Graves. "Nor no rats, neither. He was set upon by a large dog for sure, but why? And who would do such a thing in broad daylight?"

"One may do the strangest things in London, Graves, and the citizens would pass on by without a care."

Graves rose, wiping his hands on his coat. "Constable Prendergast, we shall arrange for the body to be removed for further examination." The young constable nodded. "In the meantime, I want an inventory of all who work here at the theatre and their comings and goings. I need a list of all those who may have used this alley." He looked up. "What lies beyond those windows, Kitty?"

Raising her eyes upwards, Kitty found the time between her sobs to form a sentence. "They are dressing rooms mostly. The very top one belongs to the chorus and musicians."

Graves nodded to Prendergast. "Let's see if they remember anything suspicious," he said.

"Yes, sir," Prendergast replied, attempting to peel the young woman from his arm. "I'll set another constable at the mouth to the alley. Got to keep the crowds at bay."

"Good man!" Hicks clapped a hand on the man's shoulder with more force than was necessary. "Now then," he continued, turning to Sergeant Graves. "Might it be time for a spot of supper?"

As the party moved back through the alley to the rope, a small boy with a floppy felt cap and gravy on his chin stood aside to let them pass. He had watched the whole drama unfold, and thought he knew just the person who would want to know that two detectives were investigating the discovery of the body in Vinegar Yard.

III

Big Tam

If you knew Gravesend, it was said, you knew Big Tam. A native of Glasgow, he had moved south in his youth and had a knack of making his presence felt. At full stretch he reached almost seven feet tall, had hands like shovels and feet like flat irons. A butcher by trade, he had found gainful employment at Milton Barracks on the outskirts of the town. It housed over five hundred soldiers and officers, temporarily held in transit on their way to overseas wars. Each week, the barracks took delivery of cattle and sheep from the market at Deptford, brought alive to be slaughtered at the abattoir. Big Tam was happy in his work, and particularly happy when spending the proceeds of it. Having no family, he had none to please but himself and would do so every night at one of the many taverns Gravesend had to offer. As he stumbled from The Three Daws after a night at its long bar, he rose to his full height and let out a belch. A shout from an upstairs window bid him be quiet at such an ungodly hour, but Big Tam felt nothing but pride as it echoed off the walls around him. Pausing only to pass water by the old wood yard on the corner, he made his way unsteadily down Crooked Lane towards his lodgings in Ordnance Road. A few lights burned in the boats that bobbed on the Thames. The moon lit the road beneath his feet. Spying a feral dog by the roadside, Tam bent to pick up a stone. Swaying as he stood, he held the projectile for a moment between a thumb and forefinger then, taking aim, he let it go. He rejoiced with a song and a dance as the stone hit its mark, drawing blood from the unfortunate creature's leg. The dog ran on with a yelp, its flank twitching with pain. Big Tam planted his feet on the road and launched a chorus of Daisy Bell to the heavens, the wind whipping his hair about his head. His broad Glasgow accent reverberated across the river to Tilbury as he stood, spreading his arms wide to embrace the night. Perhaps it was the noise that was his undoing. Perhaps it was his size. Either way, Big Tam had made himself conspicuous to the two men in the brougham behind him.

The man at the reins was tall and angular. He was swathed in a black cloak, his broad-brimmed hat pulled low over his heavy brow so that only his beak of a nose was visible. The man beside him melted into the dark as they sat, tensed with the anticipation of a fight. They had been careful to pick a quiet hour, when the sensible citizens of Gravesend would be in their beds. With muffles on their hooves, the horses had made their way stealthily along Crooked Lane, pulling the carriage ever closer to its quarry. Almost silently, the two men lowered themselves to the road, the taller of them stilling the horses with a hand to their muzzles. Pulling a sack from his cloak, he held it high above his head to bring down upon their prey, motioning to his companion to proceed with caution.

Big Tam finished his song, cleared his throat and spat phlegm to the floor where he stood. It had been a good night, he mused drunkenly, and he had no doubt there would be another tomorrow. Cruelly, his assailants chose that very moment to strike. Tam gave a cry as he felt the sack thrown over his head. His arms pinned suddenly to his side, he kicked out desperately, making contact with the shin of one of his aggressors. The man gave a howl of agony and fell to the road, rubbing furiously at his leg to relieve the pain. Seizing the advantage, Big Tam bent at the waist, turned and barrelled into the man who held the sack, his head making contact with his belly. He felt the sack loosening about his neck and knew that, with a few sharp movements, it would fall from his head completely. As drunk as he was, it would take more than two men with a hessian sack to subdue him.

He had incapacitated one already, he knew. The kick to the man's shin had produced a resounding crack. The one who had held the sack had let go now, no doubt with the force of Tam's head meeting his belly. He stood a chance. With a roar, he straightened up to his full height and swung his arms about him, his mighty fists clenched tight in anticipation of making contact with flesh and bone. A man was on his back now, his arms squeezed tight about his neck. As Tam struggled to shake him off, he felt his eyes begin to bulge. Barely able to breathe, he summoned all his strength and bucked and reared to try and dislodge the man. Eventually the man fell from his back with a thud. Big Tam charged about the road with as much force as he could muster in his drunken state. Where the devil was he? The answer came in the form of a splintering crack to his skull. For a moment, the darkness was shattered into a thousand glittering shards. It seemed he could see the stars. He struggled to regain his balance. Blood ran from his head, stinging his eyes and tasting bitter in his mouth. He could feel he was falling. His legs buckling beneath him, Big Tam swayed dangerously, then crashed to the ground with no less force than a felled oak split at the trunk. Their quarry subdued at last, the two men stopped for breath.

"You all right, Bracewell?" rasped the tall man with the beaked nose.

"Just get the bastard in the carriage," replied the man in the road, clutching his shin awkwardly as he staggered to his feet.

"Give him his credit, he's a strong'un," offered the tall man as he bound Tam's hands and feet with rope from the brougham. "Should fetch us a pretty penny."

"Credit be blowed," spat Bracewell as he limped to the carriage. "I'd rather see him bound and chained so I could have a proper crack at him. He fair near broke my leg."

"I'm sure that can be arranged." With a dry laugh, his companion heaved Tam's limp body onto the seat, covered him with a greasy blanket then took his place at the reins. Bracewell heaved himself aboard. With barely a sound, the brougham turned in the road and proceeded back up Crooked Lane. The only witnesses to their night's work were the stars in the sky and a stray dog by the roadside who barely looked up from licking its wound as they passed.

IV

Marks Of Interest

The morning was struggling to assert itself. The wind had calmed but left debris on the streets. Scraps of paper, food and even clothing lay in drifts with sticks and branches as Graves and Hicks walked briskly down The Strand. Graves had met Ignatius Hicks at The Silver Cross and prised him from his breakfast. As they rounded the corner into Agar Street, Graves took the time to look around him. The morning was his favourite time of day and he felt his spirits lift as he watched the city come to life. Baskets of fruit were emptied onto carts for sale, shop shutters were thrown open with a clatter and storefronts were filled with produce to entice passers by. Carts and private cabs rattled past in the wide road, their wheels splashing up dirt and detritus as they passed. Frock-coated gentlemen tipped their hats to acquaintances across the road. A knot of urchins gathered at a corner to discuss their strategy for the day. They scattered at the sight of the two detectives, Ignatius Hicks in particular cutting an all too recognisable figure.

Charing Cross Hospital had stood at its present site for sixty years. It presented a neat facade to the world but in truth it had become a sprawl. Much of the hospital had been extended and enlarged over the years so that it now held over a hundred and fifty beds, three children's wards and accommodation for fifty medical students. Clean, Palladian lines and a portico at the entrance gave it an air of solid authority amongst the squat and ramshackle buildings that surrounded it. Five storeys of windows stared blankly out onto the street. Two drunks asleep on the front steps were woken from their stupor by a porter. They swore and spat as they shuffled further up the street, only to settle and squabble together in another doorway that took their fancy.

Passing a donations box fixed to the railings at the entrance, Graves led the way through the impressive wooden doors and into the large, airy space beyond. A flurry of nurses bustled before them, their soft crinoline skirts and full aprons billowing around them as they hurried about their duties. A rather stiff-looking man stood at a desk in the centre of the hall, his starched collar buttoned up so tight that his neck brimmed over the top. Turning to their right, the two men descended a flight of steps to the bowels of the building. The daylight faded behind them as they left the terrestrial world and sunk deeper into the Earth, their footsteps echoing off the tiled walls. Gas jets lit their way to a subterranean corridor where few ever trod. Graves peered in at each open door as they passed. Shelves of jars and instruments adorned every room. In one or two, doctors were bent at their work, their starched white aprons streaked with unknown substances. A sinewy man of inestimable age shot the visitors a look of irritation and closed a door with a slam, but not before Graves got a glimpse of a cadaver upon the table, its chest cavity open so that the inner organs were displayed. Finally reaching the last door in the row, Hicks announced their presence with a sharp tap of his pipe on the frosted glass. It was opened by a thin bird of a man with a pair of spectacles balanced on the end of his nose. Strands of white hair were trained across his balding head, and his overall expression was one of disdain.

"I expected you earlier," snapped Doctor John Crane, MRCS. His Scottish burr lent him an air of patient civility quite at odds with his sentiment.

"Inspector Hicks was busy at his breakfast and loath to be torn away," offered Graves with an apologetic shrug.

"Best meal o'the day," thundered Hicks. "And it mustn't be rushed." He raised an admonishing finger to the young sergeant. Graves refused to rise to the bait, however, instead following Doctor Crane to the table in the centre of the room. There, laid out like an offering, was the body from Vinegar Yard. It lay on its back, its clothes having been removed. The matts of bloodied hair and clothes that Graves had noticed in the alley had gone, but the poor man was now adorned with grislier signs of injury. Great, fresh scars ran the length of his abdomen, across his stomach and up his chest to his throat; the signs of the doctor's investigations.

"I've cleaned him up as best I could, but it was no easy task," Doctor Crane intoned with a professional detachment. "He certainly came out of his encounter much the worse for wear, didn't he?"

"I'm presuming he was got at by a dog?"

"You'd be correct in your assumption, sergeant. The tooth marks here and the stretch of the jaw indicated by them would suggest a breed similar to a bull terrier. I've seen such marks before."

"What can you deduce of the man from his remains, doctor?" Hicks stood with his hands on his hips, gesturing with a nod of his head that Graves should make notes. The sergeant shrugged his coat off and hung it on a coat stand by the door. Pulling a notebook and pencil from his waistcoat pocket, he stood by the unfortunate man's naked feet, primed to make a record of the doctor's findings. Doctor Crane bent to take a pair of long-handled tweezers from a tray of medical instruments. Graves could see serrated blades, clamps and syringes amongst them, but also bottles and vials of strange fluids.

"We have before us the body of a male, some thirty years old." Graves scratched at his notebook as the doctor continued. "The subject was in good health."

Hicks threw back his head and let forth a peal of laughter. "Exceptin' he's dead," he guffawed.

"He was in good health *ante mortem*," the doctor continued, lifting his spectacles to glare at Inspector Hicks as if he were a naughty child. He cleared his throat pointedly before continuing. "Although evidence of opiate dependency may be seen in the bloodshot eyes, the mottling of the skin about the mouth and the scratches to the chest."

"Scratches?" Graves lifted his pencil from his notebook.

"It is common enough to those in thrall to the drug," sighed the doctor, seemingly irritated at the interruption. "The results of the agitation and even hallucinations that are concurrent with its use." His clipped Scottish vowels made him sound more brusque than ever. Graves nodded in understanding.

"He clearly died of his wounds, particularly the laceration of his jugular vein, here," Doctor Crane pointed to the man's neck with the tweezers, lifting a flap of skin to reveal a tubular vein the width of a child's little finger. Looking closely, Graves could clearly see it was torn in several places. "Although there is evidence of previous injury to the head, namely the zygomatic bone," he pointed to the man's cheek with his tweezers, "the mandible," he pointed to the jaw, "and various bones in the skull."

"He's certainly been in the wars, then?" offered Hicks. His interjection was roundly ignored by the other two men in the room.

"There are several other points of interest," continued the doctor, pushing his spectacles back up his nose the better to continue his examination. "Most noticeably here on the hands."

Doctor Crane lifted the man's hand from the table and spread his fingers wide. Graves peered closer. They were big hands for sure, but Doctor Crane was clearly alluding to something more. "The knuckles are scarred." Doctor Crane looked up to see what effect his words had had. Inspector Hicks was stroking his beard in an attempt to look thoughtful.

Graves was scratching his head. "Are they recent scars?"

"Now that is an interesting question," teased the Doctor. "In point of fact, they are scars upon scars." He lifted the other hand to display a deep cut across his knuckles.

"They look recent enough to me," harrumphed Hicks.

"That is the site of my investigations, Inspector Hicks. The cut was made but half an hour ago." Thinking he'd have more luck with Graves, the doctor turned to the young sergeant in front of him. "The scar tissue is thick and calloused and runs right to the bone," he explained. "Indeed there are signs of trauma to the metacarpals themselves."

"What might have caused such a thing?"

Doctor Crane fixed Inspector Hicks with a hard stare, plainly disappointed at his lack of perspicacity. "Their size and location would suggest to me at least, that we are in the presence of a pugilist."

"A boxer?" Graves" smile spread across his face.

"And experienced too, from the depth and quantity of the scars. This would also explain the trauma to the head and jaw."

"Took a beating then, did he?" Hicks had his fists raised before him.

"I think it's fair to say he gave as good as he got, Inspector Hicks."

"What do we have there?" Graves was pointing at an area of raised skin on the man's chest. "Looks like a blister."

"It's a design formed from the blistering of the skin," confirmed the doctor. Peering forward, Graves could indeed make out a strange shape made of hard, yellowing tissue. It was a circular design representing a crude, demonic face. Its eyes were slits and two horns extended from the top. Doctor Crane pinched the bridge of his nose between a forefinger and thumb as if the effort of explaining was too much. "To put it bluntly, sergeant, this man was branded."

"Branded? Like a heifer?" roared Hicks.

"Or," interjected Graves pointedly, "like a slave."

"And recently, too," continued the doctor. "Or at least within the last few weeks."

Graves drew a deep breath. "Anything else?" He licked the end of his pencil and held it poised midway between lip and paper.

"Yes, sergeant, there is something else." Doctor Crane was clearly enjoying the theatrical nature of the proceedings. "Take a look at this." Using his tweezers again, Doctor Crane leaned forward over the body to lift a flap of skin at the throat. A bluish, grey tube protruded from the man's neck. "Ignore that, sergeant, we're not interested in the trachea." As Doctor Crane pushed the ribbed tube away with his tweezers, Graves was sure he saw Inspector Hicks turning away to stare at a nondescript chart on the wall. "This is where I would direct your attention." He was holding apart another chamber of the neck, this more red and sinewy. "The oesophagus is inflamed." Looking about him, the doctor could tell he would be obliged to continue. "It may be caused by the fluid of the stomach extending beyond the lower oesophageal sphincter and irritating the oesophageal wall. Now, that in itself may not be pertinent. I should imagine there are many such men throughout London who suffer with a reflux, but look at this."

Perfectly orchestrating proceedings so as to follow a clear line of thought, Doctor Crane again lifted the man's left hand from the table. "Might I invite you to examine his fingertips, Sergeant Graves?"

Lowering his notepad for the moment, Graves leaned in. Hicks, too, had found the strength to peer closer.

"They're yellow." Hicks' eyes were wide.

"Indeed they are, inspector," purred the doctor.

"One may see such stains on the fingers of a smoker," mused Graves.

"Very good, sergeant," Doctor Crane was clearly enjoying himself now. "But these are not tobacco stains. If I might trouble you to hold this, Sergeant Graves?"

Doctor Crane held the man's hand a little higher, the better for Sergeant Graves to take it from him. It was cold and hard, the flesh unyielding. The doctor took a flask from the tray of instruments near the table, using a pipette to draw a small quantity of fluid. "Now, sergeant," he instructed, his voice clear and precise, "hold the fingers up, if you would."

Graves held the fingers as requested while the doctor applied drops of the fluid to each fingertip in turn.

"It's turning brown," exclaimed Hicks, his eyes wide in a simple wonder. Graves could see that he was right. The yellow staining beneath the fingernails in particular was turning a reddish-brown.

"Indeed it is, inspector."

"What does that tell us, Doctor Crane?" Graves had the feeling the doctor was reaching the denouement to his demonstration.

"There is only one substance that may cause inflammation of the oesophagus if ingested in quantity, turns reddish-brown in the presence of an alkaline solution," he held up his pipette. "And has such a distinctive smell when activated."

Graves took a moment to smell the air about him. There was an exotic odour of ginger and orange which turned bitter in the mouth. He smacked his lips, trying to distil the scent. It had a familiar taste.

"Is that - " he began.

"Yes, Sergeant Graves," affirmed Doctor Crane, his voice rising in triumph. Lifting a finger in punctuation, he rolled the word around his mouth as if he were tasting the very substance itself. "Turmeric!"

V

The Clockwork Man

The man with the heavy brow and beaked nose had disguised himself well. A shapeless jacket hung from his shoulders. A pair of filthy docker's overalls covered a torn collarless shirt and threadbare corduroy trousers. A cloth cap was pulled down to his eyes and a neckerchief pulled up over his chin to his nose. His great hobnailed boots stomped through the dirt as he made his way to St. Katharine Docks, a large knapsack thrown over his shoulder. He knew he wouldn't look out of place. Every one in ten men employed at the docks was dressed just so. Already, as he passed Dock House onto Upper Smithfield Street, he could hear the hiss and grind of the steam engines employed to keep the water level in the two great basins above that of the tidal Thames. Standing at the iron gates at the entrance opposite Norwich Court, he could see the docks were a bustle of activity. Around him rose the great brick warehouses and wharves, some five or six storeys high. Ropes and pulleys lifted loads from carts. Men meandered here and there with sacks of grain or spices on their shoulders. Traction engines pulled great loads of produce from the ships berthed in the East Dock, weaving their way between horses and drays laden with hops or barley. Steam rose from the Red Lion Brewery to compete with the clouds, and strange and exotic smells wafted on the light April breeze. Unnoticed and unremarked amongst the throng, the man with the beaked nose strode purposefully through the gates and past the customs sheds to his left and right. He knew exactly where he was heading. It would be a symbol, he had been told. He was to strike right at the heart of the dock.

He crossed the courtyard and walked onto the causeway that separated the two basins, East and West. The air was full of cries, the ringing of bells and the clatter of rigging in the wind. Ducking low, he slipped into the central warehouse and swung his bag from his shoulder. All around him, shelves stood from floor to ceiling, groaning with sacks of flour and corn, bundles of timber and haphazard stacks of masonry and brick. Bobbing behind a central aisle, he set his bag down by the farthest wall. Looking through a grimy window, he saw the central basin and system of locks that gave out to the river. Beyond them, on the south side, stood Shad Thames and St. Saviour's Dock. He knew they were in for quite the display.

With a look of concentration on his face, the man applied himself to his deadly task, pulling at a clasp to open the bag. Reaching inside, his fingers found and removed a bundle of cylindrical sticks, each the size of a large cigar. Dynamite. There were half a dozen in all, bound together with string; five sticks surrounding a sixth. Taking hold of two lengths of copper wire that protruded from the central stick, he reached inside the knapsack to find the timer mechanism. He pulled a simple, mechanical clock from the pouch, its internal workings exposed. Attaching the wires as he had been shown, he placed the device carefully beneath the window for maximum effect. Any nearer to the sacks of grain behind him and the blast would be mitigated. Looking about him for a final time, he swung the bag back over his shoulder and walked to the main thoroughfare through the warehouse. Lifting his hat to wipe the sweat from his forehead, he ducked back out the door into the morning. Finally, affecting as casual a manner as possible, he made his way back through the iron gates at the entrance and onto the streets beyond.

Bowman knew he had been side-lined. His posting to the docks at Shad Thames had been a demotion in all but name. He had baulked at the public nature of Hicks' pronouncement in The Silver Cross the night before and had felt his face flush under Graves' gaze. Was he the laughing stock of the Force? He was conscious of sideways looks and nudges amongst his colleagues that previously, perhaps, he would have dismissed. Since his release from Colney Hatch, however, such looks had been heavy with meaning. Did they still trust him? He cared not for Hicks, but was sad to think he had lost Graves' respect. They had worked together well, he thought, as he ambled from London Bridge Station to Bermondsey.

Turning at a row of ramshackle stables he entered Willow Walk, immediately lamenting his decision to walk alone in such a questionable area. The street was lined to one side by the railway depot. He could hear the railwaymen and depot workers trading obscenities beyond the high brick wall. The depot serviced the line known as the Bricklayers' Arms Branch, and Bowman could see the steam rising from a locomotive from within. A sharp whistle pierced the air, answered by a pack of dogs that gathered in the dirt by a tannery. Bowman looked around, cautiously. A gaggle of urchins played at the corner with Alscot Road. A tall man in a threadbare suit stood plying them with matches for their cigarettes. He looked up as the inspector passed, plainly concerned to see a stranger in the neighbourhood. Bowman noticed the man seemed only to have one good eye, the other a ghastly, milky white. His stubbled cheeks were ruddy and his lips thin and cracked. Lifting his fingers to his mouth, the man gave a loud whistle that echoed off the walls. Bowman suddenly felt very exposed. The near empty street ahead seemed heavy with a nameless threat. He quickened his step, wishing now that he had hired a cab at the station. Casting his eyes to the slums to his left, he noticed windows being thrown open. At one, a shirtless man leaned out to survey the scene. At another a woman hurled her laundry water to the road, missing Bowman by mere feet. A scuffle from behind alerted him to the fact he was being followed. Turning back as he walked, he saw the gang of boys from the corner, aping his gait. They followed him, step for step, giggling amongst themselves and occasionally spitting into the street. The urchins, he could handle. A cuff to the ear and a stern word were usually enough to send them on their way. What he saw ahead worried him more. Three burly men blocked his path into Upper Grange Road. They stood shoulder to shoulder, one chewing on the stump of a cigar, one scratching at the road with his boot and the other with his hands in his pockets. None of them seemed disposed to polite conversation. From the grease on their faces and the coal dust on their hands and clothes, Bowman guessed they were railway workers. He slowed his pace. The children behind him scattered.

"Lost?" The older of the men held the cigar end between his fingers, squinting at Bowman through mean eyes.

Bowman swallowed hard, trying not to betray his sense of disquiet. "Not lost, no." He felt his neck burn beneath his collar.

"Visitin' then?" laughed the junior of the men. "Come to pay your respects to your mama?" This last was said with a forced over-pronunciation.

Looking down at his wingtip brogue shoes and waistcoat, Bowman felt suddenly conspicuous. He had drawn attention to himself merely by his choice of dress. He should have been more careful.

"I am here on business," he offered.

"Business?" spat the man with the cigar. "The only business to be had round here is with the Kaiser." The other two men cackled to each other.

Aside from being the title for the German Emperor, the name meant nothing to Bowman. He doubted Wilhelm the Second had any interest in Bermondsey. "I am here on police business."

"Are you now?" The man took a step nearer. Bowman could smell alcohol on his breath.

"I am expected at the police house. I believe I am close." Bowman's moustache twitched.

"Oh, you're very close. So close, you can probably smell it." Much to the delight of his companions, the man lifted his nose to the air and took several sharp breaths. "There it is, the smell of mutton shunter." The men shared a nudge.

"Will you let me pass?" Bowman felt small in front of the three railway workers.

"Filth, are ya?"

Bowman turned. The man with the clouded eye had joined them now and, passing in front of the inspector, stood with the rest, his arms folded across his chest. Perhaps this was the Kaiser the man with the cigar had mentioned, mused Bowman. And then he caught his breath.

Some distance beyond the men, just at the corner with Upper Grange Road, stood a figure. The image seemed to coalesce before him, still some distance away. The yellow dress and tumbling chestnut hair were unmistakable. Bowman's heart thumped against his chest.

"George," she was saying. Her voice sounded so close that Bowman was convinced she whispered in his ear, yet several yards separated them.

"Anna?" he whispered.

The woman held her hand out to him, like a mother might to a child. "George," she said again. Even from so far away, Bowman could see her smile.

"Anna!" he called, oblivious to his assailants now.

The men looked around for the object of his anguish. "What's he up to?" said the younger of them.

"Oi, filth! What's got into you?" The man with the cigar was stepping back.

Bowman was insensible to them now. His eyes were for Anna only. The breeze carried her scent towards him. Pushing his way through the railwaymen, he stumbled on the road as he pursued her. His eyes strained to keep her in sight. For every step he took, she seemed to move an equal distance from him.

The men behind him shifted their weight uncomfortably, hiding their chagrin with bravado. One swore after him, another stooped to the road for a stone and sent it sailing past Bowman's ear. The man with the chewed cigar simply shook his head in mock sympathy.

"Let him go," he jeered. "The man's not up to dick."

Laughing between them, they each turned to go about their business, leaving Bowman to stagger blindly down the road towards his quarry.

As he rounded the corner to the police house, Bowman could no longer feel his feet. There was a ringing in his ears and his vision was fading to a single, bright point. He could just about make her out in front of him, but he knew she was leaving him again. She seemed somehow insubstantial, a reflection in a mirror. He pitched forward into a man with a cart.

"You all right, mate?" Sensing Bowman was far from being all right, the man guided him to a low wall that he might sit down. "Rest yourself there," he soothed. "Be right as rain soon enough."

As the man walked on, pushing his rickety cart before him, Bowman sat with his head in his hands. His vision was clearing. Looking about him, he fought to clear the fog in his brain. Anna was gone, leaving behind her a nagging question in Bowman's mind. How was it that, nearly a year after she had died, he had just seen his wife on a London street?

VI

Arrival

Bermondsey Police Station was set back from the road, inconspicuous amongst a row of plain, three-storey terrace houses. It comprised two properties surrounded by a wrought iron fence. Steps from the street led to doors surrounded by imposing porticos. Detective Inspector Bowman slowed his step as he approached. The only thing that distinguished the police station from the neighbouring houses was a sign on a battered notice board proclaiming the property to be part of the Metropolitan Police Ambulance Service. As he stood at the bottom step looking up, two police constables ambled from the building. One straightened his hat on his head as they meandered down the road in the direction of the river. Bowman took a breath to steady himself. He had been shaken by the events of the last half hour and, try as he might, he was finding it difficult to turn his mind from them. He knew it was all the effect of his fevered brain. He also knew there was a word for it. A word he hadn't heard or seen since first reading it on his patient record at Colney Hatch. *"Prone to delusions"*. There was no other explanation but that he had experienced a delusional episode. Bowman was a rational man and able quickly enough to dismiss any notion of spectral visitations. And yet, she had seemed so real. He put a hand to his breast to steady his heart then ascended the steps to the police station.

Inside, all was a riot. The cramped reception area was full of children. Some lounged on the deep sills, absently drawing on the windows with their fingers. Others sat patiently on wooden benches by the walls. Most, however, careered about the room at speed, tripping and pushing each other in sport. Their cries were deafening. Among them, Bowman recognised the urchins who had followed him down Willow Walk. He had to muster all his strength not to turn tail back to Scotland Yard at once. As he stood at the door trying to make sense of the scene, there came a crack. A silence descended.

"Where is Mr Babbington?" The voice belonged to a fearsome young lady who stood at the reception desk. She held a long cane before her, just above the tabletop. She was tall Bowman noticed, perhaps as tall as him. Her lithe frame was draped in a grey pinafore that reached to the floor. Most of her hair was tied up in a bun upon her head, but Bowman noticed stray ringlets dancing about her face as she held court. On the table before her lay a ledger and her matron's hat. "I shall ask again," she was saying, slowly. "Where is Mr Babbington?"

The boys sniggered. One of their number, clearly the bravest among them, walked carefully to a cupboard door. Reaching out with a grubby hand, he turned the key to release the lock. With a flourish, he pulled the handle and sprang aside to let the door swing open. There stood Mr Babbington, his face flushed, his hair plastered to his forehead with perspiration. He was a man in his fifties but old before his time. White bushy eyebrows stood out prominently from his forehead, framing blue-grey, rheumy eyes and reddened cheeks. Bowman could see he had a drinker's nose. As the poor man staggered out from the cupboard, it was clear the woman at the desk was trying hard to suppress her laughter. Taking their cue from her, a few boys in the room started to snigger.

"Mr Babbington," began the woman. "Would you be so good as to return your charges to the workhouse? I had rather see them put to work than walking the streets again."

Mr Babbington gave her a surly look, straightening his cravat at his collar before replying. "Miss Beaurepaire," he mumbled, trying to salvage what dignity he could, "I am grateful for your interventions. Do offer my thanks and highest regards to your constables." Placing a battered hat upon his head, Babbington turned his feet to the door, bidding his charges follow him. Clearly sensing they'd had enough mischief for the day, the boys fell into line behind him and, one by one, they marched from the room. Some of the last stragglers loitered by the door until a sharp look from the woman at the desk sent them on their way.

"They're from St. Olave's," she explained to Bowman as she caught his eye. "He has no authority over them, so they roam where they will." She was tidying the contents of the cupboard as she spoke. Babbington had clearly been in a state of agitation whilst within. Papers and books had been pulled to the floor and maps and ledgers lay dishevelled on the shelves. Shutting the door behind her, the young woman blew an errant hair from her face and held out a hand.

"Alma Beaurepaire," she offered by way of an introduction.

Bowman took her hand. "George Bowman, Scotland Yard." He swallowed hard, blushing at his inadvertent use of his Christian name.

"Yes, George," she replied, briskly. Bowman swallowed again. "You are to accompany me to St. Saviour's Dock where I shall place you under the auspices of the loading officer." She was reaching for her hat at the desk.

"Have you been matron here long?" asked Bowman, removing his hat from his head.

"These last three years."

Bowman played nervously with the rim of his hat, turning it this way and that as he spoke. "And you are placed here on account of the children?"

Alma stopped to look the inspector up and down. "It's an unusual thing to find a female in a police station is it not, George?" Bowman blinked. Her continued use of his first name was both disarming and unsettling. "Unless the woman in question is either inebriated or has been beaten by her pimp," she continued, fixing her mob hat to her head with a pin. Bowman blanched at her forthright language. "But there is such a great number of workhouses in the area and we have more than our share of errant children." She slammed the ledger shut at her desk in preparation to leave. "Your commissioner, in his wisdom, has decreed that the fairer sex are better suited to the task of policing them. So, George, here I am." This last was said barely inches from the inspector's face.

"Miss Beaurepaire," he stammered, "would you be so kind as to escort me to the dock?"

A smile played over her face. Bowman sensed he was being toyed with. "My, but aren't we the stuffy sort?" Alma clapped him on the shoulder, "Hold your fire, Inspector Bowman. It doesn't do to rush a girl." With a smile playing about her lips, she walked briskly to a flight of stairs heading down to the cells. "Samson?" she yelled, her hands on her hips. "I'm headin' out to the docks with my new friend George." She flashed Bowman a smile. "Be sure to man the desk while I'm gone!" Not waiting for a reply, Alma Beaurepaire swept from the reception room, pausing at the top of the steps to turn to the inspector.

"You comin'"?

Swept up in her wake, Bowman dutifully followed her into the street, accidentally dropping his hat at the top of the steps as he did so.

In the few minutes he had been in the police station, Upper Grange Road had become busy. Doors had been thrown open onto the street, letting forth a multitude of men in shirtsleeves, tattered trousers and hobnailed boots. Each house seemed to be home to several of them, piling out as they struggled into overalls and aprons. Turning from the slums, they moved as one towards the river. The air was full of oaths and cigarette smoke. As Bowman walked with his companion, he felt part of a movement of men.

"There's a boat come in," Alma explained. "There's goods to unload."

Terrace after terrace of crumbling slums lined the way to St. Saviour's Dock, broken only by the occasional appearance of chapels and dye, glue and Indian rubber works. The streets were awash with humanity.

"Twice a day they try their luck at the docks," Alma was saying as they followed the throng into a thoroughfare known as Neckinger. "If they're hired, there's half a day's pay in it."

She had an easy gait, her long arms swinging loosely by her side. She plainly felt at ease here amongst the grime and filth. Bowman envied her for it. As Alma turned to him, she caught Bowman looking at her and raised a quizzical eyebrow. He looked quickly away.

The closer they got to the docks, so the more filthy the streets and houses became. Stinking ditches ran between the slums now, their smell rising to mix with the odour of spice and steam emanating from the wharves ahead. Faces peered from broken windows. More than once, Bowman saw them spit into the street.

"How do you come to be in London, Miss Beaurepaire?" Bowman asked as they picked their way carefully through the fetid streets.

"Misfortune," she replied, matter-of-factly, stroking an errant ringlet from her eyes. "My mother died in Australia, when I was just five. My father had died four years earlier. He was the governor of a penal colony in New South Wales. I spent some time in an orphanage then found myself a passage home." Bowman threw her a questioning look. "My father's family are from Sussex. Of course, they had never known me, so they shunned me. I was on my own." She shook her head at Bowman's look, "Don't feel sorry for me, George. I've found my place in this stinking city. Believe you me, the Outback has got nothing on Bermondsey."

Bowman pulled his coat about him as a wind whistled through the alleys on their route. The river was in sight now as they emerged from Rose Court. "Do all these men work at the dock?" Bowman was casting his eyes at the masses about him. Each man had a look of hunger in his eyes, a desperation to find employment for the day. The inspector was jostled and shoved as he walked.

"It's a monster," Alma laughed. "It'll chew 'em up and, at the end of the day, it'll spit 'em out. If they're lucky."

As they rounded the corner, St. Saviour's Dock lay before them. A great gouge in the Thames shore, it cut into the south bank of the river like a scar. The Thames was swollen at the height of its tide. Gentle waves lapped at the wharves that rose from the water. They soared over several storeys, great escarpments of brick and mortar. Printed across each in black painted letters of four feet high were names such as Meriton, Shuter and Hamlyn; each wharf large enough to hold unimaginable quantities of spices, coffee and tea, flour, grain and other goods to be consumed by the voracious city. Passing along Dockhead and into Shad Thames, Bowman saw a foreman posted outside the entrance to each of these great warehouses. It was towards these men that the pressing throng was headed. In a moment, they were overcome with bodies pressing to be first in the queue for work. Shouts echoed off the walls, arms were held aloft and Bowman even saw some punches being thrown in pursuit of a morning's employment. It was a scene of desperation. Barrows and carts were commandeered and brought to the wharves. Looking through the open wharves to the dock beyond, Bowman noticed wooden gantries being swung out over the water in anticipation of an arrival. In just a moment more, Bowman saw a great, three-masted clipper breaching the Thames wall. A swell of water preceded it, which swept through the length of the dock and, at parts, onto the narrow walkways. As the clipper lowered her sails, ropes were thrown ashore to be secured on the quayside. Men shouted orders from the decks to those below. Extra ropes were thrown. Bowman could even see sacks of produce being thrown prematurely to the wharves. Here they were stacked or loaded onto waiting carts and pushed away; rice to the rice mill, hops to the brewery. The wood that clad the iron skeleton of the ship groaned and creaked as she was brought to bear. Bowman could see deckhands scrambling to bring in the sails and fold them away. Hatches were flung open in anticipation of the great disgorging of goods. All was activity.

"Let's leave them to it," Alma said as she turned to the inspector. She was amused to see him so interested in the processes of docking a ship. "I need to take you to the loading officer."

Stepping deftly between the hordes, they made their way down Shad Thames. The clipper now secured, the carts and barrows were brought close and loaded with large sacks and wooden chests. A musty odour escaped the open hatches and mingled with the sweat and tobacco that hung in the air. Bowman recognised it as tea. The ship and its cargo had clearly come a long way. Walking down some steep steps towards the river, the inspector took his opportunity to look out over the Thames. His view to St. Katharine Docks on the north bank was obscured by ships and boats of all sizes, each awaiting their turn to berth. Clippers and schooners were moored alongside rowing boats and ferries in the middle of the river.

"Some of them have been there for days," Alma was saying as they walked. "That's why we need the likes of you, George." Bowman flinched and looked around. For her to use his Christian name in so public a place was quite inappropriate. "To guard the tea for the British."

Turning his gaze upriver, Bowman took in the brutal majesty of Tower Bridge. Still under construction, it resembled nothing less than the skeleton of some great beast dug up from the mud of the Thames. Two great scaffold towers had been erected on massive piers sunk into the riverbed. Inside them, Cornish granite obelisks were rising, solid and immutable, topped with Portland stone. A gantry was slung between them at their tops and suspension cables were slung to the riverbanks on either side. If he squinted against the spring sun, Bowman could make out some of the four hundred men employed in its construction, scurrying from one side to the other or climbing the impossible height to the gantry unaided. It was little wonder people referred to it as the Gateway to the Empire, though Bowman thought it looked more like a gaping mouth, eager for satisfaction. London's appetite was endless, he mused, and he wondered if even the ships now moored in the Thames would be enough to sate its hunger.

"It'll be the end of us, that's for sure."

Bowman turned to see Alma Beaurepaire staring up at the bridge with him. "You cannot halt progress, Miss Beaurepaire. Especially when there's an Empire to feed."

Alma flashed him a smile and an enigmatic look that Bowman couldn't read.

His thoughts were interrupted by a scream for help. Suddenly alert, Bowman looked around to find the source of the distress. As he bounded back up the steps onto Shad Thames, his eyes scanned the length of the wharves. Amongst the bustle at Corder's Wharf, he saw a man lying on the ground near the water, his face a mask of agony. In a flash, Alma was next to him, marshalling those around her to get help. Trying to make sense of the scene, Bowman saw a cart upturned next to the man, its cargo of sacks spilling onto the dockside. Some had split as they fell, releasing puffs of a yellow spice that dissipated on the wind. Alma was kneeling now, offering such comfort to the man as she could. As Bowman approached, he could see the man's leg was crushed between the clipper and the dockside. Men leaned against the great ship's side, trying to heave it away from the dock wall as the unfortunate wretch on the ground writhed and grimaced in pain.

"The cart rolled into me, knocked me over," he was panting. "I lost my footing."

"Get that cart back on its wheels," Alma was commanding. "Let's sling him on it and get him to The Sisters Of Mercy."

Bowman was impressed with her calm demeanour. "There's a convent nearby," she was explaining to him. "They have an infirmary."

Bowman sprang to help some men right the cart, brushing it clear of dirt and dust as best he could. Laying some sacks across it to offer some comfort, his thoughts turned to the poor man's version of events. Looking at the flagstones that lined the floor in Corder's Wharf, he could see they were level. In order for the cart to have rolled into the man, it would have to have been pushed. Easy enough amongst this number of men, he thought, for it to have happened by way of an accident. Looking about him, Bowman saw one still point in all the activity. Halfway up the dock, a man was leaning nonchalantly against a door, drawing on a pipe as he watched proceedings with a calm detachment. Bowman recognised him at once. It was the man with the clouded eye from Willow Walk. Quickening his step, Bowman rounded the cart in pursuit. Finding his progress along the dock impeded by the sheer crush of men, he called out to stop the man. A few heads turned in response. As he neared the doorway where the man had stood, he found his path blocked by a horse and cart. He slapped the beast on its flank in frustration, trying in vain to peer round its sweating hide. By the time it had moved, Bowman had lost sight of the man. Puffing out his cheeks in exasperation, Bowman swung his hat from his head to wipe his brow on a sleeve. His frown cut deep into his forehead. What was the name the man with the cigar had mentioned on Willow Walk? Bowman searched his thoughts. The Kaiser. Was that the man with the clouded eye? He heard a struggle behind him. Turning, he saw a small party employed to remove the injured man from the dock. Under Alma's calm direction, they were hoisting him onto the cart, cradling his shattered leg as best they could. Bowman could see it was nothing more than a mulch of blood and bone. His screams echoed off the wharves and warehouses as they lowered him onto the soft sacks. As the man clutched at the air in agony, his body convulsing with pain, something about his hands caught the inspector's attention. Stepping a little closer, he could plainly see his fingertips and nails were stained a bright yellow.

"What will become of him?" he asked Alma as the cart was maneuvered through the wharf to the streets.

"He'll never work again, that's for sure," she panted, her exertions showing in her flushed face. "If he's lucky, he'll finish his days in a workhouse for the invalided." Bowman's moustache twitched. "He's no use to the Empire now, is he?"

With a strange look that Bowman couldn't quite interpret, she turned and led him back down the steps to the Thames. As they neared the river, Bowman saw a man walking towards them. He was decked in a smart frock coat and top hat to denote his station among the dock's employees.

"Inspector Bowman," he was calling above the din. "I had word to expect your arrival." He had an officious look about him and walked with a pronounced limp. "As you have seen, there is never a dull day at St. Saviour's." He shared a look with Alma who raised a thin smile in response. The man was holding out his hand in greeting. "I'm the loading officer for St. Saviour's Dock," he was proclaiming.

"You have me at a disadvantage," Bowman ventured, shaking the man's hand.

"Of course, forgive me," replied the official with a smile. "My name is Bracewell. Cornelius Bracewell."

VII

A Wolf In Sheep's Clothing

The Tower Subway had lost some of its allure. Opened to great fanfare as a narrow gauge railway over twenty years before, it had spent the first months of its life propelling the wealthier citizens of London beneath the Thames in cable-hauled cars, twelve at a time. The lack of profit produced by so erratic and unreliable a transport, however, saw the discontinuation of the service within a few months. Now, at the presentation of a ha'penny, all of London could traverse the width of the river on foot. It had the appearance from within of a cast iron intestine, reaching through the mud from Tower Hill on the north side to Vine Street on the south.

A small knot of intrepid pedestrians stumbled into the gloom, their fingers reaching for the greasy sides of the tunnel. It seemed to breathe and sweat with the movement of the river above, and the ground was given to mild tremors as they walked. Some found they had to duck, and hats were removed on account of the low ceiling. As they began their perambulations, one of their number broke rank and began to run the length of the tunnel. Holding his hands out to steady himself, the tall man with the beaked nose ran with his head low. He stepped carefully over the iron ribs of the tunnel that threatened to trip him at every turn. Where his hands brushed against the wall, he found them to be damp. Water condensed against the cold metal and ran in rivulets to the floor, mixing with the dust to make a stodgy, sloppy mess. Breathing hard, he at last reached the tunnel's furthest end, bounding up the sloped entrance until the muscles in his legs burned with the effort.

He emerged onto Pickle Herring Street, already pulling his coat from his shoulders. Walking at a pace, he passed up Potter's Fields and through the churchyard at St. John's, always careful to avoid the tide of men sweeping to the dock for employment. He knew full well that some would recognise him and so, his hat pulled low over his eyes, he slunk back into the shadows as they passed. Finally, he rounded the corner onto Upper Grange Road.

Pulling his hat from his head and his kerchief from his neck, he took the steps two at a time. He breezed through the reception area, nodding at Samson at the desk. The portly sergeant nodded back. The hook-nosed man was relieved to be back. Taking a breath to calm himself, he walked purposefully to the back of the building and down a flight of stairs. Taking a key from his pocket, he opened a cupboard and reached up to a shelf, pulling a bundle of clothes from their place.

Doing up the last of the buttons on his coat, the man caught Samson's eye as he passed back into the reception area. The desk sergeant, busy scratching at his ledger, gestured with his pen in greeting.

"Constable Thackeray," he said, airily. "I trust you passed a productive morning?"

Thackeray smiled in response and ducked through the door, placing his policeman's hat on his head as he descended the steps to the street.

VIII

The Devil In Bermondsey

Bracewell had an iron grip, noticed Bowman as he shook the loading officer by the hand. He was a compact man with a barrel chest, his ruddy face shining in the morning sun. Though he affected an easy manner, he was betrayed by his clenched teeth and narrow eyes. Bowman had the sense that the man was in pain.

"Thank you, Miss Beaurepaire," he was saying silkily. "I shall show Inspector Bowman the ropes."

Alma shrugged her shoulders and threw Bowman a disarming smile. "See ya later," she chimed. Gathering her skirts, she walked carefully from the dock. Watching her go, Bowman saw her turn at least twice to see that he was looking. Both times, he felt his face flush and his neck burn beneath his collar. He turned away quickly so as to avoid her eye, but not so quickly that he didn't see a mischievous smile play about her lips.

"Each clipper carries in eighty tons of tea and similar quantities of spice or opium," Bracewell was intoning, clearing his throat to catch the inspector's attention. "They unload here twice a day when the tide is at its highest."

Bowman turned to face him. The loading officer was standing tall, conveying as best he could the sense that he was master of all he surveyed. Bowman noticed a bead of sweat escaping from his hairline.

"What will be my duties here?" Bowman asked.

"Your presence alone is valuable to us, inspector. We lose stock by the day to thieves." He motioned that Bowman should join him as he walked up Shad Thames. All around them, the unloading of the clipper continued at a pace. Men shouted to each other or passed sacks along a line. Carts were loaded and wheeled away. Spillages were swept up as if every grain or leaf was precious.

"The owners make these wharves as secure as they can, but still they hold precious cargo. This one here, for example." They had stopped outside a tall warehouse. Men came and went through its open gate, pushing sacks of produce on ramshackle carts. "This is Crown Wharf. At this very moment, it holds within its walls over thirty thousand pounds' worth of coffee, saffron and turmeric." He pointed back at the clipper as it rose and fell with the swelling tide. "The tea in this shipment alone will be worth some one hundred thousand pounds. It makes us quite the target."

They had reached the end of the dock now, and the two men turned back from Tooley Street to view the scene before them.

"Of course, if I had my way, we'd hang 'em all." Bracewell turned to the inspector. Bowman wasn't sure if he was smiling or not.

"They'd hang pirates on this very spot, inspector. The river here is called the Neckinger on account of all the hangings. It means the Devil's neckcloth."

Bowman looked about him with fresh eyes. St. Saviour's Dock was evidently once a barbarous place.

"Are there devils here, Mr Bracewell?" he asked, pointedly.

"Look around you, Inspector Bowman," Bracewell held his arms wide as if to encompass the whole of the dock. "You'll certainly find no saints." He threw his head back and laughed at the very idea.

Bracewell's mirth was interrupted by the arrival of another man. The constable was a tall, angular man, and Bowman couldn't help but notice the heaviness of his brow and the prominence of his nose. "Ah, Constable Thackeray," Bracewell was leaning in to shake his hand. "I trust you can show Inspector Bowman round the wharves? He is in charge here now."

Bowman thought he saw a flash of something pass across the constable's eyes. What was it? Annoyance? Resentment? "Of course," the man replied, bobbing his head in deference.

"Perhaps you could show him your itinerary?" Bracewell prompted.

"We use the Customs House as our base," the constable explained. "We could start there."

As Bracewell made his retreat, Bowman saw him take a fob watch from his coat to study the dial intently. Snapping it shut, he stopped at the mouth to the Thames to gaze absently out to the far shore.

Thackeray led Bowman down the opposite side of the quay to the Customs House. As they walked gingerly through the maelstrom of activity, Bowman couldn't help but notice the constable glancing at the clock on the wall of the rice mill behind them. Finally, they turned off the dock into an alley. A plain and weather-beaten door stood back from the passage with a sign nailed to its peeling exterior; 'St. Saviour's Dock, Customs House'. As the constable unlocked the door to admit him, Bowman felt him pause on the threshold.

Away from the hustle and bustle of the dock, the little room in which they found themselves seemed an island of calm. A shelf groaned with papers, files and ledgers, while a simple table and two chairs stood at its centre. Charts and maps lined the walls. The room seemed to ring with silence.

And then it was broken.

A thump and a crack echoed from across the river, the sound glancing off the sheer walls around it. Bowman felt it in the pit of his stomach. There were shouts and cries from the dockside and the sound of running feet. Thackery ran from the room, Bowman sprinting after him in hot pursuit. Coming to a halt on the bank of the Thames, the two men stood breathing hard as they stared out over to the far shore. All around them, the dockworkers jostled for the best position from which to view the spectacle. They pointed, shielding their eyes against the sun, trying to make sense of the scene. Across the water, Bowman could see a ball of smoke rising to the heavens. Even at this distance, it was possible to make out the figures of men running in fear. Flames licked at their ankles as they fled. One man, set alight from the blast, threw himself at the mercy of the River Thames. Smaller explosions came like afterthoughts and it was possible to see buildings falling in on themselves. Great plumes of smoke belched into the sky until it was a smudge of dirty grey to rival the river.

"St. Katharine Docks!" one of the men was shouting. "It'll be flattened!"

His heart in his mouth and his mind reeling at the thought of what he might find there, Bowman knew at once that he had to get to the north bank.

IX

Inferno

As he approached Tower Bridge from Shad Thames, Bowman knew it was his only option. Even if Bracewell had secured him the services of an oarsman, to row the river would take too long. With St. Katharine Docks aflame, it was even doubtful they would find a safe mooring once across. The nearest crossing upstream was the Tower Subway. Bowman knew that would put at least another twenty minutes on his journey so he stood, breathless from his exertions, on the approach to Tower Bridge. The hammers were silent. Carts of material and tools had been abandoned. The explosion on the north bank had aroused much excitement and interest amongst the workforce. Almost to a man, they crowded to the east side of the bridge to stare agog at the unfolding scene. As Bowman picked his way swiftly along the bridge, he looked around at the spoils of construction. Great lumps of steel lay ready to be lifted into position by ropes and pulleys. His progress was punctuated by piles of masonry and vats of grease. Barrels of steaming pitch bubbled and popped. The road surface - such as it was - was strewn with rivets, hammers and debris. Above him, men swung from their footholds to gaze across the river, calling out to each other from their great height. Bowman threw his eyes ahead, focusing beyond the span of the bridge to the north shore. A fire was raging at the heart of St. Katharine Docks. The flames leapt from warehouse to warehouse, further explosions rattling across the Thames as their contents combusted. Already, Bowman could see measures being taken to try and subdue the conflagration. Hoses and pumps had been turned on the fire and great flumes of water arced through the air.

"Hey! Watch yer step!" The cry caught Bowman mid-step. Up ahead, he could see a blustering foreman with his hands on his hips. "What do you think you're doin' here?"

Bowman fumbled for his papers. "Detective Inspector Bowman, Scotland Yard," he called, holding his identification before him.

"Oh?" sneered the man, his filthy face alight with mischief. "And I'm a monkey's uncle."

"I need to get to St. Katharine Docks."

"Putting on quite a show for us, aren't they?" The foreman twisted his head over his shoulder to gaze at the blaze on the north bank. The acrid tang of smoke hung in the air.

"Who?" Bowman squinted against the sun to size the man up. He was dressed in tattered work clothes and heavy boots, a grubby hat jammed on a thatch of greasy hair. As he turned back to face the inspector, Bowman could see he had several missing teeth and a scar that cut across his mouth.

"The Fenians, o'course," he rasped. Several workers turned to nod their heads in agreement.

Quickening his pace, Bowman strode past the man. "I am hoping a man may cross this bridge in safety?"

"A man may," replied the foreman with a knowing grin to his comrades. "I don't know about a detective inspector."

The men at the makeshift balustrade had turned now, the entertainment on the bridge proving to be of more amusement to them than that on the riverbank.

"Send 'em 'ome to Ireland when you catch 'em!" called one to a resounding cheer from his fellow workers. "I've a sack o' potatoes at home I'd gladly send with 'em!" The men around him fell about at this and clapped him on the back, their shoulders heaving with laughter. Further up the bridge, a knot of scaffolders and labourers spat on the ground. Their faces were flushed with anger.

"Keep your ruddy potatoes, Fraser," shouted a man with a peg leg and a broad Irish accent. "You'll be needin' 'em for when the revolution comes."

Leaving the two groups of men squaring up for a fight, Bowman ploughed on with half an eye on St. Katharine Docks. As he proceeded across the bridge, he heard the plaintive cry of the foreman behind him; "Stop ya gawpin'! This bridge won't build itself!"

The inspector found himself in the middle of the bridge now, where the two leaves of the bascule met. The river was clearly visible through the unfinished surface beneath his feet. At one point, the road narrowed to the width of the three or four girders that were slung below him. He slowed his pace, not daring to look too closely at the swollen Thames beneath. The wind whipped about his coat as he lifted his gaze to the end of the bridge.

And there she stood. Diffuse as smoke at first, she soon seemed as solid as the steel and stone around her. Bowman stopped, his heart racing. Shaking his head, he fought against the feeling of suffocation. Trying to call her name, he felt the word catch in his throat like a barb. There was a ringing in his ears. He looked behind him at the construction workers. Surely someone else could see her? They continued with their work, seemingly oblivious to the woman in yellow only yards away, the only distraction to their labours being the belching smoke on the north bank. As he lifted his head again, he saw she was beckoning him. He fell to his knees, the rough, unfinished surface of the road chafing at the skin through his clothes. The yellow of her dress was blinding now, and he had to raise his hand to shield his eyes.

"Hey, watch yer step!" the foreman shouted from behind. Bowman summoned his strength, trying to see beyond the apparition. He shut his eyes tight and willed her away. A sudden blast tore through the air. Looking to his right, Bowman could see the whole of the central warehouse had been torn apart. Shards of wood and glass spiralled to the ground, narrowly missing the stevedores as they ran for safety. Ahead on Tower Bridge Approach, Bowman could hear the bells of an approaching private ambulance. A carriage drawn by two horses rounded the corner and turned into Upper East Smithfield, its driver urging the team on with a crack of his whip. The commotion had brought Bowman to his senses. Standing again, he focussed on the way ahead. There was no sign of her now. Lucid once more, Bowman mused how he could be so convinced of her appearance when in the thrall of a manic episode, yet appreciate its sheer implausibility when free from it.

Stepping from the bridge, he inspector took the shortest route to the docks. Taking the steps down to Little Thames Street two at a time, he followed the river round to the dock entrance and the locks that kept the Thames at bay.

He was confronted with pandemonium. Men were running from place to place, shouting orders or crying for help. Bodies and body parts lay scattered about the warehouse precincts. Casualties lay dazed on the walkways awaiting help. Their faces and limbs were burned and blistered. Charred corpses floated in the water in a slick of blood. Ships of various sizes bobbed on the water, caught in the middle of discharging their loads. Cranes had been abandoned and carts neglected in the melee. Steam fire engines sprayed water pumped straight from the Thames. With the East and West Docks either side of the warehouse, the flames were being held at bay. In the midst of it all, a chubby man in a grubby waistcoat and corduroy trousers was conducting proceedings. Bowman could see another ambulance joining the first. It was to him that the drivers turned to be directed to the casualties that most needed help, and so it was to him that Bowman directed his feet.

"Inspector Bowman, Scotland Yard," he announced, squinting through the smoke.

The man gave a look of exasperation. "Heaven save us!" It was not the reaction Bowman had hoped for. "What I want is ambulances!"

Looking behind the man, Bowman could see another private ambulance rattling into the dockyard, its two horses whinnying in alarm at the scene. Bowman ran to give assistance, taking bedding and dressings from the ambulance and looking around for who he might help first. All around, men were returning to their injured colleagues as the flames were beaten back.

"Mr Tremont, sir!" called one. The chubby man in the waistcoat wheeled round to face him. "It's Sheridan, sir. He's alive, but won't last without help." Bowman ran to the man's side, calling for others to render assistance. As three others approached, their hobnailed boots skidding on the walkway, Bowman took command.

"Strip him to the waist, but carefully. You," he pointed to the man who had first called out, "take off your neckerchief." As the man removed the kerchief from his neck, Bowman ran to the dockside, grabbing a bucket from a pile of discarded equipment. He filled it at the waterside and ran back, kneeling beside the wretch on the ground. He was shivering violently now, screaming as the men removed his shirt.

"It must be done now," explained Bowman, "or it will only be done later, and that will be the worse for him." Bowman took his companion's kerchief and rinsed it in the water. "Press this to the burn," he ordered. Lifting his face to the wind he called to those around him. "Any man with a burn must be cooled. We are surrounded by water, so use it!" Several workers left their injured colleagues to find a receptacle and run to the water's edge. Bowman could see the ambulance workers were loading men onto the back of their carriages, but with so many injured their removal was likely to take time.

Bowman walked back to Tremont. He noticed he was looking out across the Thames to the south bank, a haunted look on his face.

"Mr Tremont," began Bowman, "Do you have any idea what happened here?"

"This will ruin us for sure," uttered Tremont, his face a picture of dejection. "Things have been bad enough with Tilbury, but this'll put a cap on it, you mark my words." He looked wildly about him. He had the look of a scared man, thought Bowman.

"What was in the warehouse?"

"Nothing beyond comestibles and building materials," Tremont shook his head. "No explosives."

"Might a man have gained access with a bomb?" Bowman chose his words carefully, looking for any reaction on Tremont's expressive face.

"He might," he began, wringing his hands in desperation. "But why might he do such a thing? I'm of the opinion it was only an accident." Tremont hollered to a fire engine to redirect its hose to the roof of another warehouse.

"I saw the blast, Mr Tremont. That was no accident." Bowman wiped his face with a hand and noticed it was covered in a skein of ash and grime.

"Then you know nothing of a docker's trade, Inspector Bowman." Tremont turned to the inspector, a look of indignation on his face. "We handle explosive material as a matter of course. Accidents are but a hazard of the trade."

"You said the warehouse contained nothing beyond comestibles."

"And such material is prone to combust. Sometimes with no external aggravation."

Bowman stroked his moustache, doubtfully. "I find that – "

"It was an accident, Inspector Bowman, and that is that." Tremont pulled himself up to his full height. "It is my job now to care for my employees and their families as best I can. What is yours?"

With that, he strode purposefully away, leaving Bowman to stare thoughtfully across the Thames to St. Saviour's Dock on the south side.

X

The Mark Of The Devil

The blast had woken Big Tam. He lay in a confused state at first, trying to make sense of his surroundings. A dull fog lay behind his eyes. A sharp pain throbbed at his head. As his eyes grew accustomed to the dim light, he realised he was looking at his own hand, curled in a fist on the ground before him. Shifting his weight to restore feeling to his arm, he flexed his fingers with a tremendous effort, first one then another. Then he realised he had been stripped to the waist. The floor felt hard and cold at his shoulder. He winced as he rocked himself onto his back, his head pulsing in pain at the exertion. He tried to lift his hands to his head but found his right hand was secured by a chain to the wall behind him. He pulled at it hard, but succeeded only in chafing his wrist on the metal cuff that held him. Lifting his feet, he shuffled closer to the wall that he might rest his back against it. The sound of his boots scuffing against the floor resonated in the space around him. Tam had the impression he was in a large, empty room. He felt a stab of pain and set his teeth against the agony. As he sat, gasping for breath, he squinted into the gloom. A fierce, red glow lit a far corner. Blinking the sweat and dirt from his eyes, he saw it was a brazier, its coals throwing heat and a little light into the vast room. Lifting his eyes, he found the ceiling was too high to see. Instead, a black gloom hung where the roof should be. Looking around him now, he saw nothing but shadows. The floor was covered in grease and dirt and the walls that he could see were streaked with grime. Next came the smell. It was an industrial stench, metallic and sharp. Big Tam had been in enough warehouses to know how they smelt. Slowing his breathing, he turned his mind to the question of how he had got here. A strange collection of memories jostled in his head; drinking at The Three Daws, setting out to walk by the river to Ordnance Road, a dog and then? Darkness. Pain. And then he was travelling in a cart. He had come too just once on the journey, he remembered now, but only to vomit his guts up in the sack they had placed back on his head. He had no idea how long the journey had been, nor in which direction. In short, he realised with a flash of despondency, he could be anywhere. Using his free hand, he wiped the sweat from his brow and felt round to the back of his head. His hair was a matt of blood. Feeling beneath the clot, he could discern a split in his skin. The whole area felt tender to the touch and Tam winced in pain. Struggling to focus again, he lowered his hand and noticed a puncture wound on his forearm, just above a vein. That would explain the fog in his brain, he thought, and the parched feeling in his mouth. With a mighty effort, he rocked to his knees. The chain on his arm was long enough to allow him to stand, but not much more. Gripping it tight between both hands, he tugged furiously at the tether. It was fastened good and strong. Bracing a foot against the wall, he levered all his eighteen stones against it. Still, there was no movement. His eyes accustomed to the gloom now, Big Tam looked around for tools. In a corner maybe twenty feet away stood a large pedal lathe, its metal parts reflecting a fiery red from the brazier. On it lay a hammer. In order to escape the chain Tam needed that hammer, but in order to reach the hammer he would have to escape the chain. Even in his befuddled state, Big Tam still found it within him to let out a dry laugh at the dreadful contradiction.

He was brought up sharp by a sound. Some distance away, he could hear doors opening. For a moment, a chink of light filtered under a doorway in the farthest wall. So it was daytime, at least. Crouching low, he sunk into the shadows as best he could, settling his large frame against the wall. His breathing slowed. His hearing alive to every sound, he heard the clink of keys and the releasing of a lock. There was a scratching, scuffling sound at the ground by the door. It swung open, sending funnels of dust whirling before it. Tam cast his eyes feverishly about him, looking for anything that might aid him in his escape. If this was one of the two men who had attacked him last night, he reasoned, he now had the advantage of not having a sack over his head. The door was closed. Footsteps echoed around the empty warehouse as a figure drew nearer. But there was something else. A low, guttural sound. The growling of a dog. As it stepped into the fierce, red light of the brazier, the figure took on a shape that Tam could distinguish. It was wearing a long, loose coat that hung about the ankles and a cowl pulled over its head to confound any attempt at identification. The dog stood obediently at its side, its squashed nose sniffing at the air. Tam recognised it as a bull terrier, a breed with which he was familiar from the many dogfights he had attended. He knew them for a vicious animal and would never have wished to face one in such a position. For a while, the figure stopped, regarding Big Tam in an eerie silence.

"What d'ya want?" Tam rasped, his great Scottish voice echoing off the wall' "You'll kop it when I pull myself free." To demonstrate just how dire a threat that was, Tam pulled at his chain with a roar.

The figure tipped its head to one side in a gesture that caused Tam's heart to race. Terrifyingly, it was a look of amusement. The figure turned under Big Tam's gaze and walked to the brazier, the dog sitting patiently to one side. Its tale was wagging with excitement, its tongue lolling from one side of its mouth. Tam crouched on his haunches, the sweat on his torso glistening in the red light. "What d'ya want from me?" he pleaded.

The hooded figure was at the brazier now, reaching forward with a gloved hand to take hold of a long metal rod resting within. The coals spat and sparked as it was pulled from the blaze. As the figure turned, it held the rod at arm's length. The tip was aglow from the heat of the fire and fashioned into a shape. As it danced in the air before him, Tam could see it was a circular design like a simple face, with slits for eyes and horns protruding from the top. With a lurch, he realised he was to be branded with the sign of the Devil. The panic rose within him and he pulled at the chain again.

"You'll have to get near me first," he spat, swinging his free arm wildly in front of him.

As if in response, the cowled figure reached into the folds of its coat and drew out a heavy cudgel. The dog was on its feet now, salivating wildly. Tam kicked and thrashed in desperation, his eyes wide in an animal fear. The figure was crouching low, weighing the balance of the cudgel and the brand in either hand. In silhouette against the brazier, it shifted its weight on its feet, swaying in anticipation of the right moment. As Big Tam swung again, his free hand bunched into a fist that seemed to whistle through the air, the silhouette seized the moment. Tam was caught off guard and off balance. As his arm swung wide in front of him, it was met with the crack of wood on bone. The cudgel had been slammed down against his forearm. Tam roared at the pain as it travelled up his arm to his shoulder and neck. The dog joined him in his wailing, lifting its head to howl and bark. As he looked down to his shattered forearm, he was met with a kick to his face. Precisely placed, it cracked his teeth. His head snapped back instinctively, and Tam felt his old wound throb as it made contact with the wall behind him. He fell to his knees with a thud that seemed to shake the ground, his breathing laboured. Finally, the cudgel was pushed against his chest and Tam fell back, a heap of shattered bones. His vision was fading and his head felt split with pain. He knew now what must come. His fervent hope was to lose consciousness before the deed was done. The dog was quiet now, almost in anticipation of the inevitable. The tip of the branding iron swung before him; a glowing, disembodied head in the darkness. Then, ominously, it dipped out of view.

He smelt it first. It was a smell he had known before at the farms and charnel houses where he had found employment in his youth. It was the smell of burning, blistering flesh. As the steam rose before his eyes, he suddenly felt the pain. The figure seemed unmoved, uncaring as it busied itself about its work. Even as Tam screamed, it seemed unconcerned whether he would be heard, or if he was heard, whether anyone would care. It was a torture meted out with impunity. The dog threw its head back again, the sound of its howling a grisly chorus to proceedings. As Big Tam fell into a feverish oblivion, his final thought was that he would never be saved, and he would never be missed.

XI

Clutching At Straws

"Anarchists!" Hicks bellowed to anyone who would listen. That the bluff inspector was so forthright in his views was bad enough, thought Bowman. That he was sat in Bowman's favourite chair by the fire was worse. The Silver Cross was busier than he had ever seen it. The booming construction works in the city had seen an influx of labourers who all, much to the landlord's delight, needed feeding and watering. Harris was even offering lodgings in his upstairs rooms, Bowman had heard. The workers were happy enough to share three or four to a room, and Harris was happy enough to take their money. Casting an eye through the smoke to the bar, Bowman could see Harris busy at the pumps, his long, lank hair plastered to his forehead with the sweat of his toil. He had never looked happier. There was barely any room to be had in the small saloon area of the inn. Men were pressed five deep at the bar. Tankards and jugs of beer were passed over heads with practised aplomb. Bowman could see one man already in his cups, the only thing keeping him upright being the crush of men about him. Alarmingly, he seemed to be in the midst of a deep, drunken sleep, supported as he was by his fellow men. Bowman shifted his weight. His legs were feeling stiff from standing so long at the fireplace.

"Anarchists!" chimed Hicks again from Bowman's chair, his pipe clamped between his teeth. Bowman turned to face the bloated detective. "They've become emboldened," Hicks was musing, surrounded by the detritus of his dinner. "Too many European revolutionaries have sought refuge here and we've been daft enough to give it them. They care nothing for the law, or the Empire."

Bowman ignored the remark.

"According to The Standard," Sergeant Graves interjected, his blue eyes shining in his enthusiasm, "It was the Fenians." He pulled a newspaper from his pocket, shaking it flat to hold up in the light. The whole of the front page was given over to the explosion at St. Katharine Docks. Above several columns of typically alarmist newsprint screamed the headline, 'IRISH BOMBS AT LONDON'S HEART'.

Bowman smoothed his moustache with a finger. "The dock master was convinced it was not a bomb at all."

"Not a bomb?" roared Hicks, unaware or unashamed of the beery froth that clung to his moustaches. "We heard the blast from Drury Lane. Anarchists, Bowman, you mark my words."

Bowman raised his voice to be heard over the surrounding mayhem. "I would caution you to wait until you are in full possession of the facts before coming to a judgement."

"Never stopped him before." As Graves raised his beer, a sudden shout came from the bar.

"Put that filth away, will ya?" It was delivered in a broad, Irish accent. The hubbub died away to an uncomfortable silence. "I said, put that filth away before I pitch it into the fire."

The crowd in the saloon parted to reveal a short, wiry man in scruffy clothes. His skin had the appearance of one who leads an outdoor life, and Bowman noticed his hands and fingers were swollen with blisters and calluses. A threadbare kerchief hung at his neck and at least half the buttons were missing from his waistcoat. Most incongruous of all, however, was the wooden peg leg that extended from the man's right knee. Bowman recognised him as the disgruntled workman from Tower Bridge.

Sergeant Graves gulped in sudden realisation that the man was addressing him.

"I was merely reporting the day's news," he explained, gathering the paper from the table as he spoke.

Harris had made his way through the hatch at the bar and stood behind the man, his body tense. With a hand at his shoulder, he attempted to calm the labourer.

"Steady now, O"Brien," he soothed. "These men are from Scotland Yard."

"I couldn't care less if they'd come from Buckingham Palace," O'Brien jeered, shrugging his way from beneath Harris' appeasing hand. "If Victoria herself stood before us there with that filth in her hand, I'd say the same."

The drinkers at his back laughed and clapped at his remarks. Harris threw Bowman an apologetic look.

"We built this Empire with our own hands," continued O'Brien.

"Aye, and I know some who gave their blood for it, too. You'd do well to remember that before you show such a thing to your friends." With a gnarled finger, he pointed at the folded newspaper beneath Graves' arm.

"It'd be just like an Irishman to build a thing then blow it up for spite," shouted a voice from the crowd. There was more laughter at this, and some raised their glasses in agreement. O'Brien turned to face the mob.

"Me and my lads are building you your precious bridge. And who do you think raised old Nelson on his column?" He was having to shout to be heard above the cheering now. "Who laid your roads?"

"Who drunk our whisky?" called the voice again. At this, the room became a roar.

Detective Inspector Hicks rose up from his chair and spread his arms wide. "What of the Underground Railway bombs of Praed Street and Charing Cross?" His booming voice brought the room to a quiet stillness. Bowman rolled his eyes.

"And I suppose Britain is a land of saints?" O'Brien replied, his chin jutting forward in defiance. "With the Commissioner of Scotland Yard as its patron?"

All eyes were on Hicks now. He rubbed his hands together, blinking furiously as he searched for a response. "You can ask him yourself when the Special Irish Branch comes knocking at your door." This brought a smattering of applause.

"I've no fear of Scotland Yard or its detectives," drawled O'Brien, daringly.

"Ireland would be in a better fix with a law keeper or two." Hicks held his lapels in a vain attempt to appear intelligent. He succeeded only in looking pompous.

"Didn't you hear? St. Patrick himself had all Scotland Yarders banished," O'Brien was stamping his wooden leg on the floor to punctuate his words. "Along with all the other snakes!"

The crowd at O'Brien's back took up a chorus of hisses in response, then laughter erupted again. Like the breaking of a squall, the collective mirth cleared the air. Sensing the storm had passed, Harris pushed his way through the crowd back to the bar. With fresh calls for drink, his hands were soon busy at the pumps.

"Inspector Hicks," began Bowman once he sensed all eyes were off them, "I would caution you to have a few more facts at your disposal before you engage in such sport."

"The Evening Standard says it was Fenians. I say it was Anarchists." Hicks leaned forward conspiratorially, as if he was to impart some ancient wisdom for Bowman's ears alone, "Perhaps it was Fenians *and* Anarchists!" With that, Hicks whipped his empty tankard from the table and waddled to the bar.

Bowman sighed. It was unfortunate that the editor of The Evening Standard was seeing fit to whip up a public panic before the facts were known. It was dismaying that a detective inspector from Scotland Yard should be complicit.

"The man's a menace," Bowman growled.

"He is that," agreed Graves. "And he's never knowingly bought a man a drink. Which makes him the worst of men in my book." Graves sported a wide smile that Bowman couldn't help but find disarming.

"What news from Drury Lane?" Taking advantage of Hicks' absence, the inspector was lowering himself into the recently vacated chair by the fire.

"A mauling by a hound, that much is clear." Graves took a slug of his ale. "The wonder is he didn't make himself and his predicament known to the police. Drury Lane is thick with them on account of the pickpockets and cutpurses."

Bowman sighed. It was a sad fact that, even with the advances of recent years, the police were still not trusted by the public at large.

"We're yet to identify the man but there are certain pertinent details which may be of help," continued Graves, hitting his stride. "We are to telegraph all stations and divisions in London to check against missing persons records."

Bowman shook his head. "If such records exist."

"It's a start." Graves flashed his smile again. "Doctor Crane suggests the man might be a boxer. That's bound to narrow the field."

"Then I would concentrate your efforts on the East End, Graves. They have a surfeit of boxing dens; some legal, some less so."

Graves nodded enthusiastically. "Just my thinking too, sir. If they could help with the poor man's fingers it would be a boon."

Bowman held his tankard halfway to his mouth. "His fingers?"

His frown cut into his forehead.

Graves nodded. "There was a yellow powder beneath the poor man's fingernails. Doctor Crane professed it to be a spice. Turmeric, he said it was. How might a man get turmeric beneath his nails?" Graves drank from his glass, clearly at a loss to explain.

Bowman was on his feet now, all action. "If such a man worked at the docks he might." He snatched his hat and coat from the hook by the fireplace and headed for the door.

"How's that, sir?"

Bowman turned. "I was witness today to an event which was presented as an accident. I have my doubts. The man in question had a yellow powder beneath his nails and on his fingertips."

"Might he be connected with my man at Drury Lane?"

"He might well be, Sergeant Graves." Bowman was shrugging on his coat. "But I won't know until I ask him."

"In a hurry, Bowman?" Hicks had returned from the bar, his tankard dripping with a beery foam.

"I must to the docks."

"Ah, security matters?" Hicks threw him a condescending wink.

"More spiritual than material, Inspector Hicks. I am to see The Sisters Of Mercy, and a man they have in their care." With that, Bowman breezed through the door, his hat on his head and his coat buttoned up against the evening chill.

Inspector Hicks turned to Graves, uncomprehending. "Well now, that is a shame," he bluffed. "I was just about to buy the man a drink."

XII

A Night At The Theatre

Sergeant Anthony Graves pulled his coat around him as he stepped from The Silver Cross. He left Inspector Hicks to his beer and his opinions and rounded the corner onto Trafalgar Square and The Strand. Looking up at Nelson on his column, the young sergeant couldn't help but wonder of the things the admiral might see from so lofty a position. Trafalgar Square was busy with people. Children ran and played amongst Landseer's lions, ladies in long dresses promenaded around the fountains, some arm in arm with smart young men in formal coats. Hawkers and sellers displayed their wares at stalls or on trays. Soft, dimpled oranges and rosy apples were offered alongside roasted chestnuts and liquorice root. Match sellers sang out across the square, their rough melodies rising high into the air where Nelson himself stood in judgement. Graves had learned to see through the surface appearance of things. As an insect might skate upon the water of a pond oblivious to the threats that lay beneath, so many people, he thought, lived their lives without the appreciation of the danger just below the surface. There in the corner of the square, a group of ruffians were gathering, their eyes alighting keenly on the rich pickings about them. Purses were carried with abandon, pockets were left agape. A swift hand could cheat the eye and a lady may be robbed in a moment. Looking up towards St. Martin's Church, he saw several drunks spilling into the road, fighting amongst themselves over a bottle of gin.

"You all right, dearie?"

Graves turned to the source of the voice. He was confronted by two women dressed quite inappropriately for the cool air. They were each squeezed into a bodice, one decorated in black brocade, the other in red pleated cotton. Their full skirts were tattered and torn. One wore her hem tucked into a garter revealing an ankle and a calf that, Graves noticed, was capable of turning heads from across the street.

"Spending your night alone, are you?" Graves looked to the woman who had spoken. Her face was heavily made up with an opaque, white powder. A tatty, blonde wig was pulled too low over her forehead and obscured her eyebrows. A row of ramshackle teeth peeped through her painted lips. Her companion hovered at her shoulder, a good few inches shorter and a few years younger. "You could have us both if you could afford it," the taller woman was saying. Graves looked to her more demure companion. She still had her natural beauty, he noticed. Her large eyes looked up at him as she twirled her hair in her fingers. "She's deaf and dumb, dearie," the older woman was grinning, the air whistling through her teeth as she spoke. "So, you can call her what you like and she'll be quiet as a mouse in return. How d'you like the sound o'that?"

At this hour, Graves considered himself officially off duty. He shrugged the women off with a coy smile and continued his progress up The Strand. Around him, the evening light was fading. Lamplighters were about their work, stretching their tapers up to the gas lamps at intervals along the street. The road was a bustle with those leaving their places of employment for the evening and those arriving for their entertainments. The proliferation of gin palaces, coffee houses, hotels and theatres made The Strand and its environs a magnet for those with a mind to be amused.

The pavements had been subject to many recent renovations, but still there were areas that remained little more than damp and muddy walkways. Graves watched as many a lady lifted her fine skirts to prevent them being caked with mud. The road itself was rutted and churned by the passing carts and cabs. Horses kicked up dirt behind them. Graves knew that, even though his intended destination was but a few minutes' walk away, he would be brushing dust from his coat for the rest of the evening.

The Strand once stood as the bank to the Thames itself. Now it provided a tide of its own in the shape of the vagrants and visitors who crowded between its pavements. A deluge of humanity, it swirled in at the shop doorways and hotel concourses. It swept through the alleys and spilled into the yards. And everywhere it went, Graves knew, lay the potential for crime. Pockets were picked as a matter of course, handkerchiefs stolen, shop fronts robbed. Foolish was the storeowner who wasn't alert to such goings on.

Between the road and the river, where large, imposing houses had once fronted the Thames, the Victoria Embankment now held the tides at bay. The great embankments were to ensure London's place as a civilised and prosperous city, though Graves doubted they had achieved much more than pushing the stink of the river some five hundred yards further from the noses of the shoppers and passers by around him.

Great houses sat back from the road, once home to dukes and abbots. They were now occupied by government departments, merchants, shipping offices and grand hotels of which The Savoy was the most recent. At the eastern end, St. Mary le Strand stood sentinel against the hordes of Mammon, its steeple pointing up to a heaven forsaken or ignored by the drunks that sheltered in its doorways.

Amongst the filth, fine gentlemen resplendent in their Astrakhan coats and silk top hats picked their way carefully to the theatres, sweeping the dirt from the road with their canes. Ladies clutched their handkerchiefs to their noses as they navigated the fetid pools and horse dung that littered the thoroughfare. The smells from the chophouses mingled with the aroma of the bad water that lay in intermittent pools along The Strand's length. If ever there was a sharper picture of the divide between those that have the most and those that have the least, then Graves had yet to see it. The streets and shop fronts that provided a diversion to some, were home to others. A man with one arm and a tattered eye patch begged for money by Somerset House, a drunken woman rolled in the road by the newly built Terry's Theatre. Wherever Graves cared to look along the street, he was presented with London life in all its variety.

The sergeant was in an unusually circumspect mood. There was something about the Drury Lane murder that troubled him beyond the condition of the unfortunate man's body. Graves wouldn't consider himself a particularly religious man. Beyond his habitual Sunday attendance at his local church in Stanmore, he considered himself no more pious a man than any he knew. His natural exuberance enabled him to enjoy the singing of hymns and he had even been known to take a turn at the chapel organ if the occasion demanded. Beyond this, however, he paid not much heed to the iconography and tenets of the Christian Church. And yet, he was troubled. Troubled by the detail he had omitted to mention to Inspector Bowman in The Silver Cross. Troubled by the image of the Devil, branded onto the poor man's chest. It was unlikely he had caused the wound himself or come by it as the result of an accident. Sergeant Graves was sure it had been inflicted as a badge of ownership, as a farmer would brand his cattle. The thought that there was, somewhere, someone who would consider humanity in the same light caused a shiver to pass down the young sergeant's spine.

Turning into Catherine Street, he lifted his eyes to The Theatre Royal. The large, square building was surrounded by a crush of people. Some elbowed their way through the crowd, others waited patiently to be allocated their tickets for the evening's performance. Smart broughams discharged their loads onto the pavements; elegant ladies and gentlemen dressed in their finery, eager to see a play and to be *seen* to be seeing a play. Graves had no doubt they would be shown directly to their boxes by the theatre manager himself, there to enjoy a convivial glass or two before the show.

As a particularly well-dressed dowager stepped beneath the ornate portico at the theatre's entrance, Graves noticed a young boy in a floppy felt cap keeping to the shadows, his keen eyes alert for any opportunity. Receiving a cuff to the head from a smart attendant in a red frock coat, the lad moved to the other side of the street to watch proceedings, his grubby hand reaching into his pocket for some tobacco. Turning into Vinegar Yard, the sergeant stepped carefully through the scattered debris on the ground. All sign of the day's activities had been removed now, save a stain of blood on the pavement by the stage door. He had felt sorry for the stage door lass at their earlier meeting in the yard and, his conscience had pricked at not giving her more attention. He wanted to call upon her now to make amends. He was sure she would be at her employment at this, the busiest time of the evening.

As he approached, he saw a gaggle of theatrical types gathered at the doorway. An array of wigs was piled on heads and rouged cheeks shone in the evening light. The gossip was of the body found not three yards from where they stood.

"Gives you the shivers," said a young man in an elaborate frock coat with extended lapels. "At least they moved him before the evening performance."

"There's no one safe," declaimed an ancient actor in a footman's

THE DEVIL IN THE DOCK

costume, his wrinkled nose turning up at the depravity of it all. "To think he died where we stand."

They turned as one to Sergeant Graves as he approached. "I'm looking for Miss Kitty Baldwin," he said with an engaging smile.

The actors looked to one another with raised eyebrows. "I'm sure you are, dear," the elderly footman insinuated.

Graves smiled all the wider, his eyes twinkling in the face of such arch amusement. "Is she at work tonight?"

"She is," the older actor responded, resting on his hip. "As she is every night. She's working out the Kaiser's share, you'll have to wait your turn." Graves was nonplussed at the name.

"Might we know who calls upon her?"

Graves regarded the powdered faces before him as the actors leaned forwards in anticipation of his answer. "Detective Sergeant Graves," he said, breezily. The effect was immediate. The older actor looked in at the stage door, swallowing in his obvious discomfort. Another of them cleared their throat.

"Then, Detective Sergeant Graves," began the younger actor, keen to move the conversation on, "perhaps your time would be better spent catching whomsoever killed the poor man here in Vinegar Yard today, rather than catching the bit of skirt what found him."

The other actors sniggered. Graves thought the young man's opprobrium might have been all the more effective if he hadn't been wearing a full theatrical costume and makeup.

"What's the show tonight?"

"The same as the last twelve weeks," snarled the old footman. "The Prodigal Daughter."

"Then I must make a note to see it," said Graves winningly.

"Make all the notes you want, we close on Saturday." There was another round of sniggers.

"Well," began Graves, "It's been a pleasure to talk to you." As he made his way through the stage door, the young sergeant made a mental note never to seek out the company of actors if he could help it. What he couldn't have seen is that, as he entered the theatre, the small boy with grubby knees and a jaunty felt cap had observed the whole encounter.

Once inside the theatre, Graves was met with a maze of cramped and dingy corridors. The musty air was thick with tobacco smoke

67

and the smell of sweat. The sound of a tuneless piano percolated through the walls. Somewhere, someone laughed. In a corner, a large woman stood sewing an elaborate costume with needle and thread, her face a picture of careful concentration.

As he stood, letting his eyes grow accustomed to the gloom, Graves was suddenly confronted by a tall, angular man who was plainly in a hurry to leave the building. He jostled with the sergeant in his haste, mumbling under his breath. In the short time they stood face to face, Graves couldn't help but notice the man's heavy brow and prominent nose. Graves mumbled an apology and the man was gone as quickly as he had appeared, fumbling with a large, faded carpetbag held under his arm.

Turning to his right, Graves was met by a low counter that gave into a small office. One wall was entirely given over to small compartments holding keys, papers and personal effects that Graves guessed belonged to the actors and theatre workers around him. Gas lamps had been lit and filled the room with an orange-yellow glow. On a stool by the counter sat Kitty. Her wide eyes were bloodshot and her delicate fingers picked nervously at a thread on her dress. Seeing Graves standing at the counter, she rose slowly to her feet, clearly surprised to see him. She wiped her eyes with a delicate handkerchief. "You were at Vinegar Yard this morning," she began. "With the larger gentleman."

"Sergeant Anthony Graves, Kitty," Graves held out his hand. "I was passing by and thought I might call upon you. You seemed understandably distressed at our last meeting."

"I have never seen such a thing before, Sergeant Graves. I was overcome, that is all." She was clearly embarrassed at her earlier demeanour.

"Are you fit to work this evening, Kitty?" Graves was concerned at her downcast expression. She seemed as fragile as a bird.

"It's work what's keeping me sane. I have to work, sergeant. I got rent to pay."

"Then perhaps you'd like some company on your walk home tonight?" The words were out of Graves' mouth before he knew it. His eyes shone with a kindly humour and Kitty was taken with him at once.

"That would be nice." For the first time in their conversation, Graves saw her lift her eyes from her hands. "I will be finished once the first act is done, then you can walk me to Marylebone." Kitty paused, her hands wringing nervously at her handkerchief. "Do you know any more about the man?"

Graves wished he could offer her more comfort. "We don't Kitty, but it's early days." She cast her eyes down again. "There are some marks about the body that may prove useful. We are in the processes of establishing an identity. That would be of great help in our investigations."

"Then it is not even known who he is?" She blinked at her inadvertent use of the present tense.

"Not yet, no."

"Poor man." In that moment, Kitty looked more delicate than anyone Graves had ever seen.

"Tell me of the show," he beamed, intent on lightening the conversation. Kitty looked up again.

"Oh, it's a silly thing. Not a patch on the pantomime." She opened her eyes wide. "Would you like to see it? Or the first half at least, before I leave?"

Graves was intrigued enough to acquiesce. "How would I get a ticket?"

"Oh, ticket be blowed. I'll show you through." With that, Kitty threw a shutter down over her counter and grabbed a key from the table. Locking the door behind her, she called to the actors at the stage door. "Nathaniel, Thomas, you've got five minutes. I'm taking this gentleman through front of house so you're on your own."

"I've never been known to miss an entrance," purred the older actor in the footman's costume.

"He's right," volunteered another. "It's getting him off again that's the problem!"

"Come with me." Kitty beckoned the young sergeant to follow her as she set off through the maze of passages towards the stage.

As they walked, Graves was struck by how dark and dingy the corridors were. Faded playbills had been pasted to the wall. Where they had flaked away, they lay in drifts on the floor exposing crumbling brickwork and peeling paint. The floor itself was uneven and, in some places, slippery with a skein of water. Gas jets were placed at intervals along the wall, their yellow light lending an eerie glow to their journey.

Passing down some steep, narrow steps, Kitty turned to her guest. "We're going under the stage," she explained. "This passage will lead us back up the other side to the pass door."

As they passed through the subterranean corridor, Graves saw dressing rooms to his left and right. The first was home to a gaggle of actresses in wide skirts and even wider wigs. One was at her mirror applying thick daubs of makeup. Another lay upon on a low day bed, smoking a long cheroot.

"Five minutes, ladies," Kitty chimed as they passed. Graves noticed large, wooden flats leaning against the wall, painted with pastoral views and townscapes, pots of paint lined up carefully beside them. A knot of stagehands hung about at a corner, one stripped to the waist in anticipation of the evening's work. At last they ascended another flight of stone steps, twisting back upon themselves as they climbed. And then Graves heard it. A faint murmur at first but, as a door was opened to the side of stage, it grew to a roar. An impatient audience were in their seats. Immediately before him, Graves was presented with huge painted flats, stretching twenty feet up beyond the top of the proscenium arch. It was clear the first scene was to occur in the parlour of a large country house. The glassless windows gave out to a painted backdrop of a formal garden rendered so exquisitely, Graves almost thought he could smell the flowers. Heavy drapes hung either side of the windows, tied back with elaborate sashes. A loveseat stood centre stage, upholstered in plush, red velvet. Bookcases and ornate tables were placed carefully for effect. Graves noticed a roll top secretary desk was primed with paper and quill, the use of which would, no doubt, result in hilarious consequences. All in all, the effect was to present the perfect stage upon which a comedy of manners might be performed. Looking up, Graves could see the scenery was suspended by a series of ropes and weights to a network of gantries high up in the roof. There he saw other huge flats waiting in their place to be lowered, one featuring a cliff edge and seascape, the other, improbably, a man on a throne suspended in the clouds by a flock of swans.

"The fly tower," said Kitty as she noticed Graves' awed expression in the gloom. "One of the highest in London."

Burly men lounged against a lattice of ropes that hung to the side of the stage. Graves guessed they were awaiting a cue to haul the next flat down from its position in the fly tower. They regarded him with expressions of sublime disinterest. Looking out to the front of stage, Graves saw heavy curtains pulled across the proscenium. Two actors stood to one side, their heads inclined towards each other in gossip. There was a sense of anticipation in the air. And all the while, beyond the curtain, the audience were taking their seats. Peels of laughter rang out occasionally and the odd scream punctuated the general melee. Graves felt caught in a moment of potential, the air full of a strange, crackling energy.

"After you." Kitty was holding open a door set in the side of the proscenium arch. Stepping through, the sergeant was suddenly in another world. This was a world of light, colour and opulent comfort, quite remote from the dark and gloomy underworld he had just passed through. The corridor before him was carpeted in a rich, red Worcester. The walls were papered in a luxurious flock. A brass handrail stretched the whole length of the corridor, above which were affixed play bills and faded daguerreotypes of esteemed and august actors. Names of previous productions sang out from framed programmes, including those of The Theatre Royal's famous pantomimes; Dick Whittington, Jack And The Beanstalk and Robinson Crusoe.

Kitty was pulling a curtain across the opening to an alcove. "Here you go, Sergeant Graves, you can watch it all from here."

Sergeant Graves stepped into the box and looked around him. It was furnished with four exquisite side chairs, each with a tasselled cushion on their seats. Gas lamps burned at the wall, illuminating portraits of Queen Victoria in the guise of the three muses. Her Majesty was known to be a keen supporter of the theatre and indeed was patron to many. The box hung out into the auditorium above the stalls. Moving to a chair, Graves looked out over the unruly audience. He hovered above a sea of heads, all bobbing animatedly before him. The noise was a roar now. Graves could see a woman being escorted from the theatre by attendants. She was plainly drunk, swinging her hat about her head and singing loudly at the top of her voice. Looking back, Graves could see a well-dressed man with his head in his hands, now sat next to an empty seat. Elsewhere, another man lay across the laps of three of his companions. Looking up, Graves beheld the ceiling. An impressive chandelier was set into a richly decorated ellipse edged in gold. It gave the impression of a large eye staring down from the heavens. The murmur that the sergeant had heard backstage was now a raucous and unbridled roar, and he wondered that a play would be able to quieten the crowd at all. His concern was addressed, quite suddenly, by the striking up of a band from the pit beneath the stage. The audience took to their seats and diverted their attention to the curtain. Slowly but perceptibly, the hubbub subsided. Sitting in anticipation, Graves noticed that the lights were dimming. A single, wide spotlight lit the curtain until, with a great crescendo from the band, it faded and the curtain rose with a cheer.

XIII

Visiting Hours

Inspector Bowman couldn't deny he felt a subtle thrill at the prospect of his inquiries. He had felt redundant at St. Saviour's Dock until the explosion across the river. Now, he was in the throes of an investigation once more, he couldn't but admit it made him feel vindicated. More than that, it made him feel useful. He had learned the lesson of his previous encounter on Willow Walk and had, this time, caught a hansom cab from Whitehall.

The Sisters Of Mercy Convent was an overtly monastic building. Its high forbidding walls loomed over the road in the dark, its crenellations and spires pointing the way to heaven to any in the area who were disposed to look up. It was only fifty years since the foundation stone had been laid, but it had the appearance of a medieval building; all tapered arches, mullioned windows and buttressed walls. It stood opposite a tannery, one of several within a small radius, that belched steam and smoke into the sky at every time of day or night. The pungent smell of damp leather hung in the air.

As the hansom rattled to a halt, Bowman was surprised to see a familiar figure striding down Parker's Row towards him. In her long matron's dress and mob cap, the inspector recognised Alma Beaurepaire at once.

"Hey, George!" she called as Bowman paid the driver. "Couldn't keep away, huh?"

Bowman blushed as the coachman threw him a knowing smile.

"What're you doing back in Bermondsey?"

"I am come to see the man who was injured at St. Saviour's," Bowman began by way of explanation. He was reluctant to say too much. "You said they would bring him here." The driver cracked his whip and the hansom clattered away towards the river and Shad Thames.

"Then you're in luck," Alma grinned "That's just where I was going, too."

Bowman tried to hide his consternation. Perhaps it was as well to have a representative of the local police at his side during questioning, but he couldn't help but think Miss Beaurepaire might hamper his investigations.

The door was opened by a tiny woman in nun's vestments. Her face was as smooth as a shiny pebble and her eyes gleamed behind little, round spectacles. She listened intently as Bowman made his introductions and gave his reason for visiting at such an unsociable hour.

"There was a man brought here earlier from the dock," he began.

"Jonas Cook, Sister Vincent," Alma interjected. "He was brought here from St. Saviour's." Alma was plainly known here. Perhaps Cook wasn't the first man from St. Saviour's to have required the sisters" ministrations.

"Ah yes," Sister Vincent replied. "The poor man and his leg." She spoke with a soft Irish lilt and tutted as she led them deeper into the convent. "He is in our infirmary, but there's not much we can give him beyond rest and prayer. We have cleaned his wound as best we can and given the poor man opium. We will see in the morning if he will keep his leg."

Bowman's frown cut deep into his forehead at the news. "You mean he may lose it?"

The sister stopped mid-step and turned to the inspector. "If it turns bad, it'll have to come off." The sister affected a tone more suited to reassuring a child. "With God's blessing it will not be so."

As she turned to continue their journey, Bowman glanced at his companion. Alma Beaurepaire had an easy confidence about her that Bowman envied. Perhaps that came from her early life in the colonies, he mused. At any rate, she seemed well able to take any circumstance in her stride. She had been impressive on the dockside that afternoon, taking control of the situation with élan, and now she appeared equally at home in a house of God. Her eyes were downcast in an attitude of respect as she walked, cap in hand, through the dimly-lit passageways of the convent. Their footsteps echoed off the narrow walls around them and once or twice, the two visitors had to duck to pass through a doorway.

"The sisters came here from Ireland," Sister Vincent announced. "Our mission is to help the poor and the sick. We find enough of both in Bermondsey to keep us busy, as you might imagine." Bowman nodded sagely in response. "Several of our sisters gave assistance to Florence Nightingale at Scutari." It was clear that

Sister Vincent was glad of the company. "But I feel there is a war to be fought here, inspector, on the streets of Bermondsey."

Bowman couldn't help but agree. As the Empire stretched its arms around the world, so its eyes often missed what was happening here at home.

"He's in no trouble is he?" The little group had stopped before another low door and the sister regarded Bowman through her spectacles with beady eyes. "We minister to all who need it, Inspector Bowman, but if the man's a criminal - "

"Jonas is in no trouble," Alma interjected. "And he's no criminal for ought I know."

"I am simply investigating the circumstances of his accident, that is all," added Bowman, choosing his words carefully.

"And it takes a detective from Scotland Yard to do that, does it?"

Bowman swallowed. He couldn't let Alma know he was investigating other matters. For all she knew, he had been posted to St. Saviour's Dock on a matter of security. He would prefer it if she was kept still in that mind.

"I happened to be at the scene of the accident this afternoon."

"Hmm," the sister's eyes narrowed. "How fortuitous." Sister Vincent turned to open the heavy, wooden door before her. "He's in here, inspector. I'm not sure how much sense you'll get from him."

The first thing Bowman noticed was the smell; a pungent mix of wet, sweaty sheets and festering wounds. Someone was coughing; a painful rattling rasp. Six beds were arranged along the longest wall, each occupied by a patient. As Bowman looked along the line of patients, he saw some were plainly in worse health than others. An elderly lady lay completely still, mouthing silent words to the ceiling. Next to her, a small boy was curled up on his bed counting his fingers. Excepting the wooden crucifixes that hung above each bed, the walls were bare. Candles burning at two windows offered the only light so the room was engulfed in a stultifying gloom. Sister Vincent led them to the farthest corner, to a young man sat staring balefully at the wall opposite. His pale skin was pricked with sweat. He was evidently fighting hard to keep his eyes from closing. Periodically, he would give an inadvertent shudder, then wince with pain. The lower half of his sheet was stained with blood. As each spasm passed, he would cast his eyes up to the crucifix on the wall and offer a prayer of thanks.

"He's a pious man," beamed Sister Vincent proudly. "The Lord will be kind to him."

"This man is in a lot of pain," Bowman remarked, plainly.

"Jonas," Sister Vincent was cooing. "Jonas, there's a gentleman here to see you. From Scotland Yard, no less."

Bowman felt the atmosphere change in the room. Suddenly, all eyes were upon him. The man in the bed next to Cook spat a lozenge of phlegm to the floor then wiped his mouth on the back of his hand. The young lad near the furthest window sat bolt upright in his bed, curious to see just what a Scotland Yard detective might look like. Evidently disappointed with the tall, slender figure with the careworn face and neat moustache, he sunk back into his pillow with a sigh.

"Jonas, how are you?" Alma bent low over the bed, scanning Cook's eyes for signs of comprehension.

"I'll leave you to your investigations," Sister Vincent purred. "But don't tax him beyond his capabilities." She patted Cook on the hand, crossed herself, then walked the length of the room to the door, distributing beatific smiles to the afflicted.

"Jonas, this is Inspector Bowman," Alma continued. Bowman's moustache twitched as he felt the man in the next bed glaring at him. "He wants to ask you some questions."

Cook's response came by way of a scream. His eyes swivelled in his head and he clutched at the sheet with his shaking hands.

"It's all right, Jonas," Alma soothed, lifting a stray strand of hair from her eyes, "He's here to help." Reaching down to a basin, she rinsed a cloth in some water and applied it to the man's forehead.

"Jonas," Bowman began awkwardly. "Can you tell me what happened this afternoon?"

Cook took great gulps of air to try and settle his breathing. His words, when they came, were faint and halting.

"I fell," he gulped. "The cart. It ran into me."

"Was the cart not pushed?" Bowman inquired, softly.

"It was but an accident." Cook winced again as a spasm passed through his leg. He lifted it from the bed with a pained expression, grasping the bed frame until the agony subsided. Bowman caught sight of the dressing now and saw that blood had seeped through from the wound, sticking to the sheet where it touched.

"But the ground is level there, how could it roll?"

Cook was silent, breathing through gritted teeth in short, sharp gasps. "It was God's will."

Bowman shook his head in disbelief. "That you should be harmed?"

"He said it was an accident," Alma was saying. "Perhaps it is best not to press him."

Bowman peered closely at the man's hands. They had clearly been bathed by the sisters but, even in the dim light, he could see the man's nails were stained a yellow colour.

"What do you do at the docks, Jonas?" Bowman leaned in closer that he might hear the man's response.

"I work when I can," he whispered, gesturing to his dry lips with a trembling hand. Alma rinsed the cloth again and put it to his mouth. He nodded in thanks, then continued. "Twice a day I join the line, most days I work. I know the men at Corder's Wharf. They know I work hard."

"How long have you worked at St. Saviour's?" Bowman was keeping his voice low.

"Since I was a nipper. It's all I know." Cook gave an involuntary shudder.

"And what do they take in at Corder's Wharf?"

"Tea and spices," Cook coughed. "Lately Turmeric from India. Raises quite a stink."

Bowman nodded. He could tell from Cook's face that he was struggling to remain conscious. The inspector didn't have long.

"Jonas," he began, moving closer to the patient. "Who would want to see you hurt?"

Cook swallowed hard, shaking his head. "No one hurt me, it was an accident."

"I don't believe it was, Jonas. I find it difficult to explain the events that led to your injury without ascribing it to a human agency."

"Don't push him, George," Alma cautioned, placing a hand at the poor man's forehead. "He's hot as burning coals."

Bowman pressed him again. "I saw a man at St. Saviour's. A tall, thin man with a clouded eye."

Cook shook his head.

"Sounds like Sallow," offered Alma, a puzzled expression on her face. "Ichabod Sallow."

"Would Ichabod Sallow want to see you hurt, Jonas?"

"No. Why would he?"

"You tell me." Bowman's heart quickened as he awaited Cook's response. He could see hesitation in the man's eyes. He licked his lips, bending low to deliver the question he had been building to. "Jonas, is Ichabod Sallow the Kaiser?"

The effect in the room was immediate. Bowman felt the air thicken with a heavy silence. Alma snapped her head round, her expression inscrutable.

"You're pushing too hard, inspector," she snapped. There was an edge to her voice Bowman hadn't heard before.

"Sister!" The man in the next bed had propped himself up on his elbows. "Sister!" he called again. The boy at the end of the row had thrown his covers over his head. Were these people scared?

"Who is the Kaiser?" Bowman demanded of the room.

"Inspector Bowman," Alma had rounded on him now, her eyes burning. "Will you leave these poor people alone? If this is how you do things at Scotland Yard, it's no wonder you're held in such contempt."

The words stung. Bowman blinked, lost for a response. He appealed directly to Cook. "Jonas, I don't believe you came by your injury through accidental means. I believe you were harmed by Ichabod Sallow. Why?"

"What evidence do you have?" Alma asked, boldly.

Bowman paused. He could see Cook was locked in a struggle to stay conscious. A moment more and he would sink into his own personal oblivion. As he opened his mouth to push the matter further, Bowman was interrupted by Sister Vincent at his elbow.

"Inspector Bowman, would you have the decency to leave us all in peace and vacate this place?" Her soft round features had hardened.

Bowman leaned his hands on Cook's bed, desperate to get some sort of answer before the man slipped into unconsciousness.

"Who is the Kaiser?" he hissed. "Why are the people here in thrall to him?"

"Get this man out!" The man in the next bed was visibly angry at Bowman's intrusion and pointed to him with a trembling, bony finger. "He's filth."

Sister Vincent had him by the sleeve now and was dragging him forcibly from the room. "This is a place of God, inspector," she was saying. "And a place of rest. The corporal works of mercy bid us welcome strangers but you have overstayed your welcome, sir."

The sister bundled Bowman back down the passage by which they had entered. Turning one last time, the inspector saw Alma Beaurepaire standing in the door to the infirmary, her arms crossed, her look severe.

"I would thank you to complete your investigations elsewhere, inspector. You had no business to bring distress to my patients."

Bowman straightened his coat about him. "May I come again tomorrow?" he asked.

"You may not," the sister blustered, closing the heavy, wooden door behind her. Bowman stood alone on the grand porch to the convent, gnawing at his lip, deep in thought. With a sigh, he turned into the night and contemplated how best to effect a safe journey home.

Pulling his collar up and his hat down, he stepped back onto Parker's Row. He'd taken just a few steps when he noticed a smart, black brougham carriage waiting at the junction with Oxley Street. Slowing his step, Bowman looked around for any signs of trouble. The street appeared deserted. As he neared the brougham, he could see the driver perched on top. He was glaring directly at him. He was a severe looking man with a long, equine face that seemed quite in keeping with his employment. As Bowman stopped, the coachman lifted his hand and beckoned that Bowman might step nearer. The inspector hesitated. Somewhere, a dog barked. As Bowman was musing on how best to proceed, he became aware of movement behind him. Turning on his heels, he saw three burly men approaching from beyond the convent, blocking any chance of retreat. Bowman recognised them from their encounter on Willow Walk. He wondered that the man with the white eye, that he now knew to be one Ichabod Sallow, wasn't with them. As he turned back to the brougham, he saw that its door had swung open. The coachman was gesturing to it with his outstretched hand. Without a word being said, Bowman was given to understand that he was expected to climb on board. Trying to escape would be futile, he knew. He didn't know these streets at all and guessed the residents wouldn't be particularly sympathetic to a Scotland

Yarder. If his reception in the convent was any indication, Bowman and his type were regarded with contempt at the very least. As he stepped closer to the carriage, all the while keeping the three men in his sight, Bowman was reminded of Miss Beaurepaire's comment upon their first meeting. This did indeed feel like a lawless town. The Outback had come to Bermondsey.

As he stepped aboard the brougham and settled back into his seat, Inspector Bowman felt an arm reach across him to close the door. The figure tapped on the roof with his cane and, with a jerk, the carriage moved into the road. Turning to face him, Cornelius Bracewell tilted his head in greeting.

XIV

Presumed Missing

Detective Sergeant Anthony Graves had no clue what was going on. In the previous hour and a half, he had watched from his vantage as a succession of bizarre characters had paraded before him, declaiming to the galleries and falling over one another in a series of heavily rehearsed and highly improbable pratfalls and high jinks. The plot, as far as Graves could understand it, hinged on a young girl determined to marry below her station and against the wishes of her widowed father. Multiple scenes were played wherein the young man in question was hidden in cupboards and beneath furniture and even, for one particularly excruciating episode, disguised as a woman to escape the ire of his prospective father-in-law. All this, Graves noted, was greeted with hoots of laughter from the audience, in particular those who sat directly beneath him in the stalls. As the curtain fell for the interval, there was much wiping of eyes and shaking of heads amongst them and, as they headed to the various bars for their interval drinks, much re-enacting of favourite scenes from the play. The young sergeant sat for a while in the box, nonplussed. He would, he thought as he scratched his head, have been much happier with an evening at The Silver Cross. The entertainment there seemed more honest somehow, and certainly less contrived. Resolving to walk Kitty to his favourite inn at once and there spend the rest of the evening in her company if she'd let him, Graves swung his legs from the chair and ducked through the curtain to the passage outside. Unsure of the route back through the stage, he turned into the throng and headed for the foyer, his intention being to make his way out the building and round to the stage door in Vinegar Yard.

The going was slow. It seemed the world and his wife had come to see The Prodigal Daughter, and now they were in need of a drink. As he made his way downstairs to the theatre entrance, Graves saw the more genteel members of the audience were gathering in the better class of bar. Gentlemen in top hats and frock coats drank champagne and chattered with ladies in their wide dresses and tiaras. The further downstairs he went, so the noisier the bars became. The stalls bar, which stood at the theatre entrance, was crammed with a crowd already half drunk. No wonder, mused Graves, they were enjoying the play so much. Youths in their caps and waistcoats drank to impress the women in their company. Wiser, older men watched from the bar as their younger comrades squabbled and competed for attention. Calls for more beer echoed into the street and hawkers and traders took their chances with their trays of oranges and pies. Tankards of ale and colourful, sweet confections were passed back and forth over heads as the crowd swayed, as one, back and forth. It was all Graves could do to keep moving. More than once he trod on people's toes in his efforts to reach the doors.

In the street at last, he was glad to feel the cool air on his face. The shops around Russell Street had closed their shutters for the night, but now there was a free for all. Barrows of fruit, bread and roasted chestnuts assailed the nostrils of passers by, their attendants singing loud to promote their wares. Graves shouldered his way through the crowd and turned into Catherine Street. As he rounded the corner, his gaze was drawn to a young lad in a large, felt hat leaning against a doorway. His tousled hair hung into his eyes as he regarded the sergeant with a smirk. Graves remembered seeing him at Vinegar Yard that afternoon. This was clearly the boy's patch, he thought and he felt a pang of sympathy at his plight. The urchins that Graves had met in the course of his duties had always seemed happy enough, but he knew they led lives of severe deprivation and misfortune, often prey to older men with few scruples.

Graves picked his way carefully up the alley. At this hour, it was already home to several vagrants. Three or four had lit a fire at the furthest end and they huddled round for warmth as they drank their gin, swearing and spitting amongst themselves. They paid no heed as the detective sergeant made his way to the stage door, carefully avoiding the fresh piles of excrement at his feet. The smell was almost intolerable; the stink of ordure and urine. Half way along, he almost stumbled over a prone body on the ground, its arms spread out at an awkward angle across the alley. Bending to confirm the poor soul was still alive, Graves lifted the wretch by the coat collars and propped him up against the wall, placing his half-empty bottle beside him. The stench of vomit rose from him and Graves had to hold his breath. The poor man's clothes were stained and greasy, his hair and skin caked with the filth of the alley. He mumbled something then sank back into his stupor, his head rolling onto his chest. Graves wondered how Kitty coped with such sights every day.

Stopping at the stage door, Graves peered round the corner, expecting to see the young lass pulling down the shutter at the end of her evening's work. The shutter was still up. He stepped inside, gingerly, knocking at the open door for attention. Nothing. Confused, Graves headed down the corridor to the under stage. He was stopped on his way by the large lady he had seen sewing in the passage. She carried a large basket of costumes that Graves recognised from the first half of the play.

"I'm looking for Kitty," the sergeant said. "She said to meet her at the stage door at the interval."

"Oh, I think she's long gone, dear," said the woman, barging through with her basket. "I dare say you got here too late."

"Where do you think she's gone?" Graves' blue eyes blinked in bewilderment.

"Home, I expect." The woman threw the basket onto her shoulder as she retreated into the wardrobe rooms. "If she's got any sense."

Forlorn, Graves made his way back down Vinegar Yard. Why had Kitty not waited? She had said she would look forward to having Graves' company. Perhaps she had changed her mind. Shrugging at this strange turn of events, he emerged back onto Catherine Street. There, still standing in the doorway opposite, was the young boy in the floppy, felt hat. Just as Graves was about to cross the road and talk to the lad, he gave the sergeant a toothy grin and a knowing wink. Graves stopped. What did he mean by that? Did he know something? Graves opened his mouth to ask, but, before he could engage him in conversation, the boy pulled his hat down over his forehead and ran off into the evening crowds, his eyes alert for easy pickings.

XV

A Rendez-Vous

Cornelius Bracewell had remained silent for the whole journey. His narrow eyes regarded Bowman closely as the smart brougham careened through the streets of Rotherhithe and Deptford. Resting his hand upon his cane, he had the appearance of one out for a Sunday drive. Bowman noticed that he was dressed formally beneath his coat, in a wing collared shirt and white bow tie.

Street after street rattled past the windows, often separated by vast tracts of marsh and wasteland. Bowman knew, however ghastly these vistas were, they were still home to some. Occasionally he would see a vagrant or two wandering beside the road, plainly drunk, their eyes wild. Once, the carriage swerved to avoid the body of a woman in the road. Whether she was alive or dead was not clear, and Bowman could see the driver had no inclination to stop and find out.

Bowman had no wish to engage his companion in conversation. He was uneasy at the means of his abduction. How long had he been watched? For watched he must have been if they knew where to find him. Where exactly was he going? He felt in no immediate danger now and guessed he was being taken to a rendez-vous, but with whom? The crease of a frown deepened on his forehead as he contemplated his situation. Bracewell was surely armed, he reasoned, rendering any attempt at escape quite futile. Besides, Bowman didn't know these streets. If he had managed to escape the carriage and run, they would surely find him. He resolved to sit and wait.

After twenty minutes or so, Bowman felt the carriage begin to slow. Looking out into the darkness, he was conscious of a lack of houses. An open space lay before them, and Bowman guessed they were passing one of the great Royal Parks. Considering they were still south of the River Thames and had been heading east, the inspector hazarded a guess that it was Greenwich Park. It was not an area he knew well, but he could swear the air felt cleaner here. Soon, they were passing smart villas with trim cupolas sat proudly on top. Large, imposing buildings were set back from the road, the street lamps lending an opalescent pallor to the white Portland stone. The streets were busier now. Boys and girls of indeterminate ages stood in doorways, inviting strangers to join them in their rented rooms. Gangs of youths spilled onto the street. Here and there, pot-houses were marked by the presence of two or three lads sitting on their steps, staring insensibly into space.

The carriage turned off the main road. Bowman saw they were passing down the side of the Royal Hospital School towards the Thames. Even by night, the masts and rigging of several boats could be seen swaying in the breeze on the river, lamps burning on their masts like stars in the sky.

They stopped before an impressive, red-brick building with solid, white pillars. An elaborate cupola framed the large, wooden doors at the entrance. As more carriages unburdened themselves at the roadside, Bowman watched as liveried doormen welcomed their occupants with a curt nod. A brass plaque beside the door proclaimed the place to be The Trafalgar Club.

The door to the carriage snapped open, and an efficient looking doorman wished Bowman a good evening. Standing to one side, he gestured that the inspector should alight and make his way into the building. Looking to his left, Bowman saw Bracewell nodding slowly. All the while, he kept one hand ominously beneath the folds of his coat. The threat was implicit. Slowly, Bowman lowered himself from the brougham and crossed the path to the grand entrance. Bracewell was at his side at once, limping slightly as they made their way through the doors.

"Do not distress yourself, Inspector Bowman," he purred. "There is none here that wish you harm." His ruddy face shone in the lamplight. Bowman swallowed hard and fought the urge to resist.

The reception room to the Trafalgar Club was an opulent affair. The marble floor was inlaid with the club's motto in an antique font; A Mari Usque Ad Mare, From Sea To Sea. A representation of a ship that Bowman recognised as HMS Victory lay at the centre of the design, its sails billowing in the wind. The high, panelled walls were adorned with large oil paintings of seascapes and famous ships, some presented in calm seas or storms, others in the heat of battle, their guns blazing. They were displayed in lavish frames featuring carved motifs of warfare; muskets and rifles, swords and cannon. Great gilded pots held ferns and fronds that reached halfway to the ceiling. Here and there, rich ornaments were displayed in cabinets. Stuffed animals from far-off climes were mounted under glass for curious eyes to inspect, their claws pinned to rock or branch before vistas of distant lands. Bowman recognised marmosets and lemurs, birds of paradise and reptiles among so many more strange beasts. Great map books were opened upon tables with instruments of navigation laid upon them. There was a gentle hum of convivial conversation and, from one of the two corridors that led from the foyer, the clink of cutlery on china. A large reception desk stood at the foot of a sweeping staircase, manned by a wiry man with bushy eyebrows and a disdainful manner. Bracewell approached the desk, his cane tapping against the marble floor.

"Good evening, sir," sneered the concierge, barely concealing his contempt. "How may I be of assistance?"

"We are here for dinner," replied Bracewell curtly. Bowman raised his eyebrows in surprise. "We are to join Chief Inspector Callaghan at his table."

Inspector Bowman reeled at the news. That they were to meet a member of the Metropolitan Police Force after such a journey seemed scarcely credible. He hadn't heard of Callaghan, but then the ranks of The Force were far too large for any one man to have an intimate knowledge. Looking at Bracewell with fresh eyes, he wondered just how trustworthy a dinner companion he would be. Suddenly roused from his thoughts, Bowman realised he was under scrutiny. The man behind the desk was regarding him with a withering stare.

"Your... overcoat, sir," he searched for the word as if the garment were beyond description. "May I hang it in the cloakroom?"

It was clear Bowman had no choice. As he shook off his coat, the concierge returned from a large cupboard beneath the stairs. He held a smart frock coat before him, and bade the inspector put it on.

"Club rules, sir," he smirked.

Bowman felt all the more uncomfortable in his oversized frock coat as he was led with Bracewell to the dining room. It was a large hall with a high ceiling studded with candelabra and frescos of seascapes. Twenty or so round tables were laid for dinner and a good many of them were occupied. Each was covered with a pristine, white cotton tablecloth on which stood cut crystal glasses, fine bone china plates and silver cutlery. Carafes of wine and decanters of brandy stood sparkling in the lamplight. All around them as they walked, Bowman heard whispers of polite conversation. It was only after a few moments that he realised all the dinner guests were male. Each was dressed in formal dinner suit and tie so that, despite the addition of his smart frock coat, the inspector felt himself distinctly underdressed. Older gentlemen peered at him through their spectacles and monocles while their younger companions smoothed their hair in the large mirrors that hung around the room.

The concierge led them to a table by the fire. A lone man sat at his dinner, a napkin tucked into the collar of his shirt as he sipped from a bowl of soup. He had a fine head of hair for a man his age, fashionably styled with pomade. A pair of impressive mutton chop sideburns graced his cheeks and when he looked up, he did so with a pair of steely, grey eyes.

"Your dinner guests, sir," the concierge announced, giving a sharp bow whilst maintaining the impression that such a thing was below him.

"Thank you, Jenks," replied Callaghan in a crisp voice, dabbing at the corners of his mouth with a napkin. "Gentlemen, please take a seat."

The concierge deigned to pull out their chairs and the two men sat, each facing Callaghan across the round table. Places had already been laid before them. Before they had even had the chance to pull themselves to the table, an efficient sommelier was topping up their glasses with claret.

"I must apologise for the nature of your journey, Inspector Bowman," Callaghan said through a half smile.

"It is not the nature of the journey to which I object," snarled Bowman, quietly seething at the guile of the man. "But the nature of my abduction at its start."

Callaghan took a sip of his wine. "Despite appearances, inspector," he began, "I am a busy man. This evening marked the only opportunity to meet with you. Mr Bracewell was kind enough to attend to the details, for which I apologise."

Looking to his companion, Bowman could see Bracewell

seemed not in the least apologetic for his actions, but rather sat grinning in his seat, his napkin already tucked over his collar in anticipation of his dinner.

"I had not thought to end the evening in conversation with a Chief Inspector of police," Bowman drawled. "Or perhaps I would have dressed more appropriately."

"No matter," Callaghan waved his hand. "It is understood you are my guest." As he spoke, Bowman and Bracewell were each presented with a bowl of brown soup. Bracewell smacked his lips, picked up his spoon and slurped noisily as he ate. Bowman raised an eyebrow.

"Will you not eat, Inspector Bowman?"

"I'm not hungry," Bowman snapped. All around him, fine gentlemen were continuing with their evening, raising glasses to toast a venture with their colleagues or sitting alone to enjoy a peaceful meal. Sporadic peels of laughter rang out from a large table in the corner, echoing around the room and causing much turning of heads. They were clearly in the midst of some celebration, as there was a regular clinking of glasses and the occasional, short oration from the older members of the company. Bowman turned his attention to the suave man in the chair opposite. There was not a hair out of place on his head. His face, though lined about the eyes, was smooth and youthful looking. His bow tie was knotted expertly around a starched collar, his waistcoat discretely fashionable. As the chief inspector placed his napkin delicately on the table, he lifted his eyes to meet Bowman's gaze.

"Perhaps I should explain." Callaghan shifted back in his seat. He looked, thought Bowman, perfectly at ease in these rarefied surroundings. "Inspector Bowman, I must ask you to cease your enquiries at St. Katharine Docks."

There was a pause.

"What do you know of my enquiries?" asked Bowman, carefully.

"I know that you are jeopardising years of intelligence gathering and diligent investigation on behalf of my colleagues at the Special Irish Branch."

Bracewell slurped on his soup, clearly unconcerned at the revelation.

"Why is Special Irish Branch at St. Katharine Docks?" Bowman was leaning forward on his elbows, his voice low.

"There is no need to be so clandestine, inspector," Callaghan chuckled. "The Trafalgar Club is the very epitome of discretion."

Bowman looked around at his fellow diners. Some sat barely ten feet away and could easily have overheard the conversation if they wished. He cleared his throat.

"What is your interest at the dock?" he repeated.

"We have seen an increase in Fenian activity. Their desire to see an Ireland free from British interference is driving them to ever more desperate means, and violent."

"The bomb?" offered Bowman.

"Just the latest stage in their campaign," said Callaghan. "We believe there is a Fenian cell operating from St. Saviour's Dock. We have planted an asset among them that must not be disturbed or exposed."

Bowman sneered at the chief inspector's choice of words. He assumed Callaghan meant there was an undercover agent at work. One who could gain the trust of the group, act like them, perhaps think like them but, ultimately, betray them. Bowman had had experience of such men before. Indeed, Detective Inspector Treacher had proven invaluable during the affair with the head in the ice. Bowman's thoughts turned to those he had met at the docks. Was Bracewell Callaghan's informer? Looking at him now, he doubted it. There was nothing subtle about the man, and Callaghan had given no indication that he was in any way in cahoots. Constable Thackery he had only met briefly, so he was very much an unknown quantity. If Jonas Cook was Callaghan's man, laid up as he was with The Sisters Of Mercy, then the game was up. One other came to Bowman's mind. He had clearly made himself a part of the community around the dock, even a feared one. He would be well-placed to infiltrate a Fenian cell. Bowman was sure they would welcome a tall, rangy man with a clouded eye and a belligerent personality to their ranks.

"Ichabod Sallow is our man, Inspector Bowman," Callaghan confirmed. "Operating within our remit."

And perhaps outside of it, mused Bowman, his thoughts on the incident with Jonas Cook.

"Your enquiries are placing our investigations in danger, and I must ask you to desist." There was a note of threat behind the kindly smile and Bowman detected a hint of steel beneath the outwardly smooth exterior Callaghan presented to the world. He thought it best to say nothing of his suspicions in regard to Sallow's part in Cook's injury.

"Then you will need to speak with the commissioner," the inspector said, simply. "I am at the docks at his specific request."

Unnervingly, Callaghan laughed, the sardonic chuckle of one who feels superior to his company. The chief inspector sat further back in his seat, lifting his hands to pat his hair.

"Inspector Bowman, you and I both know that you were sent to St. Saviour's Dock on matters pertaining to security and that is all. I believe that you have strayed beyond that path into matters that do not concern you. Indeed, you are placing the whole of London under threat with your actions."

"I am pursuing my enquiries in my duty as a police officer."

"Your duties do not include the scuppering of a delicate investigation, inspector!" Callaghan had raised his voice in an unguarded moment.

Throughout all this, Cornelius Bracewell had been busy at his soup. Cleaning the last dregs from his bowl, he dabbed at his lips with his napkin and leaned back in his seat, content.

"Just how is your investigation proceeding?" Bowman demanded.

The chief inspector took a moment to regain his composure. "Mr Bracewell here," he began, "has been of particular assistance." Bracewell gave a humble shrug. "He has enabled us to detain a Mr Tremont, the master at St. Katharine Docks, under suspicion of collusion."

Bowman found that difficult to believe. "You think Tremont guilty of bombing his own warehouses?"

"I do not deal in beliefs, inspector, but facts."

Bracewell sat forward, his wide face looming towards Bowman as he explained himself. "I know many men on the north bank," he said. "Indeed, many of them are my men, too. Work is at a premium at the docks, inspector, and the smart man will make himself known both sides of the river."

As he spoke, an efficient, young waiter in dress jacket and bow tie cleared away the empty bowls. Bowman motioned that he should take his too, gesturing that he had no inclination to finish it.

"I have men in particular," continued Bracewell, flecks of soup appearing at the sides of his mouth as he spoke, "who have attained such a position that they have been granted access to Tremont's offices and effects. Under the guise of going about their business, auditing accounts and so forth, they have been able to acquire certain documents from Tremont's belongings."

"These documents complete the case against Tremont for being a Fenian sympathiser and responsible for the deaths of many." Callaghan looked pleased with himself as he concluded his case.

"To what end?" demanded Bowman.

Bracewell cleared his throat, "My men found evidence to indicate Tremont has benefited financially." Bowman turned to his dining companion, eyebrows raised. "We believe him guilty of false accounting. His records have revealed several financial anomalies which might bear more investigation."

"You *believe* him guilty?" echoed Bowman, pointedly. "I thought you dealt in facts."

"Subject to due process, of course." Bracewell gave a supercilious smile.

"They indicate that Tremont has been concealing the origins of illegal Fenian funds," continued Callaghan, eager to take control of the conversation.

"How so?" Bowman was picking his way through the implications.

"The Fenians need money to fund their activities, buy their equipment, rent property and so forth. And in large amounts, too. These funds are attained through criminal means, but must be presented as legitimate when spent so as not to arouse suspicion."

"The papers taken from Tremont's office indicate he has set up a complex web of financial and commercial systems through which this tainted money may be processed," added Bracewell. "And then he takes his share."

Bowman nodded. "I should like to see this evidence."

Callaghan fixed him with an unnerving gaze. "Inspector Bowman, I have brought you here to insist you interfere no further in the work of my department, not to ask your opinion on the matter."

Bowman was troubled. Tremont had not presented himself in any other way than as a victim of horrible circumstance during their interview at the docks.

"Where is Tremont now?" asked the inspector.

Callaghan sat back as his next course was presented before him. An older waiter placed a plate on the table, covered with a silver cloche. It was removed with a flourish to reveal a pile of vegetables arranged around a small, roast bird. "We have him in a cell on Bow Street," Callaghan continued, apparently unconcerned at the prospect of the waiter hearing. "There to remain while we build our case against him."

"It does not seem to me that your case is robust," said Bowman, boldly. "I have spoken with Tremont, and he gave every indication of being at the mercy of events rather than the master of them."

"A subterfuge, Inspector Bowman," said Callaghan through a mouthful of partridge.

"Why would Tremont plant a bomb in his own warehouses?"

"To place a strangle hold around the city's neck?" Callaghan conjectured. "To spread fear?"

"These are mere suppositions," blustered Bowman, indignantly.

"At any rate, inspector, I must insist you confine your investigations to matters of security as the commissioner willed it. If you do not, the consequences would be grave for you."

"What do you - "

"Leave well alone, Inspector Bowman!" Callaghan banged the handle of his knife on the table by way of punctuation. His grey eyes were glaring with a ferocity that betrayed him. Bowman sat stock still, his moustache twitching in the face of such bellicose behaviour.

"You should know, inspector," continued Callaghan, an eerie calm to his voice, 'that I hold some sway with the commissioner." Bowman narrowed his eyes. "I'm sure he would be very interested to hear of your confrontation with Sallow and his men on Willow Walk." Callaghan swallowed his food and lifted his glass to his lips, keeping his eyes fixed on Bowman all the while. "I think he would be interested to learn of your eccentric behaviour following the encounter."

Bowman's neck itched beneath his collar. He felt his palms begin to sweat.

"Your man Sallow is quite the informer," he said quietly.

Callaghan paused at his meal, resting the knife and fork on the plate as he spoke. "It is hardly a secret, Inspector Bowman, that your behaviour has been somewhat erratic. I understand the commissioner is unsure how to deal with a man of your sensibilities. You present him certain challenges."

Bowman glanced to his side to see Bracewell was staring at him with renewed interest, a look of bemusement on his face.

"I am fulfilling my duties as an inspector."

Callaghan scoffed. "Barely. Your career sits on a knife-edge, inspector. I must ask you again to tread carefully at the docks, lest the commissioner be informed of your irregular behaviour."

"The commissioner takes advice from others more infinitely qualified than Ichabod Sallow," spluttered Bowman.

"You refer of course to Athol Wilkes." There was a weary tone to Callaghan's voice. "The superintendent at Colney Hatch?"

Bowman's shoulders sunk in defeat. "You know Wilkes?"

"I make it my business to know everyone, Inspector Bowman." Callaghan was at his meal again. "Wilkes dines here once a month with benefactors to your lunatic asylum." Bowman bristled. "I know him well enough to have his ear on matters pertaining to The Force. I think he would be easily swayed. A word or two should suffice."

Bowman felt trapped to the left and the right. He had no doubt Chief Inspector Callaghan had sway over the commissioner, and if he were to influence the superintendent's report, Bowman's position at Scotland Yard would be untenable.

"So, I make this final appeal to your better judgement," Callaghan poured a little more gravy from an ornate jug on the table. "Steer clear of St Katharine Docks and it will be the better for you." The chief inspector added a little salt to his food. "If I were you, I would stick to matters of security."

Beside him, Bracewell was at work demolishing the bird on his plate. A waiter approached with Bowman's meal.

"Now, inspector, you must either join us for dinner or I shall have Mr. Bracewell's man drive you home."

Bowman sat, dejected, in the back of the smart brougham as it rattled through the dark streets of Greenwich. He had made a hasty retreat from the Trafalgar Club, eschewing Callaghan's offer of dinner. The concierge had returned him his coat as he left, holding it at arm's length as if it might expose him to some dreadful contamination. Bowman had given instruction to the driver to take him to his rooms in Hampstead and now the carriage approached the Woolwich Ferry, the means by which they were to cross the river.

The Gordon was a side-loading paddle steamer of some five hundred tons. Painted in a red and green livery, she could carry twenty vehicles on her broad upper deck and a thousand foot passengers besides. Her use, alongside two other such craft, had necessitated the building of approaches and pontoons for the benefit of those living within the eastern reaches of the Thames. Opened some three years since, it provided a free service to those who lived far from the great bridges of London, offering opportunities for passengers and trade on both banks of the river.

As they traversed the gentle swell of the Thames, Bowman sat with his thoughts in the back of the brougham. A gentle rain fell against the window, smudging the lights of the north bank and running in rivulets down the glass. Following his conversation with Chief Inspector Callaghan, several questions had persisted. If Ichabod Sallow was a Special Irish Branch agent, why had he put Cook in hospital? Why was Callaghan so insistent that Tremont was responsible for the bomb at St. Katharine Docks? And exactly what was Bracewell's part in the investigation? It was not unheard of for the police to involve the public in their operations, but Bracewell seemed to have unprecedented knowledge of proceedings.

As the carriage disembarked and began its journey back along the north bank to the city, Bowman had the distinct feeling that he was being played. By whom and to what end he couldn't tell, but the evening's events had left him feeling out of sorts. Whichever way he pursued the arguments, one thing troubled him above all else. None of this could adequately explain why at precisely eight o'clock, the very moment the bomb blew, he had seen Cornelius Bracewell staring across the river towards St. Katharine Docks, as if in expectation of the event.

For the first twenty minutes, the journey had been uneventful. Bowman had finally relaxed into the rhythm of the wheels on the road, determined to put his thoughts to one side for the night. His eyes ran over the interior of the cab as he fought to calm his mind.

A stud, he noticed, was missing from the leather upholstery. His fingers ran absently over some stitches in the canopy fabric where a hole had been mended. He had gazed out the window, trying to make sense of the streets as they flashed by. The weather had kept many indoors, he noticed. As a result, the roads were emptier than usual and progress was swift. Soon they were passing through Canning Town and over the Isle Of Dogs. Staring blankly through the glass, Bowman noticed the street names flashing passed. As they turned onto Commercial Road, he caught his breath. He knew exactly where they were. His mouth dried. His heart raced. Bowman tapped on the roof to bring the carriage to a halt. His breathing returned, but quicker now and irregular. His head swam. Opening the door, he staggered from the brougham. The driver, supremely indifferent to Bowman's condition and evidently pleased to be relieved of his duties, cracked his whip at once, steering the carriage away from the main road and off into the distance.

Bowman stood alone in the rain. Turning his feet to Adler Street, he found himself walking in familiar territory. The wet, narrow streets glistened in the lamplight. The silhouettes of well-known buildings loomed above him. Passing into Brick Lane, Bowman's blood ran cold. The air became thick and viscous. His legs were heavy as lead. His progress had slowed, each step seeming to require a huge effort of will. He blinked rain from his eyes and felt it drip from his hat down the back of his neck. Bowman turned a final corner and lifted his head to read the sign affixed to a corner wall. The very words struck dread to his heart and he fought for a moment to keep his balance. Quite by accident, and almost a year after events there had seen him locked away in a lunatic asylum, he found himself back where it had all began.

XVI

Hanbury Street

Bowman held his breath. All around him, the streets were quiet. The buildings were bathed in the soft, sickly glow of lamplight. The air was a prickle of energy. He felt both there and not there. Feeling the comfort of the ground beneath his feet, he fought to anchor himself in the present. His head was reeling. There was a ringing in his ears. He looked fearfully around for help but the narrow streets were empty. He opened his mouth to call for assistance but his throat, dry as it was, made no sound. Leaning back against the damp wall behind him, Bowman knew he had no choice but to submit to the mania, as one resigns oneself to being caught in a storm.

He could hear her now. Her soft, plaintive voice was calling his name. He screwed his eyes up against a sudden pain in his head, lifting his fingers to press at his temples. Her voice came again, stronger and close to his ear. And he could smell her scent. He opened his eyes slowly, expecting to see her standing next to him. Improbably, she stood further down the street. The rain was heavy now and Bowman could hear it slapping against the road. It stung his hands as he reached out to her.

"Anna."

But she couldn't hear him. She seemed frozen in time, her foot suspended above the ground as she stepped from the kerb to the street. He could see the Women's Refuge set back from the pavement opposite and knew he was to relive the events of her death again.

Then he heard the hooves. Time was in flux and Bowman passed between the now and the then. Moments before, he had watched as the carriage had swerved close to the kerb by the workhouse, a line of urchins waiting to be admitted for their day's work. The driver was muffled against the cold in a thick scarf that would also thwart all attempts to identify him. As the carriage clattered closer to the pavement, a door had opened and a man leant out, his coat trailing perilously close to the wheel. With an outstretched arm, he had plucked a young waif from the queue. The child had kicked and screamed, but all to no avail. In a matter of moments he was gone, the door to the carriage snapping shut behind him. The driver cracked the whip and the carriage had rattled away.

"Here they come," said a voice behind him. "Be ready now." Turning on his heels, Bowman saw Sergeant Williams had joined him, just as he had on that fateful night. His voice was low. His thick, Welsh accent gave his words an edge of urgency.

Bowman glanced to Anna and saw she was still caught mid-step between kerb and road.

Impossibly, Sergeant Graves was at his side too, his body poised for action, his muscles tensed. He looked to Bowman with a serious expression.

Bowman heard the hooves get louder, accompanied now by the rattle of a carriage. He turned to confront what he knew he must see, but saw nothing. Where the carriage should be was only empty air. Bowman was moving in time, fading between present and past. He was aware of the now, of the buildings and the rain, but cognizant also of that dreadful moment from the past, unfolding before him.

"Halt!" Williams was screaming.

The sound of the wheels clattered away down Spital Street. Bowman felt his heart racing. He blinked the rain from his eyes. Involuntarily, he felt his right hand close around his revolver. The handle was warm to the touch. He curled his finger round the trigger, lifting the gun to take aim.

As he squinted down the barrel, Bowman saw with horror that his sight was trained on his wife. This wasn't right, he told himself. This wasn't how it had happened. Graves was standing beside him now, a look of encouragement on his face. Williams was shouting into his ear. "Stop that carriage!" Bowman felt locked in position. Try as he might, he couldn't shift. He felt his finger tighten. He gritted his teeth, trying to resist the urge to fire.

Anna was moving now, slowly crossing the street to the Women's Refuge. She was intent on her journey, blissfully unaware of the catastrophe to come.

Then Bowman saw the carriage. Hooves thundered on the cobbles as it rounded the corner back on to Hanbury Street. The horses strained against their harnesses. The brougham swayed dangerously out of control, its driver slumped at the reins.

"No sir!" cried Graves, a look of alarm on his face. "It's too late!" This was all out of sequence, thought Bowman as he tried to avert his hand. Still, his finger squeezed at the trigger. Still, Anna was in his sight. Events were beyond his control now. He felt at a remove from proceedings, as if he watched another in his place. He squinted down the smooth, cold barrel of his revolver.

Anna had seen him. Her eyes were open wide in expectation, the beginnings of a smile on her lips. "George," she was mouthing. Her face lit up at the sight of him, and Bowman felt tears prick behind his eyes. Two words were caught in his throat. He had been hiding from them for the best part of a year. If the words were said, he knew, they would unleash a torrent. He had leaned against them for months as one leans against a door. They were pushing back against him now, and he knew he would have to relent. He found his voice as his finger tightened.

"I'm sorry," he said. And he fired.

The scream of a train's whistle brought him to his senses. He was on his knees in the rain, his coat tails dragging in the road around him. It was impossible to know how long he had been there, but he saw that he was several yards away from where he remembered standing. He pressed a hand against the road and caught his breath. The ringing in his ears was subsiding. Staggering to his feet, he saw a young man standing, watching from a doorway. He had a look of alarm on his face. Bowman held up a hand to indicate he was well, but the man took to his heels. Casting his eyes around, the inspector got his bearings. Soaked to the skin and with a heart heavier than it had ever been, Detective Inspector George Bowman pulled himself up to his full height, wiped the rain from his face and shuffled off into the night.

XVII

A Course Of Action

Overnight, April tipped into May and the morning brought clearer skies. The streets around Whitehall came slowly to life as Bowman watched from his office window. Looking down onto Victoria Embankment, he could see a woman feeding the pigeons with seed from her pocket. She was wrapped in a large, dirty coat that had clearly once belonged to someone else. Bowman noticed she had no shoes upon her feet. She swore as a young lad ran past, upsetting the birds and causing them to fly up and over the river to Westminster Bridge and beyond. Bowman peered beyond the buildings of state that clustered for safety around Whitehall and off towards Trafalgar Square and the West End. What villainies had occurred overnight, mused Bowman. What discoveries would be made today in the filthy alleys and dark corners of the city? Only just in view, Nelson's Column rose in the thick of it all. The morning air was so clean and Bowman so high, he felt he could reach out and touch it. His eyes were drawn momentarily to his own reflection and he saw with a start what a picture he was presenting to the world. He had neglected to go home last night, but rather found himself wandering the streets of Whitechapel until dawn. As the streets had woken around him, he had been subject to many strange looks and suspicious glances and so had resolved to find a hansom cab to Scotland Yard. Peering at his image in the glass, he could see the consequences of having spent such a night with no rest. His eyes were bloodshot. His hair hung lank upon his head. He smoothed his moustache between his finger and thumb in a vain attempt to appear more presentable. He succeeded only in noticing he had neglected to shave. Bowman sighed and raised the glass of brandy to his lips. He knew it was perhaps too early to drink, but he needed a restorative after a night on the streets. Turning to replace his glass at the bureau that stood across the room, he was surprised to see Sergeant Anthony Graves standing at the open door. How long he had been there, he could not guess.

"Morning, Graves," Bowman muttered as he crossed the room to the bureau. He was acutely aware of his unkempt appearance and absently brushed at his waistcoat with the palm of his hand. As Bowman shambled across the room, Graves saw the decanter was emptier than he remembered.

"You wanted to see me, sir?" the sergeant offered, tentative.

"Yes, sit down Graves." Bowman was staring up at the map that adorned the wall above the bureau. The whole of London was within his gaze, from Plumstead Marshes in the east to Mortlake in the west. Narrow streets and alleys were marked and named in a neat, calligrapher's hand. Even individual houses were indicated. Hundreds of souls could be encompassed within the span of a hand, each with their own secrets.

"You'll have to get a new one soon, sir." Graves was sitting in the chair before Bowman's desk. The inspector could tell he was fighting hard to resist putting his feet upon it.

"How's that?" Bowman turned to face his companion.

"The map, sir. London's changing at a fair old pace these days. You're a couple of bridges missing for a start."

Graves was right. The pace of change was alarming. The London skyline would be unrecognisable to anyone who may have last seen it even ten years ago. Bowman moved thoughtfully to the window and rested against the sill. He caught Graves' expression as he turned into the room and felt he was being scrutinised. Graves was clearly taking note of his dishevelled state, from his mud-spattered shoes to his creased shirt cuffs and bedraggled hair. The young sergeant had an open face that could be easily read, and Bowman could see concern writ large.

"Sergeant Graves, I have a proposition for you."

Graves leaned forward on his seat, his blue eyes shining in their eagerness. "Oh yes, sir?"

He was interrupted by a rap at the door. Looking up, Bowman saw Ignatius Hicks filling the frame with his bulk, clearly pleased with himself for having remembered to knock.

"Yes, Inspector Hicks?" Bowman sighed.

"Had a rough night of it, Bowman?" the rotund inspector roared as he strode into the office. Graves looked away, embarrassed at just how brazen the inspector was.

Bowman stuttered for a moment, then considered the best way to deal with such a remark was to ignore it. "What do you want, Hicks?" he retorted.

"I bring news," the inspector proclaimed, holding his hands wide as if performing to an audience at the theatre. Bowman rolled his eyes to the ceiling. Sergeant Graves stifled a smile. "Specifically, news pertaining to our body in Vinegar Yard."

Bowman stood straighter at the window. "Your investigations have borne fruit?"

"The ripest sort," winked Hicks, pulling his pipe from his pocket. Graves stood to face him. "He is Harry Pope, a labourer from Chiswick. Reported missing from his place of work seven weeks ago by the foreman of works." Hicks' eyebrows were raised in expectation of praise for his findings.

"What more do you know of him?"

"Only a physical description," blustered Hicks, tamping down the tobacco in the bowl of his pipe. "Came in from a station at Turnham Green. It fits our man to a tee."

"Right down to the tattoo?" asked Graves.

"Tattoo?" Bowman's eyebrows were raised.

"He had a tattoo, more of a branding, on his chest," explained Graves. "A strange design like the face of the Devil."

Hicks felt the wind being taken out of his sails. "There was no mention of his tattoo."

"Then he may have come by it since he disappeared," suggested Bowman from the window.

"Oh," continued Hicks as he struck a match. "And he was a keen boxer, skilled too. It seems he's just one of many men disappeared from their job of work over recent months. I've seen reports from all over London, and they are all of a type; large, brawny men."

"May I see those reports, Inspector Hicks?"

"I didn't think to bring them, Bowman, as you're not with us on the case." This last was said pointedly, marked Bowman.

"Then, where has he been these last seven weeks?" Graves asked, scratching at his blond curls.

"That is not for me to say," blustered Hicks. "But to have an identification is surely progress?"

"Progress it is, Inspector Hicks," agreed Bowman. "And I have a thought as to where he has been held."

"Held, sir?" Graves turned to the inspector.

"Almost certainly, Sergeant Graves." Bowman turned to face the window, his hands clasped behind his back. For a moment, Graves thought he detected the inspector's hand shaking, but then saw there was more to it than that. It wasn't Bowman's hand that was trembling, he realised but, strangely, the index finger on his right hand. His trigger finger. "Your description of the state in which the poor man was found ravaged," Bowman continued, "would indicate a fugitive in fear of his life. Clearly he was running from the hound."

"So, he'd escaped from somewhere," Graves said, thoughtfully. "And the dog had been set upon him."

Hicks was trying his best to follow the argument. "But escaped from where?" he bellowed.

"I was, last night, in the presence of an injured worker from St. Saviour's Dock." Bowman was treading carefully to avoid all mention of his rendez-vous with Callaghan. "One Jonas Cook. I believe his accident was orchestrated by another. He had, beneath his nails, the same yellow colour as Harry Pope."

"Turmeric!" Hicks held his pipe aloft.

Graves whistled with excitement. "That's some coincidence," he beamed.

"I believe it to be more than coincidence, Graves." Bowman sat at his chair and placed his elbows on the desk. "I believe our two cases may be linked."

"What case?" boomed Hicks. "I understood you were to be on security detail, not pursuing your own enquiries."

"This investigation was born out of my position at the docks. A man was injured at the quayside. He had about him some marks similar to Harry Pope. I would suggest the two are linked." Bowman was leaning forward. "And furthermore, that Pope was either pressed into service at St. Saviour's Dock or held there."

"But Turmeric may be found elsewhere. A man might buy a quantity at the market." Hicks clamped his pipe between his teeth.

"But not in such amounts as to stain so heavily, Hicks."

Graves was thoughtful. "Then what do you propose?" he asked, his eyes wide in anticipation.

"Jonas Cook worked at Corder's Wharf. They take in tea and spices." Bowman sat back to survey the room. "I need someone on the inside." Graves' ears pricked up. "I am known at St. Saviour's and would no doubt find many doors closed to me."

"And as we're now effectively working on the same case,"

continued Graves, rubbing his hands, thoughtfully.

"I am sure there can be no objection to me requesting your services," Bowman concluded, folding his arms across his chest.

"I suppose there can be no harm," began Hicks, puffing eagerly on his pipe. "I shall relish the chance of providing some assistance." Already, his eyes were alive with the prospect of going under cover.

"I was not thinking of sending you, Inspector Hicks."

Hicks looked suddenly downcast, but recovered sufficiently to object. "You cannot send Graves alone. You suspect this chap Cook has been the victim of something other than an accident. Things could get sticky."

"Sergeant Graves is more than capable of holding his own." Bowman chose his words carefully. "And is less likely to draw attention to himself."

Hicks gave a harrumph of disappointment and jammed his pipe in his teeth in protest, whilst Sergeant Graves sat back in his chair, eyes twinkling.

With Graves preparing for his investigations on the south bank, Bowman resolved to walk to Bow Street and speak with the desk sergeant there. With a few well-chosen words, he was sure he might be permitted some time with Tremont. Bowman still found it difficult to see how the dock manager could be wrapped up in a Fenian plot, besides which, Callaghan had failed to offer any adequate reason as to why he should want to bomb his own dockside. Having despatched Hicks for a list of those who had been reported missing around London, Bowman descended the stairs from his office to the great reception hall at Scotland Yard.

As ever, it was a bustle of activity. Footsteps echoed off the tiled floor and the hubbub of conversation rose up to the high ceiling. Ladies and gentlemen found themselves waiting on benches alongside the very lowest in society. Drunks and vagrants mixed with bankers and shopkeepers as they awaited their turn at the central desk. Here and there, police constables stood with their charges, some in handcuffs. The occasional drunken cry would pierce the air. As Bowman stepped from the stairs, he was certain that even the nobility were represented in the room. A thin, elderly lady with grey eyes and translucent skin sat stock still beneath a window. Her hands were folded over the handle of her cane, and her nose was lifted into the air in an attitude of superiority. A smile played about Bowman's lips as he allowed himself to imagine the purpose of her visit. Money was involved, no doubt. And probably a maid, too. The inspector took solace in the fact that the citizens of London were finally coming round to the idea of a professional police force standing ready and waiting to give assistance. Just as he was tightening his coat around him in anticipation of the keen May wind, he heard a voice rise above the hubbub.

"There he is!" it cried. "That's the very man."

Bowman recognised the voice, and particularly the soft Irish lilt, at once. Casting a glance at the reception desk, Bowman saw Sister Vincent gathering her skirts. The desk sergeant threw a questioning look to Bowman and the inspector waved his hand to indicate his assent.

"Sister Vincent," Bowman began, "I trust all is well at The Sisters Of Mercy?"

"No, inspector, it is not," the sister replied, matter-of-factly. In her wimple and spectacles she reminded Bowman of a small mole, blinking in the light of the high windows that graced the walls. "I came as soon as I could." She was breathless. Bowman led her to a bench and motioned that a young man in a funeral director's coat should make way for her.

"What is ailing you, sister?"

"I should have listened to you, inspector. I see it now, but I was concerned that you were disturbing the peace of the convent."

"What has happened?" Bowman sat slowly next to her, imploring her with his eyes to continue.

"Oh, Inspector Bowman, it's Jonas Cook." Bowman swallowed hard. He felt his hand begin to twitch involuntarily, so held it in a fist to hide the tremor.

"What of him?" he asked, already sure of the response.

"He's dead, inspector." The sister's pronouncement was enough to draw the eyes of those on the bench around her.

"I am sorry to hear of it. You said yourself that he was very ill."

"And so he was, inspector. But he did not die of his injuries."

"Then what are you suggesting?" Bowman asked slowly.

"That he was murdered in the night as he slept."

Bowman swallowed. "Can you be sure?"

"As sure as I sit here, inspector," Sister Vincent blinked. "I am no doctor, sure, but I saw the marks on his neck this morning as he was carried to the chapel."

Bowman shifted his position on the bench, suddenly aware that they were conducting the conversation in a very public place.

"Marks on his neck?" he repeated.

"He was strangled, Inspector Bowman, no doubt about it."

Bowman thought back to his visit to The Sisters Of Mercy and the patients he had seen in the infirmary. It would be difficult to effect such a murder with so many witnesses present.

"Who would have access to the infirmary?"

"Only the sisters and any visitors we may have."

Bowman rubbed his chin with his hand, suddenly embarrassed at the stubble he felt there. "Are your doors locked overnight?"

"Never," declared the sister, her eyes wide. "That would be to bar the way to strangers."

Bowman nodded slowly. "Then did you see anyone enter at any time?"

"I did not. Miss Beaurepaire left some time after you and from that time there were no more visitors."

The inspector raised his eyebrows. "How long did Miss Beaurepaire stay after me?"

"Just long enough to settle the patient. She was concerned you had taxed him overmuch with your questions." Sister Vincent fixed him with an accusatory stare. Bowman looked away. "I let her out myself."

"And did you then look in on your patients?"

"I did," the sister nodded. "But they were all asleep or nearly so."

Bowman thought. Was it significant that Ichabod Sallow hadn't been with the three men on Parker's Row? If word had got round that Cook was speaking with the police, perhaps Sallow would want to quieten him for good. None of which sounded like the actions of a Special Irish Branch officer.

"Sister Vincent," he soothed, "I am going to send Inspector Hicks to see you at the convent. Show him the infirmary and tell him of your suspicions." Bowman blanched at putting Hicks in any position of authority, but he had other plans for the day. "He will then report directly back to me."

As Bowman showed the sister from the building, he wondered at the events of the last two days. The commissioner had clearly wanted him out the way. He had been sent to St. Saviour's Dock in the belief that he would come to no harm. It seemed, however, that the commissioner had, quite unwittingly, placed Bowman in a web of intrigue.

XVIII

Corder's Wharf

Sergeant Graves had to admit he was enjoying himself. He had spent the previous hour being briefed by Bowman, then had availed himself of some suitable clothes from Scotland Yard's lost property room. Anything that had been held for six months or more was considered fair game, so Sergeant Graves had chosen a pair of baggy corduroy trousers, a collarless shirt and a red cotton neckerchief. He had even toyed for a while with a pair of spectacles with a cracked lens. It fell to Inspector Bowman to remind him that, as he was not known at the docks, he was not in search of a disguise, but rather an appearance that would not mark him out from his fellow workers. Graves had thrown a threadbare jacket over his waistcoat. A pair of over-sized boots was retrieved from a shelf. Inspector Bowman chose him a hat to complete the look and sent him on his way to Shad Thames.

The journey to Bermondsey had been without incident. Graves had thought it prudent to catch a cab to London Bridge Station, then walk from there. Now the sergeant sauntered down Queen Elizabeth Street, part of the throng of dockworkers anxious for employment. Looking around him as he walked, Graves saw men of every age and size, but all in a dishevelled state. Their faces marked with expressions of grim resignation, they marched to the dock in a relentless rhythm. Almost to a man, they held pipes or cigarettes between their teeth and the smoke rose in a noxious cloud down the length of the street. The houses, little more than slums, were tightly packed along the road. Dilapidated doors swung open on rickety hinges to reveal sparse parlours and bedrooms for four or more men. Rags hung from broken windows in a vain attempt at privacy. Damp clothes hung between buildings on lengths of string to dry.

Sergeant Graves had no difficulty in blending in. Few of the men spoke amongst themselves, and Graves guessed they would be used to strangers in their number. The docks drew desperate men from across London and beyond in search of paid labour. The sergeant surmised that any number of strangers could appear on any given day quite unremarked. He felt part of a tide of humanity, sweeping towards the docks.

At last, he found himself on Shad Thames. He was surrounded by wharves, warehouses, mills and factories. Steam rose into the air from tall chimneys. The tang of exotic spices assaulted the senses. Animal hides were scrubbed, degreased and soaked before being hung to dry. Grain was milled into flour between great stones turned by hand or by horse. Coopers bent wood into barrels for use at the docks. Looking up, Graves saw great metal gantries spanning the width of the road, connecting the upper storeys of the wharves together. Lines of carts traversed them from one side to the other, some empty, others groaning under the weight of their loads.

Turning to run parallel with St. Saviour's Dock, the sergeant looked up at the painted letters adorning each wall. Corder's Wharf stood just a few yards from the mouth of the dock and it was towards its forbidding walls that the detective turned his feet.

Already there were crowds at the entrance to each wharf. A press of men thronged in the street, each reaching over the other in a desperate bid to find work. Graves saw punches thrown and feet stamped upon. Shouts and curses echoed down the narrow streets to the Thames. At each door stood a foreman. It was upon them that the men pinned their hopes. Each foreman stood with a ledger and pencil, marking names as they called them.

"Siddons!"

"Rigby!"

"Havell!"

Each name was met with a cry of victory from the man concerned and a chorus of disapproval from the rest. Occasionally another cry would be heard from the foreman.

"You! Name?"

A new face would light up as he gave his name to the foreman and the stranger would be permitted to work for the morning. This would set a dozen other arguments blazing in the crowd. Graves noted that younger men would always take precedence over the elder of the crowd. He mused that Mr Charles Darwin would be happy to see his theories at work at St. Saviour's Dock. Graves drove further into the throng, setting his face to catch the foreman's eye.

"Oi, watch yer step, mate!"

Graves made his apologies to the stocky man next to him. He peered at he sergeant through deep-set eyes, his lantern jaw chewing on a matchstick. "Tryin' your luck?" he asked, his eyes narrowing with suspicion.

Graves nodded. "I am that."

"See that man over there?" The man was gesturing over his shoulder at a mean looking man in shirtsleeves and a faded cloth cap. The most remarkable feature about him was his left eye, which seemed opaque and clouded. "That's Ichabod Sallow," the man was whispering. "Watch 'im."

Graves' heart raced. Had he been discovered so quickly?

The man laid a finger aside his nose as if imparting a state secret. "He doesn't take to new faces. But if he says jump, you ask "how high?" Or you'll go the same way as Jonas Cook. Got it?"

Graves relaxed. "Thank you," he said with half an eye on the man in shirtsleeves.

"You!" the foreman bellowed. Graves realised with a start he was looking straight at him. "Name?"

"Graves!" the young sergeant called. There was little point in giving a false name.

The foreman scratched at his ledger then gestured with a sharp stab at his pencil that he should enter the wharf.

To jeers and whistles, Graves pushed his way through the crowd. The man with the clouded eye glared after him, clearly making a mental note of the newcomer's name.

The double wooden doors opened into a vast space. Many men had already been admitted. They swarmed across the flagstones to the opposite wall where a door opened to the dockside. Galleries rose the height of the room, laden with crates and sacks of produce awaiting distribution. The galleries were supported on sturdy pillars designed to withstand the great weight of their load, and lengths of metal fencing were affixed to secure the produce. A network of lifts, ropes, pulleys and trap doors provided access to the galleries. Graves could see many men leaning over the balustrade in anticipation of the morning's deliveries. Light was admitted via arched windows set, at intervals, into the nearest wall. Still, Graves noticed, this huge cavern of a room was a fog of tobacco smoke and dust that danced in the air before him.

"Get a move on!" rasped a voice from behind. Graves turned to see he was holding up a horde of dockworkers keen to start their toil. They streamed past as he stood aside, each one of them eyeing him with the suspicion always reserved for a newcomer. Graves followed the crowd through Corder's Wharf to the dockside on the other side. Already he could see a great schooner berthed at the quay ready to disgorge its load. Planks were laid from the quayside to permit access to the hatches that were now thrown open in expectation. Carts stood ready at the wharves to carry the produce inside. There, they would be emptied, their loads transferred to the great galleries around the walls, and sent out again to be reloaded. It was human endeavour on an industrial scale.

"You!" Another shout pierced the air and Graves turned to see a man in an old pork pie hat. "They need hands in the hold, get yerself down there."

Graves tugged at his cap and crossed the planks to the ship, feeling the deck shift beneath his feet as it moved on the swell of the tide.

The Eastern Star was over a hundred feet long and crammed with men going about their business. They heaved sacks onto their shoulders and scuttled across the deck like beetles. They carried heavy crates upon their heads or slung them off the boats to be caught by an accomplice. The air was full of the heave-hoes of dockworkers and many curses besides. Graves stepped nimbly between them and headed for the row of hatches that ran from stern to aft. They were thrown open to the air and the sergeant could smell the musty odours of tea and spices rising to meet him.

He waited his turn at the ladder as a stream of men poured up from the depths of the hold, each carrying a sack upon his shoulders that seemed filled to bursting. "There's turmeric on the port bow," panted one as he passed. "Grab it first before the tea."

As Graves nodded his thanks, his eyes were drawn up the quayside to the dock head. There, he saw a police constable leaning on the wall. He possessed sharp, angular features and, even from this distance, Graves could make out his heavy brow and prominent nose. With a start, he recognised the man from The Theatre Royal and, in particular, their very quick meeting by the stage door. The actors in Vinegar Yard had referred to Kitty as 'working out the Kaiser's share', and then he had seen the man leave with a heavy carpetbag beneath his arm. Had the bag contained the Kaiser's share? Graves wondered that the man should be here, several miles from where he had last seen him, but wondered all the more that he was wearing a police constable's uniform. Pulling his hat further down over his eyes, Graves turned away from him and descended into the gloom of the ship's hold.

Pungent smells assailed his nostrils and caught in the back of his throat. Dust stung his eyes and coated his tongue. From a corner, he heard the grunt and toil of men at work. They cursed as the hessian sacks chafed against their fingers or as they lifted dead weights to their shoulders. Stooping low to avoid the beams above his head, he let his eyes adjust to the darkness. He could see three or four of his fellow dockworkers by a far bulkhead, grappling with sacks of turmeric. Bracing himself against the gentle roll of the deck, Graves pushed on to the corner.

"Grab this, will yer?" A heavy sack was thrust at his chest and Graves clasped his arms around it. A spicy, citrus smell rose from the bag that the sergeant recognised from Doctor Crane's dissecting rooms. Turning again, he staggered to the ladder and out onto the deck. There, a chain of men was passing bundles of produce arm over arm to each other, cursing with the effort. Graves stepped carefully down the plank and dropped the sack onto a waiting cart by the mouth of Corder's Wharf. Rubbing the dust from his hands, he saw that his fingers were already stained an orange yellow.

"Get that cart inside!" The foreman was standing on the quayside, puffed up with self-importance. "The tide won't wait for you!"

Concerned he had caught the policeman's attention at the dock head, Graves cast his eyes up the quayside. The constable was deep in conversation with a squat man with a cane. Making use of the opportunity, Graves grabbed the cart with both hands and lugged it across the flagstones in the wharf. Once inside, he was pointed to a set of large sliding doors that were suspended from a gallery on the north wall. Graves wiped his forehead with the back of a hand. Already his clothes were damp with sweat. He pushed his way through a queue of men to the anteroom beneath the gallery, heading for an empty corner where he thought he might unpack his load. Just as he stopped, a trapdoor was flung open on the floor at his feet. He stepped back in surprise as a pair of hands reached up from the hole and scrabbled at the floor. A head that Graves recognised poked up from a cellar. The clouded eye and mean disposition marked the man out as Ichabod Sallow. Sallow fixed Graves for a moment with a ghoulish stare, then pulled himself up through the hole to his feet.

"Unload that here," he rasped, indicating to Graves' cart with a nod of his head. Graves thought it best to do as he was told. Looking around him, he saw that Sallow was being given a wide berth. The other workers in the wharf walked on by about their chores. Those waiting for work averted their gaze.

As Graves busied himself about his task, he watched as Sallow swung a rope on a pulley and lowered it into the hole. He puffed at the stump of a cheroot as he worked, seemingly not caring if he was seen. Gesturing to a fellow down the hatch, he walked calmly to the wall and swung hard at a handle fixed there. Graves watched as a wooden pallet rose from the trap in the floor. It was loaded with sacks just like the ones on Graves' cart and Sallow gestured that the sergeant should swing it away from the hole.

"Ain't seen your face afore," grumbled Sallow.

"No," said Graves, treading carefully. "I just came down today."

"Down from where?" Sallow was rolling his cheroot between his lips, thoughtfully. His clouded eye regarded Graves, carefully.

"Stanmore," Graves said, truthfully. Bowman had cautioned him that, if questioned, he should only obfuscate when necessary, the better to remember his story.

"Graves, ain't it?" Sallow spat on the floor.

"Yes."

"Can you work hard, Graves?"

"I can that."

"And keep your mouth shut?"

Graves swallowed. He felt he was being sized up. He also felt that Ichabod Sallow was up to no good. The sergeant nodded slowly, his usually expressive eyes conveying nothing.

Sallow had joined him now. "Then lend a hand unloading these, then we'll swap 'em over with today's haul."

Sallow worked quickly and quietly, swapping over the sacks of produce. Those from the cellar were piled high against the wall, those from Graves' cart took their place on the pallet. All the while, Sallow kept the sergeant in his sight. "You ain't seen none of this, right?" he said when they had finished, the threat implicit in his tone of voice, "Or it'll be the worse for you. Keep your trap shut and your nose clean and you'll fit in perfect." Graves nodded in understanding as Sallow lowered the pallet down into the cellar. Turning to see Graves still standing with his cart, Sallow fixed him with his clouded eye. "Well, be on your way then," he commanded. "The tide won't wait for you." Chuckling at his own joke, Ichabod Sallow lowered himself back through the hole in the floor and closed the trapdoor behind him.

Graves was left with more questions than answers. Just what was Sallow up to in the cellar? And why had he injured Jonas Cook? Graves guessed his answers lay beneath that trap door, and resolved to return when the day's work was done. In the meantime, he rolled up his shirtsleeves, clasped the handles to the cart and returned to his duties aboard The Eastern Star.

XIX

A Hope In Hell

Bow Street police station was a solid, inscrutable building of white Suffolk brick and Portland stone. Its high walls and slate roof stood out in stark relief against the blue May sky. Its windows reflected the busy street below.

In the bowels of the building, with his head in his hands, sat William Tremont. His portly frame was squeezed onto a solitary stool in his cell, the only other furniture being a flat and unforgiving mattress that lay on a shelf against a far wall. No natural light was to be admitted this far below ground. Gas lamps spat and flickered on the walls of the corridor immediately outside the cell. Tremont had been deprived of his coat and so sat, dejected in his shirtsleeves and waistcoat, staring at the ground between his feet.

Detective Inspector Bowman cleared his throat to announce his presence, and Tremont looked up to fix him with a baleful glare.

"I had not thought to see you again."

Bowman nodded. "I wish to speak to you, Mr Tremont."

"I have said enough." Tremont dropped his head again, rubbing his eyes with a filthy hand. "And none of that has been believed."

Bowman leaned up against the bars. Meeting his eyes again, Tremont took a moment to consider the man in front of him. His eyes were hooded, with shadows beneath them. His shoulders were slumped and there was something in his stature that indicated a man who bore a heavy load.

"Have you come to implicate me in the bomb at my own dock?" asked Tremont, sadly.

"No," replied Bowman. "I have come to help." The inspector couldn't help but note the look of cynicism in Tremont's eyes. "How long have you worked at St. Katharine Docks, Mr. Tremont?"

"Man and boy." Tremont gazed into the gloom, a wistful look upon his face. "It has always given me satisfaction." Tremont rose from the stool and eased himself over to the bars. "My work is of great import, Inspector Bowman." He clasped the lapels to his waistcoat and puffed out his not inconsiderable chest. "London must be fed and clothed and it is through my auspices that it is kept so." Tremont turned back into his cell and lowered himself to the mattress, scratching at his belly as he lay back. "Great advances have been made in the understanding of human anatomy of late, inspector." Bowman narrowed his eyes. "I have seen maps of the human body that show the vascular system as rivers and tributaries. They all lead to and from the body's beating heart, just as all trade comes through St. Katharine Docks. We are the beating heart of the Empire, inspector. Or have been so, until now."

Certain as he was of Tremont's innocence, Bowman suddenly felt a deep sorrow for his predicament. "Do you have any Irish connections?"

Tremont turned his head directly to the inspector at the bars. "Are you pedalling the Fenian lie, too?" His jowls wobbled in his distress. "The very thought is ridiculous. This is Bracewell's half-baked nonsense."

Casting a glance up the corridor between the cells, Bowman saw a rickety wooden chair by a table. Pulling it to Tremont's cell, he sat, deep in thought, to pick his way through the dock master's predicament.

"Chief Inspector Callaghan believes you may have sympathies with the Fenian cause," he said.

Tremont gave a splutter of derision. "You mean Cornelius Bracewell believes so. Or at least tells Callaghan so."

Bowman leaned forward on his chair. "What do you know of his relationship with Callaghan?"

The plump dock master shook his head, forlorn. "Only what I see. That Bracewell has seen an opportunity for advancement. I have long been in competition with St. Saviour's Dock. Bracewell has fought long and hard for advantage, lowering his port charges and importing cheap labour."

"Importing labour?"

Tremont swung his legs from the bed. "Take a look at his workforce, inspector. None of them are London men, but are brought in from the Shires and paid a pittance. I will not do such a thing to my men, and I am made to suffer for it. Then Tilbury hit us bad."

Bowman raised his eyebrows. "Tilbury?"

"Tilbury Dock has deeper basins so can accommodate larger vessels." Tremont was on his feet now, pacing with a nervous agitation. "They've made greater use of mechanisation, and they have a local workforce grateful for employment. St. Katharine Docks is not long for this world, inspector, mark my words."

Bowman nodded sagely. Everywhere, it seemed, there was progress. It was not always to the good.

"How does Bracewell make his money if he is lowering charges?"

"He finds it from other sources." Tremont looked at the inspector, darkly.

"He says he is in possession of some papers that incriminate you."

"Papers be blowed." Tremont was at the bars, looking down on Bowman. "His men are as crooked as he."

"Do you deny the papers' existence?"

"I do not, but I refute Cornelius Bracewell's inferences."

Bowman leaned back in his rickety chair, the legs creaking dangerously beneath him. "Bracewell has mentioned certain transactions designed to legitimise Fenian funds."

Tremont rolled his eyes, resigned. "Presented in a certain light, they might appear so."

"What is the truth of them?"

"The truth lies as far from Bracewell's story as might be imagined."

"I must assure you that I am not part of Callaghan's investigation. You may be frank with me and be assured that nothing of what you say shall pass beyond these walls."

"And yet you know of Bracewell's accusations?"

Bowman swallowed. "I am party to certain facts, but I am not of Bracewell's mind."

Tremont walked away from the bars, his expression one of abject sorrow. "The truth, Inspector Bowman, is that I am compromised."

"By whom?" Bowman leant forward, resting his elbows on his knees and making steeples with his fingers.

Sitting again on his makeshift bed, Tremont looked about him. How he wished to be anywhere but here. "They're known only as the Kaiser. They operate on the south bank."

Bowman's mind was drawn to the moment at St. Katharine

Docks, just following the blast, when he had seen Tremont gazing out across the Thames to St. Saviour's Dock.

"My records might well show certain discrepancies," Tremont continued. "But not as a result of any Fenian loyalty." His eyes met Bowman's in a moment of frank admission. "Rather the result of extortion."

The inspector let the words hang in the air. He could sense Tremont was grappling with his natural reticence. Throwing up his hands in resignation, he dock master continued. "For the last two years I have been threatened with retribution unless certain funds were paid. Business is precarious enough, inspector. I cannot afford anything but a smooth-running dock. I have been told to provide one hundred pounds every month or else risk a catastrophe."

Bowman's eyes widened at the sum. That was more than half a detective's yearly salary paid every month. "For how long?"

"For the last year or so. This month, I refused."

"Have you never reported this to the police? Or the Port Of London?"

"I have not. The Kaiser has men everywhere. Even, it is rumoured, in The Force."

Bowman bristled at the insinuation.

"If it was discovered that I had run for help, things would go the worse for me. I have been told as much."

"Then you have not told this to Callaghan?"

Tremont gave a hollow laugh, his shoulders heaving with the effort. "Bracewell has his ear, and I do not trust Bracewell."

"You think he may be connected to the Kaiser?" Bowman was sitting up now, his mind racing.

"Intimately."

The inspector stood as he thought through the implications of Tremont's testimony. "How does the Kaiser make contact?" he asked.

Tremont shrugged. "Through the men who work at St. Saviour's. They know little themselves, save the messages they are made to deliver. They are passed from man to man so the source remains undiscovered."

"And you have made payment every month?" Bowman's mind boggled at the sums involved.

"Every month but this, and see what a Hell I have brought upon myself." Tremont buried his head in his hands again, his chest falling with a shattering sigh. Even in the half-light, Bowman could see tears pricking at the man's eyes. His flabby face was flushed with emotion. Through all this, Bowman knew he must press the dock master further.

"How is the money collected each month?" he asked, softly.

"I leave it in person at a different location and time each month."

"Have you ever stopped to see who collects it?"

Tremont gave a mirthless laugh at the very idea. "Never, inspector. I value my life too much. And so you see why my accounts might be awry. I have tried to hide the transactions as best I could but the detail is beyond me and I have betrayed myself." It was clear Tremont was beyond hope now. "And so I languish in Bow Street awaiting my fate," he concluded, sadly.

Bowman rose from his chair and grabbed the bars with both hands. "Mr Tremont," he began, his voice sounding a note of determination, "I will make a promise to you. You will not face charges for this or any other crime." Tremont looked up from his bed and Bowman thought he saw, for a moment at least, some marks of hope in the poor man's face. "I am in the midst of an investigation which I believe will exonerate you entirely."

XX

No Holds Barred

Big Tam woke with a start. He knew he had company again. Peering into the darkness around him, he saw subtle movements in the corner of the warehouse. Straining at his chain, he rolled onto his back and winced with pain as the skin on his chest tightened. He'd forgotten about the brand on his skin. Looking down he could see the blister clearly rising from his chest, angry and red. His head throbbed. He had no idea how long he had been lying there, and could see no clue around him. The cavernous room was still shrouded in a gloomy half-light. Rubbing at his aching jaw with a hand, he squinted to the corners. His vision was swimming but there was a definite movement by the door. Now he could hear whispering too. Readying himself for another attack from the hooded figure, Tam rocked onto his knees, gritting his teeth in expectation. "Come and get me if you want me!" he slurred, his thick, Scottish vowels guttural and raw. He blinked sweat from his eyes to clear his vision and saw two shapes moving towards him. If he had not been deprived of his sight on that night by the Thames, he might well have recognised his two assailants again.

Thackeray and Bracewell moved slowly towards their prey. They knew Tam would not put up such a fight this time. He was struggling already, his great body swaying side to side in his delirium. His breathing was shallow and his eyes darted fearfully left and right. Clearly the drug had him in its thrall. Thackeray, weighing a club in his hand, gestured to his companion to swing further out to the left beyond their captive's field of vision. Big Tam was swinging his fist wildly before him. His arm felt heavy and unwieldy. His best chance of fighting back, he reasoned in his befuddled state, lay in getting to his feet. Grunting with the effort, he rocked from side to side, trying to get the momentum he needed. Just as he'd got his feet beneath him, he heard a noise from behind. He had been too intent on the tall man with the cudgel to notice his companion approaching stealthily at his back. Before he had time to react, he felt the sack on his head again. A heavy push from the cudgel and Tam fell back with a roar of indignation, his head meeting the flagstones with a crack. Thackeray and Bracewell stood back while the Scotsman thrashed about on the ground, his free hand smashing painfully on the hard floor. For a while he kicked his legs in frustration, but soon even that proved too tiring. He lay in a heap, his chest rising and falling in a painful effort to breathe. His torso glistened with a cold sweat. The two men approached, cautiously. Thackeray held Tam's free hand behind his back while Bracewell snapped on a pair of cuffs. Big Tam was helpless. Unclipping the chain, Bracewell and Thackeray lifted the subdued giant slowly to his feet. His energy sapped, Tam had no inclination to resist. His hands fastened behind his back and a hessian sack over his head, he was led, resigned, to a door in the furthest wall. Bracewell held his hands painfully up against his back. He felt the cudgel at his cheek as he walked, an implicit threat that was enough to tame him.

"Wait," Bracewell commanded, letting go his hands for a moment. Tam heard the sliding of a metal lock and a door opened. Even with his head covered, he was aware of the movement of cool air. He could smell the Thames. Daylight filtered through the rough material to such an extent that he squinted against the glare. He would have called out if he had not been certain that such an action would have resulted in a blow from the cudgel. Bracewell pushed him roughly forwards and, with a great effort, Tam placed one foot in front of the other. His breathing was laboured. His limbs were heavy and awkward. "You'll make us a fine penny tonight," hissed Thackeray in his ear. Tam wondered what he meant. He tried to throw the man a coarse word or two such as he had learned in his time at the barracks, but the air caught in his throat and he fell into a coughing fit that exhausted him. Just as he feared he could walk no further, he was brought to a halt. He heard the rasp of another lock and a door swing open on rusty hinges. A roar engulfed him like a wave, the sound of an expectant audience. It sounded like a hundred men were gathered in one place, each shouting to be heard over his neighbour. Tam was shoved forward and felt himself at the bottom of a flight of steps, the lower tread barking painfully against his shins. Led step-by-step up the stairs, he heard a great roar rise from the crowd. The air crackled with expectation. He had the unnerving feeling the roar was for him. The ground beneath his feet was springy and forgiving, giving Tam the impression of standing on a wooden platform some feet above the ground. He was commanded to stop. Another roar rose from the crowd and he was certain he had been joined by another, the floor bouncing subtly at their faltering footsteps. A slow handclap was started and feet were stamped on the ground in a cacophony of sound that seemed to come from all around. The clapping increased in speed until there was a wall of sound about him. Just as Tam felt he would go mad with the noise, the hessian sack was whipped from his head.

Big Tam found himself standing on a raised wooden stage in a huge wharf, before a baying crowd. At least a hundred were crushed in a mass before him, with yet more hanging off balconies and galleries around the walls. He stood, bemused, blinking into the light.

"He's a gonna!" yelled a man from the crowd, only to be contradicted by a louder shout, "Nah, he's a dead cert! Look at the size of 'im!" Those nearest the stage thumped on its wooden planks in the excitement, and Big Tam saw bundles of notes being held aloft. "The big man to win!" shouted the first man again and a roar of approval rose to the rafters. Many of the spectators were in their finest clothes. Gentlemen sported frock coats and silk top hats and there were even one or two ladies in their best dresses and shawls. Amongst the crowd, Big Tam saw men and women circulating with leather pouches around their waists. Periodically, they would stop to take bundles of money from the audience and place them in their pouches, offering a chit in return. "You know the odds!" called one as they moved about the room. "Three to one on the big man to win, two to nine on the Spaniard!"

Big Tam looked at the man beside him. He had a squat, powerful, physique and was hopping from one foot to the other in preparation. His bare torso glistened with sweat. His tanned skin glowed in the gaslight like burnished leather.

"He's won me the best part of ten pounds already," pronounced a fat man in the front row. "My money's on the Spaniard!"

"He's been lucky," called another. "I'm backing the newcomer!"

"Then he's a loser for sure," came the response. "If he's got an ounce of sense, he'll run a mile!"

The room erupted into laughter and abusive gestures were exchanged across the crowd. The air was a fog of tobacco smoke, and Tam saw bottles of beer and gin being passed from man to man. Slowly, it was dawning on him. Even to his addled brain, it was becoming clear he was expected to fight the brawny man beside him. Big Tam fancied himself as proficient with his fists at the best of times, but he was in no fit state to fight. Every muscle, joint and limb was aching. His head felt split from the blows dealt him by the hooded figure. His jaw throbbed with a dull pain. And he was certain he had been drugged. The scene swam before him and it was all he could do to keep his balance. He felt faint from lack of food and his throat burned.

A shout came from the rafters. "Let them fight!" The call was repeated and taken up by everyone in the room, each syllable punctuated with the stamping of many feet. Tam felt the floor beneath him shaking in time.

A whistle sounded and there was a sudden silence. Tam felt his hands being released and, looking behind him, he saw Bracewell run as best he could back to the steps, the handcuffs swinging loose in his hand. Tam flailed wildly about him, causing a roar of excitement to rise from the crowd.

"He's a feisty one!" roared a rangy man from one of the galleries. "What've you been feeding him, Bracewell?"

Big Tam turned to the crowd and roared. "May God damn ye all!"

"Haggis by the sound of it!" shouted the fat man in the front row as Tam's Scottish vowels rolled to the roof. A peel of laughter rang out in response.

As the crowd hushed in expectation, Big Tam looked around the raised dais. It was ringed by a rope, secured at intervals to posts. Bracewell was hooking up the last of the ropes behind him as he exited the ring, leaving Tam alone with his opponent. Around the platform, men were placed with cudgels balanced menacingly in their hands. Tam knew he wouldn't stand a chance if he attempted escape. All eyes were upon the two men, awaiting a signal to begin. In the silence, last minute bids were placed, the conversations taking place via a sequence of elaborate hand gestures. Tam turned to face the Spaniard. He was crouching low, his body tensed in expectation. His eyes were aflame with a belligerent menace, his fists held tight. The whistle blew again and he was upon him.

The Spaniard was quick and light on his feet, dancing this way and that. He was too lissom for Big Tam's befuddled brain. A blow was planted on his cheek; a right hook with power behind it. Tam rolled with it as best he could but still the impact was heavy. His already bruised jaw sang with pain. Ducking away, he jabbed with his left hand, making contact with the Spaniard's forehead. He headed for the ropes. Someone started a slow handclap. Tam's eyes darted around the room. The Spaniard fell about him. A hail of blows connected with Tam's head. He crouched low, bunching his hands about his face, only to be dealt an uppercut that sent him spinning backwards into the ropes. The Spaniard was a blur. Tam felt jabs to his kidneys and stomach and fell to the floor in agony. He spat shattered teeth from his mouth. The crowd roared as one, chits and money being waved in the air. Tam hauled himself to his feet. The Spaniard was at the ropes, grandstanding to the crowd, his arms raised above his head. Tam knew his only hope was his size. The extra foot he had over his opponent would give him an advantage. He knew his greater weight would work in his favour. Gathering his strength, Tam clasped his hands together and held them up over his head. Approaching the Spaniard from behind, he brought his hands smashing down on the man's head, jumping off the ground to throw his weight behind his arms as they fell. There was an audible gasp from the crowd as the Spaniard buckled to his knees. He stayed there just long enough for Tam to deal him a fearful blow with his right hand and he fell to the floor with a thud. Tam lurched to the ropes and hung there to catch his breath. The crowd was divided. It seemed half of them were delighted by the turn of events, waving their strips of paper in the air in celebration, while the other half chanted "Get up! Get up!" The chorus was hypnotic.

As Tam spat mouthfuls of blood to the floor, he saw the fat man in the front row douse the Spaniard with beer from his bottle in an attempt to revive him. Slowly, Tam saw him move. A hush of anticipation fell in the room. Slowly, the clapping started again, increasing in volume and frequency, willing the Spaniard to his feet. Tam swore to himself as he saw his opponent rise. His best chance would be to get him quick, before he'd had the time to fully come to his senses. Tam lurched from the ropes, swaying unsteadily, his focus on his opponent. The crowd shouted in warning and the Spaniard turned just in time. Jumping to his feet, he shook the sweat from his hair and lay into the Scotsman. Tam was taken by surprise and had left himself wide open. With an almighty roar of exasperation, he swung his arms around him in the vain attempt to make contact with his opponent. A particularly vicious volley left him with a gaping gash upon his eye. The Spaniard made use of his diminutive size, landing uppercut after uppercut on Big Tam's jaw. Tam felt the bone shatter as the blows landed. His head throbbed. The blood ran into his eye and down his face into his mouth. He spat in frustration, suddenly aware that he was losing all feeling in his legs. They crumpled beneath him as he reeled to the ropes. His head rolling feebly from side to side as he hung there, Tam felt something pressed into his hand from behind. It was hard, cold and metal. Looking down to his clenched fist, he realised it was closed around a brass knuckleduster; a length of jagged metal to be wound around the fingers of his right hand to produce a formidable and deadly weapon. He twisted his head round to see who had passed him the fatal prop, but saw no one beyond the men with their cudgels, standing menacingly behind the ropes. Slipping his fingers through the holes in the metal, Big Tam looked up at the Spaniard. He was winding himself up for a final charge at the Scotsman, his fists held before him, tensed for the denouement. With a roar, Tam raised his hands again, bringing his fists and the vicious metal smashing down on the Spaniard's head. As his opponent fell to the floor in defeat, there was a roar of disappointment from the audience. Looking about him, Big Tam's gaze was caught by a young man in the audience. Standing at the front, he had an open face, a mop of curly blond hair, and wore an expression somewhere between interest and alarm.

His labours finished at the dock and having worked up quite the appetite, Detective Sergeant Anthony Graves had joined some fellow workers at The Coopers Chophouse on Horselydown Lane. It was a dingy room with a low ceiling and a sticky floor. What windows there were afforded the room little light on account of the filth that lay on the glass. In a corner, a chop grill spat and smoked. The smell of burning fat mixed with the tang of tobacco and stale beer. It was just the sort of place Graves would wish to find after a hard day's graft. Ordering himself a ha'penny plate of meat and bread, he settled by the bar to down a tankard of foaming ale.

"Sallow's got his eye on you, then."

Graves turned to see the stocky man with the lantern jaw who had warned him at the dock. He was tucking into a pie. He took great forkfuls at a time, chewing at the meat as he spoke.

"Saw you with him at Corder's Wharf."

"What do you know of Sallow?" Graves wiped the foam from his mouth.

"You'd do well to watch yer step," the young man said through a mouthful of gravy. "Once he's got yer, you'll never get away."

Graves leaned his elbow on the bar as his plate arrived. "What would he want of me?" he asked innocently.

"He's recruitin'".

"For what?"

"He needs men." The stocky man looked about him, lowering his voice to a whisper. "There's a delivery Saturday night."

Graves chewed at his chop. It was more gristle than meat, he noted with disappointment. "At St. Saviour's?"

The man nodded, his deep-set eyes narrowing all the more. "You'll know soon enough if Sallow wants you."

Graves downed another draft of ale in an attempt to wash down a particularly stubborn piece of meat. "What's the delivery?"

His companion smiled a greasy smile. "It won't be tea and turmeric, that's for sure."

"Bailey!"

The man almost dropped his pie at the shout that came from further along the bar. Graves turned to see a rough looking man with a balding head and scars on his face.

"That's enough!" the scarred man growled.

Chastened, Bailey lowered his eyes to his plate.

"Sallow's business is just that, and no one else's." The bald man shot Graves a look of warning and returned to his business at the bar.

Bailey continued his meal in silence, ignoring all attempts to engage him in further conversation. Every now and then, Graves noticed, he would glance up to the bald man at the bar, only to find himself the recipient of another warning look.

The sergeant polished off his food and decided to be on his way. There was nothing more to be learned here. Now the crowds of workers had had time to disperse, he wanted a closer look at

Corder's Wharf and, in particular, the room where he had joined Sallow about his work. Wiping the grease from his mouth with the back of his hand, he made his way to the street, purposefully avoiding the ill-tempered stare from the bald man at the bar.

The road outside was quiet. With the tide out, Graves knew there would be little activity at St. Saviour's Dock. As he turned to the river, he was struck by the sweet smell of hops from the Courage brewery across the street. Tall chimneys belched their steam into the sky, their brick scorched black from the heat. Rounding the corner onto Shad Thames, Graves stopped for a moment to gaze out at the river. The retreating waters had revealed muddy banks at either side. Graves could see strange debris caught in the sediment. Clothing, great metal chains and dead fish littered the shoreline, the smell rising in the afternoon sun. If the tide had been in and the Thames lapping at the shore around George's Stairs, Graves would never have heard the sound. It was quite incongruous and, at first, Graves couldn't believe his senses. As he trained his ears to the wharves at his right, he could hear quite distinctly the cheering of many men. Following the sound, he walked up the side of Butler's Wharf along Curlew Street. The noise seemed to be coming from inside the great wharf to his side. He looked along its length for an entrance.

In just a few minutes, he found a heavy corrugated door left ajar. The noise from within was coming in waves now, by turns expressions of excitement or appreciation, then howls of frustration or disappointment. Graves was reminded of the audience he had seen at The Theatre Royal, Drury Lane just the day before. The door swung open at his touch with a squeak. With a last look around the street to make sure he wasn't being watched, the young sergeant squeezed through the gap into the cavernous space beyond.

Butler's Wharf was huge. Several thousand square feet were home to shelves upon shelves of grain, sugar, cloves, cinnamon, rubber, tea and tapioca; all imported goods awaiting transportation to the markets of London and beyond. The roof was so high as to be barely visible in the low light. The smell was a pungent mix of rare and exotic spices, tea and rubber. It was all Graves could do to stop himself exclaiming aloud at the sheer scale of it all. He marvelled at the miles these sacks, cases and chests must have travelled. The tea, stored in chests away from the spices to preserve its flavour, bore labels proudly proclaiming its origins in India or Ceylon. There seemed to be thousands of them stacked carefully as high as the eye could see. Crates of rubber from Malaya stood opposite chests of pepper from Singapore. Graves could see other crates marked as containing coffee, cocoa and sugar. In that one moment, he felt as if he stood at the very centre of the Empire. In time, much of the produce around him would face its ignominious end at the dinner tables of England, with scarcely a thought given to the industry involved in its passage around the world. Shaking his head at the thought, Graves moved slowly to the furthest end of the wharf, keeping to the shadows afforded him by the stacks of crates that loomed above him. The noise of the crowd rang in his ears as he turned a corner to a large space in which a makeshift stage had been erected. All around it, a throng of people waved slips of paper and rolls of notes excitedly in the air. There must have been upwards of a hundred of them standing before the improvised scaffold, with yet more hanging precariously from the many balconies and galleries that surrounded it.

"Where's your money goin'?" Graves turned to face the source of the voice. He was confronted by an eager looking man in a corduroy jacket, a leather pouch tied around his waist. "The Spaniard or the Scotsman?" He had to shout to make himself heard above the melee.

Graves thought fast. "What are the odds on the Scotsman?"

"Three to one," the man replied. "He's putting up a brave front. But the Spaniard's yer man." He nodded to the stage where, for the first time, Sergeant Graves saw the object of the crowd's fascination. Two men, stripped to the waist and bloodied, were smashing seven bells out of each other.

"Let me get a feel for him," blustered Graves to buy time, 'to see where my money's best placed."

"The odds'll go against you as the fight proceeds," the man cautioned. "The Kaiser's got money to make."

Graves started at the mention of the name. The man with the beaked nose, who he had but lately seen in a police constable's uniform, had been linked to the Kaiser by the actors at Drury Lane. He looked around him as the man in the corduroy jacket moved on, taking money from those in the crowd who wished to place a wager and tearing off a chit for them in return. Almost every other man in the place held a note or two in the air. Graves guessed hundreds of pounds could be changing hands. Was it all destined for this mysterious Kaiser? And to what end? Pushing through the crowd, he made his way to the makeshift stage. It had been hammered together, he could see now, from long planks of wood that were fixed on barrels for support. The rickety floor bounced with each movement the two fighters made, bending alarmingly whenever one was thrown to the floor. All around him, people were shouting encouragement at their preferred combatant, either for the Scotsman or the Spaniard. Even in the few moments he had stood there, Graves could tell it wasn't an even match. Although he had weight and height on his side, the taller of the two combatants was tiring. The smaller, darker man, whom Graves guessed was the Spaniard, was quick and lively on his feet. He seemed more practised with his fists, and more used to the crowds than his opponent.

"Tasty, ain't he?" A fat man breathed in Graves' ear, a gleam of excitement in his eye. "Over twenty fights and he's never let me down." He leaned in closer, the better to be heard over the baying crowd. "Got a bullseye on him tonight."

Graves raised his eyebrows. A fifty-pound bet would be well beyond his means as a humble detective sergeant. "That man there," the fat man continued, pointing a chubby finger at the Spaniard in the ring, "paid for my daughter's wedding!"

The men around him laughed heartily, pulling their wallets from their pockets to place their own bets in the Spaniard's favour, encouraged by the fat man's tale of good fortune. The man in the corduroy jacket was with them at once, taking their money with a practised professionalism. His eyes glinted at the fat man as he did so. Graves guessed he was a stooge, employed to talk the Spaniard up and encourage those around him to make bets of their own. Almost at once, Graves knew how the fight must end. With the Spaniard making a strong showing in the early stages, and stooges like the fat man placed amongst the crowd to talk him up, big wagers would be made in his favour. If the Kaiser was to make their money tonight, the Spaniard would lose, no matter that it was clear he was the stronger fighter. As if to confirm his suspicions, there came an almighty roar from the stage. The taller of the two men whom Graves had guessed was the Scotsman, had brought his locked hands down on the Spaniard's head. For a moment, the smaller man stood stock still, an expression of dazed indignation clouding his swarthy face. Then, almost comically, he crumpled to the floor, his face smashing hard against the rough planks of the stage. A chorus of boos rose from the crowd, the majority of whom were waving their chits angrily about them. The fat man, Graves noticed, and the man in the corduroy jacket were suddenly nowhere to be seen. Glancing back to the stage, the sergeant at last got a clear view of the two men. The victor stood, breathing hard, his eyes wild. His opponent lay prone at his feet, his head bloodied, his chest rising and falling as he gasped for breath. Through all this, Graves saw that one thing united them. Both men on the stage had the distinction of bearing a mark upon their chest. It was a mark that Graves recognised, and he caught his breath as he thought through the implications. Both men in the ring had been branded on their chests with the mark of the Devil.

XXI

The Devil's Neckcloth

"Tell me all you know of Cornelius Bracewell."

Alma Beaurepaire looked up from her ledger to be confronted by a dishevelled Detective Inspector Bowman.

"Gee, George," she purred, snapping the book shut. "Didn't get much sleep last night?"

Bowman swallowed hard and tried to run his fingers through his tangled hair. He knew he presented something of a ruffled demeanour. He had fallen asleep in the hansom on his way to Bermondsey. Indeed, the driver had had to knock hard upon the roof to alert him to his arrival. Now, his eyes felt bloodshot and his mouth was dry. He suddenly realised he had not eaten at all.

"How long has Bracewell been in place at St. Saviour's Dock?"

"Been in place?" Alma parroted. "What a peculiar turn of phrase." Her soft tone of voice lent a playful air to her words. "Perhaps we could find somewhere more comfortable to talk?"

Despite her levity, Bowman thought he detected a hint of steel behind her words. She seemed, however subtly, to regard him altogether differently since their last encounter at The Sisters Of Mercy.

Alma Beaurepaire led the inspector to a sparse but comfortable office area on the first floor. A bay window gave out onto the street below, affording them a good vantage of Bermondsey and the streets down to the river. Two small leather chairs stood either side of a desk and a wooden bookcase strewn with papers filled an entire wall.

"Cornelius Bracewell *is* St. Saviour's Dock," Alma was opining as she sat at the chair nearest the window. "There's nothing that happens there that he doesn't know of."

"How long has he been the loading officer?"

"Some ten years. He has made quite the name for himself." Alma gestured that Bowman should sit. He ignored the offer.

"In what way?" he asked.

"He is well-trusted, George." Alma leaned back in her chair, stretching her long arms above her head. "St. Saviour's is a commercial concern. It must make money."

Bowman's mind returned to Tremont's comments concerning the competition from Tilbury Docks.

"Have you had many dealings with the man?"

Alma leaned forward on the desk, a lock of curly hair falling on her forehead. "We are the nearest police station. We are here to serve all who need us. Mr Bracewell has often had need to call upon us."

"In what regard?"

Alma smiled, gently amused by the inspector's formal manner. "Mostly in matters of public order," she said, blowing her hair from her face in a manner that Bowman found most endearing. "The dockworkers are a breed apart; a rowdy bunch when in their cups. Then there is the matter of the black market."

"Oh?" Bowman raised his eyebrows.

"Wherever there is trade, George, there will be criminals. Smugglers, pirates. As I understand it, that is why you were sent to Bermondsey."

Bowman swallowed hard at the implication. Callaghan had warned him not to stray beyond his remit into matters that did not concern him. Yet, here he was. Bowman shook his head to clear it. He could not stand idly by if he thought there were criminal matters afoot. Glancing up, he noticed Alma looking at him expectantly, as if she required a response.

"And you, Miss Beaurepaire," he stuttered. "What brings you here? This is hardly the job for a woman."

Alma's eyes opened wide as she laughed at the remark. "Oh George," she began. "You and I both know it is men that rule the world, but it takes a woman to change it."

Bowman blanched. That was, he thought to himself, almost exactly the sort of thing Anna would have said. His moustache twitched at his mouth.

"Are you trying to change the world, Miss Beaurepaire?"

"Bit by bit, George." She held her hands wide. "Your Queen Victoria sits at the head of her Empire. Why cannot I sit at the head of mine?"

Bowman's eyes narrowed. "Is she not your Queen, too?"

There was a palpable silence in the room as Alma's eyes bore into him. Breaking her gaze, she looked around her as she spoke.

"This station was in disarray when I arrived, the local police held in low regard. I like to think I have assisted in its elevation."

Bowman nodded thoughtfully. Alma Beaurepaire had plainly been an asset to the people of Bermondsey. He changed tack. "Does Bracewell have any dealings with St. Katharine Docks?"

"His remit is for matters pertaining to St. Saviour's," Alma replied simply. "While St. Katharine Docks sit under the auspices of the Port Of London too, they are not Bracewell's territory."

Bowman's eyebrows rose at the use of the word. He thought it a strange one to use. Alma was looking deep into his eyes again, her gaze a silent challenge.

"And what of you, Inspector Bowman?" She used his title for the first time, he noticed, as if she was singularly unimpressed. "Will you change the world?"

Feeling suddenly awkward under her penetrating gaze, Bowman moved to the window to survey the streets below. A young child with no shoes was playing with a stray dog. An elderly woman sat by the roadside begging. He suddenly felt very hot.

"I had thought to, once. But now I rather think the world has changed me." Had Alma looked into his eyes at that particular moment, she might well have seen a greater sadness than she had seen in any man.

"But you must at least have hopes of bringing a change to the world? Or else, why rise in the morning?"

Bowman blinked. "It is a question I ask myself every day," he heard himself say.

"We all need a reason," said Alma, plainly.

"I fear I have lost mine." Bowman swallowed again, suddenly aware of the ambiguity in his statement.

Alma rose from her chair as Bowman turned to face her. "I am sorry to hear it," she was saying, a look of concern on her face. "Your wife?"

Bowman felt himself nodding, slowly. "She is dead."

"How alarming." Alma lifted a hand to her face. "Under what circumstances?"

In his mind's eye, Bowman was briefly back on Hanbury Street. The hooves thundered against the flagstones, the carriage clattering towards him. He felt the handle of the gun once more, his finger tightening around the trigger.

"She died as she lived," he whispered, barely aware of the room around him. "In the pursuit of helping others."

Alma was nodding. "Then perhaps, George, that is where you must find your inspiration." Just as Bowman was sure she would reach out to him, there came a disturbance at the stairs. Turning as one to the door, they saw a small boy enter the room, his clothes and hair dishevelled, his breathing erratic from his exertions.

"Miss Beaurepaire, you must come right away," he panted.

Alma was with him at once, crouching to place both hands on his shoulders. She looked him full in the face. "What is it, Samuel?"

"I have been sent to fetch you to St. Saviour's," he breathed, his face flushed. "The Devil has come to the dock!"

They walked so fast, they kicked up dirt at their heels. Alma had set quite a pace, and it was all Inspector Bowman could do to keep up with her. The streets were slowly filling as news of a discovery spread from house to house. Men were even leaving the taverns and public houses to see what the fuss was. By the time they were at Gedling Street, there was quite a crowd behind them and an even larger one before them. Dockhead was crammed with bystanders eager to view the sight, and Alma had to clear a path through with her elbows. Bowman noticed several women standing with their hands over their mouths, their eyes wide with shock. One was crying. Children ran from the streets and called for their parents. He heard the word 'devil' several times, carried on the breeze like a fire catching from one tree to the next. There was a palpable sense of panic in the air. At last, they were at the head of the throng, and Bowman saw the cause of the collective anxiety. There, where the road met the dock and on the very patch of land that Cornelius Bracewell had described as the Devil's Neckcloth, stood an improvised gibbet. As the crowd gathered to behold the grisly scene, their cries of anguish carried across the dock to the open river beyond. The pitiful figure of a young girl swung by her neck in the wind. Bowman took his policeman's whistle from his pocket and blew.

Slipping away from Butler's Wharf, Sergeant Graves skirted round Shad Thames with his head full of questions. He had heard the mysterious Kaiser mentioned a handful of times now. They were clearly a powerful figure, able to command both fear and respect amongst the people of the south bank and beyond. He remembered the actors at The Theatre Royal stage door and marvelled that the Kaiser's reach could stretch so far. As he mulled over the events in Butler's Wharf, he noticed the streets were emptier than usual. With the tide at its lowest, he reasoned, the majority of dockworkers would be in their beds or in the taverns and chophouses that littered the area. Now would be the perfect time, he thought, to pay another visit to Corder's Wharf. Ichabod Sallow had clearly been up to no good in the cellar and Graves was eager to learn more. His keen eyes scanning the road for anyone watching, the sergeant pulled at a side door into the wharf and slipped inside. He stood for a moment to get his bearings, his eyes adjusting to the gloom. As he had hoped, the wharf was deserted. He stepped quietly between the shelves and galleries and made a beeline for the small antechamber where he had, just two hours before, assisted Sallow with his work. Resting his weight against the great sliding doors, he pushed just enough to create a small opening. Squeezing his lithe frame through the gap, Graves slid the doors shut behind him.

There was an eerie silence behind the doors. Only two hours ago the wharf had been a bustle of men, their grunts and oaths cutting through the air. The dock beyond had been heaving with activity. Now, all was quiet. The little sunlight that made it through the filthy windows caught on the dust that danced in the air. Graves stepped gingerly over to the trap door in the floor. Crouching on his haunches, he felt through the dust to the edges of the trap. Hooking his fingers beneath the slab, he succeeded in lifting the door open on its hinges. Clapping his hands together and wiping them on his trousers, Graves peered into the gloom below. He could see a ladder descending into the darkness. Looking around, he found a lamp placed on a shelf. Pulling a box of matches from his pocket, he lit the wick and turned up the flame. The glass placed over the lamp, the sergeant stood still for a moment. He was sure there had been movement in the street beyond the window. Satisfied the disturbance had passed, Graves lowered himself slowly down the ladder into the pit below.

He was greeted by a large, cavernous space that ran the entire length and width of the wharf above. Arches and vaults supported the building, giving the space an almost sepulchral appearance. Shadows danced against the bare brick walls as the flame in Graves' lamp guttered with the subtle movements in the damp air. Holding his light before him, he saw a row of sacks propped up beneath an arch. Placing the lamp carefully at his feet, Graves tore at the hessian material, dipping his fingers carefully into the sack. He felt a fine powder between his fingers. Rubbing them together at his nose, he felt the familiar exotic smell catch at his throat. Turmeric. Turning from the sacks, he bent beneath an arch to see a large container standing on the floor. It was a squat but substantial wooden skip. Graves could see long handled paddles leaning against its sides. Lifting his lamp to peer inside, he saw it was almost empty. A film of white powder lined the walls and even gathered into drifts at the corners. Larger sacks were stacked beyond the skip, their contents indicated quite clearly by the single word stamped onto the hessian; FLOUR. The implication was clear. Sallow had been mixing the turmeric with the much cheaper flour. Such tainting of produce was illegal. It was also extremely lucrative. Graves couldn't help but think that the two things he had witnessed today were somehow linked. That the funds raised by the fight in Butler's Wharf and the income derived from the tainting of spice were being used to the same ends. Just as he mused how best to proceed, Sergeant Graves heard the whistle.

A huge crowd had gathered at Dockhead. Graves pushed his way through, eager to respond to the appeal for assistance. He was surprised to see Inspector Bowman himself with the whistle in his hand, a tall, lithesome woman standing next to him. The crowd was turned as one to focus on something above their heads, and Graves saw the inspector, too, had lifted his chin. Following his gaze, Graves beheld the object of their fascination. There, swinging from a makeshift gibbet, was the body of Kitty Baldwin.

XXII

Reflections

It came as a surprise to Bowman that Graves had known her.

"Her name was Kitty," the young sergeant explained over a forlorn pint of porter in The Silver Cross. "She was stage door keeper at The Theatre Royal." He had taken the chance to change out of his dockworker's clothes at Scotland Yard and now sat downcast with Inspector Bowman in a private booth at the back of the tavern.

"In Drury Lane?" asked Bowman, his habitual frown cutting all the deeper into his forehead.

"She found Pope's body in Vinegar Yard. I pitied the lass, so took it upon myself to drop by the theatre." Sergeant Graves toyed with his glass. Bowman regarded him in silence. His usually cheerful features were cowed, his bright eyes downcast. "I offered to walk her home but she'd disappeared."

"You suspect that was when she was abducted?" Bowman's features were clouded in thought as he nursed a glass of brandy in his hands. He had already finished two before Graves had joined him, and was both relieved and alarmed at how it had calmed his ragged nerves.

Graves cast his mind back to the grubby boy with the felt cap on St. Catherine Street. "Word was got to the Kaiser that she was keeping company with a Scotland Yarder, I am sure of it." He thought of the boy's knowing smile as he had left the theatre.

Bowman paused mid-sip. "You know of the Kaiser?"

"I have heard his name both in Drury Lane and St. Saviour's Dock."

"In what regard?"

Graves pushed his still full glass away from him, clearly not in the mood to drink. "As I arrived at the Stage Door, I was told Kitty was 'working out the Kaiser's share'. I thought nothing of it."

"What business do you think he had with Kitty?"

"That I do not know, but I saw a man leave in haste with a parcel beneath his arm. I fair near fell over him."

"'So Kitty was hanged as a warning."

"But as a warning to whom?" Graves' cheeks were flushed with emotion. "To those who would speak out against the Kaiser? Or to those who would investigate him?"

"Perhaps both," Bowman said, sadly. "I have heard much talk of this mysterious Kaiser in Bermondsey and have directed my efforts to investigating him."

"She died because of her association with me." Graves sinking into a heavy mood. "It hardly seems fair, when you have been investigating, too." He lifted his eyes to the ceiling, trying to stem the tears.

Bowman shrugged. "There's reason enough, Graves," he said plainly. "I have no one." His heart growing heavy, the inspector looked beyond the glass partition that separated their booth from the rest of the saloon. The day's work done, The Silver Cross was filling up nicely. Harris would be pleased.

Graves' eyes were shining with tears now. Bowman swallowed hard. "Tell me of your day at Shad Thames," he said by way of offering a distraction.

Grateful for the diversion, the sergeant described the events he had witnessed in Butler's Wharf. "The fighters bore the same mark upon their chests as Harry Pope," he concluded.

"And they were collecting funds at the wharf?" Bowman sat back in his chair, deep in thought.

"I was told as much."

Bowman pinched the bridge of his nose. He was suddenly aware that he had not slept in twenty-four hours. "Do you not see the pattern, Graves?"

"Pattern, sir?" The sergeant stared at him, blankly.

"Between Drury Lane and Butler's Wharf. I suspect the Kaiser may be running a protection racket in the West End."

The young sergeant followed the train of thought. "And raising funds through illegal boxing at Butler's Wharf," he agreed, the pieces suddenly falling into place. "And creaming profits from St. Saviour's Dock. I found Ichabod Sallow tainting a consignment of turmeric at Corder's Wharf."

"So we can assume that Jonas Cook fell foul of Sallow. By all accounts he was a pious man and would not have taken well to Sallow's practises."

"Sallow must have panicked when he heard of your visit to Cook at the convent."

"And he made certain that Cook wouldn't talk."

Graves' face creased in thought. "Is Ichabod Sallow the Kaiser?"

Bowman thought back to his altercation in Willow Walk. "It is possible," he nodded, downing his brandy rather more quickly than was seemly. "He is certainly feared by all at St. Saviour's."

"Then we have Harry Pope's story." Graves was suddenly energised. "Pope must have fallen foul of Ichabod Sallow at Corder's Wharf and effected his escape. But he was caught at Vinegar Yard."

"The wonder is that he ran so far without approaching an officer of the law," offered Bowman, his hands held wide. "Drury Lane is well policed."

Graves leaned forward on his seat, his eyes alert. "I may have the answer to that, sir."

Bowman raised his eyebrows, expectantly.

"The man I saw at the stage door I saw again at the dock, in a police constable's uniform." Bowman's jaw dropped at the news. "Perhaps he did not approach the police because he did not trust them."

Bowman rubbed at his forehead and smoothed his hair with a hand. "It strikes me, Sergeant Graves, that we have been working on the same case ever since you attended Pope's body in Vinegar Yard."

"It's certainly looking that way, sir." Graves reached for his drink again and took his first sip. He never felt better than when progress was being made, and his helplessness in the face of Kitty's death had been replaced with a hope that it would soon be atoned for.

"I have spent some time with William Tremont in the cells at Bow Street," Inspector Bowman was saying. "He too has felt the Kaiser's hand. He says the bomb at St. Katharine Docks was set as a warning to him."

"A warning?" Graves eyes met the inspector's.

"He has been forced to make payments under threat of such action as we saw yesterday."

"And you can be sure the Kaiser is at the bottom of it?"

"He mentioned the very name unprompted."

"This Kaiser has the whole of London in his thrall." Graves was shaking his head at the sheer scale of the operation.

Bowman smoothed his moustache between his fingers as he thought. "Tremont is being held under investigation by the Special Irish Branch, but I believe their intelligence is unfounded. He also mentioned he was being undercut by cheap labour being employed at St. Saviour's."

"Men like Pope," Graves nodded in understanding. "And perhaps the two men at Butler's Wharf. They were put to work under Sallow and forced to fight to raise money."

Bowman's face was a mask of concentration. He found it difficult to believe Cornelius Bracewell would know nothing of all this. Alma Beaurepaire had mentioned how much he knew of the dock's workings. He might even have arranged the fight in Butler's Wharf. "But why had they been branded with the Devil's mark?" he asked aloud. "And for what are the funds being raised?"

Graves took another sip and wiped the froth from his upper lip with his sleeve. "I can help you there, too, sir." He shuffled his weight in his chair, looking round to be certain he was not overheard. "There is to be a shipment."

"At the dock?" Bowman lowered his voice.

"Tomorrow," confirmed Graves.

"A shipment of what?" Bowman was thinking hard.

Graves leant back, his palms raised in a gesture of futility. "Saturday night is all I know."

The trees were bloated with blossom. Great displays of pink and white stretched over the paths. It gathered in drifts at the kerbside as Bowman made his way back to his rooms in Hampstead. The wide roads were quieter here than in the city, and the inspector was grateful for the sweeter air. He had hailed a cab at Trafalgar Square. Lulled by the rhythm of the wheels on the road, he had almost fallen asleep. He tapped on the roof to bring the driver to a halt a street or two from his rooms. The cool evening air, he hoped, would revive him. Well turned-out children played hoop-and-stick in the street in between the sporadic traffic, and Bowman saw couples out to take in the evening's sights. Smart brougham carriages stood on the roadside outside grand townhouses with immaculate gardens. Hedges had been pruned and shaped. Beds of tulips added a splash of colour to the evening.

For all its respectable finery, thought Bowman, smart London life was always ever just a step away from depravity and decline. Indeed, much of the genteel life around him depended for its very existence on the sweat, toil and exploitation of the criminal classes. Wherever there was inequality, he mused, there was need, and wherever there was need, there was almost inevitably crime. As he turned off the main road, his legs felt as heavy as his eyes. He was looking forward to welcoming the sweet oblivion of sleep.

Bowman's rooms were a shambles of discarded clothes. A screen divided the living area from the dining table and even this was strewn with unwashed shirts. With the sun retreating, Bowman lit a lamp at the dresser and sat for a moment, staring at the ceiling as if he might find inspiration there. Finally, he resolved that he should shave. Heating a little water at the range, he carried it in a bowl to the table, fetching a small mirror and razor from the dresser behind him. As he made a lather from a small bar of hard soap, he took the time to gaze upon his reflection. His skin looked paler than he remembered, the dark rings beneath his eyes more pronounced. His grizzled cheeks were sunken. As he looked down at his shaving brush, he noticed the faintest ringing in his ears. The breath caught in his throat and the room began to swim. Searching for something, anything, to anchor himself in the here and now, Bowman looked up to the mirror. He saw another man looking back.

This other Bowman was almost a year younger, and certainly healthier looking. But still, he was fearful. A hat was upon his head and his coat turned up at the collar. Bowman stared at the reflection. He felt diminished beneath his own gaze. He grabbed at the glass, raising the shaving brush to his cheek in hopes that the mundanity of the act would break the spell. The other Bowman raised a gun.

And now he could hear the hooves. Distant at first but now distinct, they clattered on the road, pulling the thunder of the carriage in their wake. His heart beat hard against his chest. His mouth dried. He tried to blink the image away but still his younger self stared back, burning onto his retina like the summer sun. The other Bowman was turning away from the mirror now and the inspector was looking at the back of his own hat. His revolver raised, Bowman was able to stare down the barrel of the gun at the retreating carriage, just as he had on Hanbury Street almost a year ago.

"Halt!" Williams was screaming. "Stop that carriage!"

Bowman winced. He knew what must come next. He was looking down the barrel, the sight trained on the retreating carriage. His finger squeezed at the trigger, and he fired.

Bowman was beyond the mirror now. He raked through the air as if he were the bullet. He saw the gun retreat into the distance and turned to face his destination. People screamed around him. Passers by jumped from the road. Now he was at the carriage and there was a crack. He had passed through the canopy, ripping through the fabric as if it were paper. And there, improbably, he stopped. Turning to examine the hole he had made he saw, just as he knew he would, a gash. It was little more than an inch in length. He knew exactly where the hole would be and how big. He knew, he realised with a start, because he had picked at its mended seam in the brougham that had taken him to the Trafalgar Club in Greenwich.

Bowman shook violently in his parlour, upsetting the bowl of water at the table. He took great gulps of air, as if emerging from the watery depths of some unfathomable sea. The mirror fell to the floor with a sharp crack. Sitting with his fists clenched and his teeth set, he struggled with the implications of his vision. His stomach churned. His heart lurched. He realised that he had, only the day before, ridden in the carriage that had killed his wife.

Fighting the urge to vomit, he staggered from the table to the decanter at the dresser. His legs were numb beneath him. As he raised his hand to retrieve a glass from the shelf, he noticed his right hand was twitching uncontrollably. He poured himself a large Madeira and took a grateful gulp, holding the glass still between both hands. Closing his eyes, he felt its warmth revive him. The room about him settled, the ringing in his ears retreated. He pulled a curtain roughly across the window and fell upon the chaise longue, placing the decanter on the floor beneath him. The turmoil had drained him. He felt more tired now than he ever had. He resolved to sleep there. He could not face his too-big bed. Kicking off his shoes, he poured himself another glass of Madeira and sank back into the unforgiving cushions. Stretching his legs with a yawn, he reached to undo the buttons at his waistcoat. And that's when he found the note.

XXIII

The Web Of Fear

As night fell over London, so terror was unleashed. To be out alone was to be in danger. To have money was to be a target. To be in business was to be compromised.

As the lamplighters went about their duties in Drury Lane, a jeweller shut up shop for the night. The early crowds had dispersed into the gin houses and theatres and, besides, Frank Jolly was tired. He had had a busy day and sold one or two items of such value that he thought he might close early and be on his way. He lifted tray after tray of rings, necklaces and brooches from the wooden display cabinets he had inherited from his father, and carried them carefully to the safe in the back room of his shop. Peering over his glasses, he took a key from his waistcoat pocket. The hefty safe was another relic from his father's time. It never failed to move Frank Jolly when he thought of how, decades previously, Frank Senior himself would be kneeling before it as he was now, his key turning smoothly in the same lock at the same safe in the same shop. The last of the trays put safely away, the jeweller turned back into his shop to pull the shutters at the windows. His face fell as he was confronted by a familiar figure.

There, in the centre of the shop, stood Thackeray. Wearing his police constable's uniform, he was holding a lit taper in one hand, a large, earthenware demijohn in the other. Frank could smell the paraffin fuel through the cork. Thackeray raised his eyebrows expectantly. Frank Jolly considered for a moment what best to do. He was too old and too tired to fight. He could not call for help. Sighing in resignation, he knew he must do as he had always done. When the Kaiser demanded payment, only a fool declined. His eyes downcast and his shoulders slumped, Frank Jolly took the key from his waistcoat pocket and bent once more at his safe.

Mr Justice Denton sat slumped in his favourite chair. He found his new Pimlico apartment most agreeable, and most in keeping with the station he had attained in life. Having shaved and changed into his finest shirt and frock coat, he was awaiting the arrival of his driver to take him to dinner at The Atheneum. Nursing a glass in his hand, he ruminated over the day's business. Oscar Berrycloth had been presented at court as a ne're-do-well. A pickpocket and a thief, he was also known as one who demanded money with menaces. Denton was in no doubt this was, in part, to fund his evident opiate addiction but there was growing evidence that he was working for another party. Tomorrow the prosecution would spell out their case, but Denton was already convinced as to the matter of the man's guilt. Berrycloth had appeared before him several times and each of those times he had been sent down for his crimes. The prosecution in this instance, acting for an old widow from Mayfair, were pleading that Berrycloth should be hanged by the neck to rid the world of him for once and for all. Denton was of a mind to grant it.

A ring at the bell broke his train of thought, and Denton downed the last of his wine. The driver was early. No matter, thought Denton. Rising from his chair, he took a moment to straighten his coat about him and admire his reflection in the glass above the mantel. He was still a handsome man, ramrod straight and in possession of a head of thick, curly hair that fell over his ears. A great, silver beard adorned his face, affording him, he liked to think, a certain gravitas and authority. Slipping into his Astrakhan coat in the hall, his eye fell to an envelope lying on the carpet by the front door. Bending to retrieve it, he saw it was addressed to him by name. Suddenly fearful, he opened the door in hopes of seeing who had delivered the envelope. Looking quickly up and down the street, he saw no one but a few passers by, some of whom tipped their hats to him in greeting.

Breathing hard, Denton closed the door behind him and leaned against it. He tore at the paper with his nimble fingers to reveal the note within, pulling it gently from the folds of the envelope. It was written in the same spidery hand that he had come to know so well. It was a simple instruction that he knew he must obey or face a dreadful cost. 'BERRYCLOTH MUST GO FREE,' the note read. 'HE IS THE KAISER'S MAN'.

Denton staggered back to the drawing room, the blood rushing to his head. There, he calmed his nerves with a steadying hand upon the mantelpiece and poured himself another large glass of wine.

"Thank you for coming at so late an hour, doctor." Mrs Fenwick was a fat lady with very few teeth. She stood in her apron at the door, beckoning Doctor Hayes over the threshold. He was, indeed, much perturbed at having been roused at such a time of night, but the address the boy had given at his door assured the good doctor that there would at least be money to be made. He had dressed quickly but properly in a sober waistcoat and charcoal trousers and now stood, Gladstone bag in hand and top hat on head, on the doorstep to Number Twenty Three, Bridge Road, Hammersmith. The house was one of the most elegant in the row, a three-storey building with high sash windows and a smart front door. Inside, however, it was all dark furniture and heavy curtains. What small light that was permitted through the heavy drapes from the lamps outside fell upon a slight figure lying, sweating, upon a daybed in the parlour. He was swathed in blankets, yet still he shivered. Doctor Hayes noticed the sheets were damp and stained. A cracked china bowl sat on the floor by the daybed, dangerously full of a thin, brown fluid. A noxious stink hung in the air.

"He's been this way for three days, doctor," Mrs Fenwick was explaining. "He took ill on Tuesday after his fish supper and could not even make it up the stairs to his room. I've done my best for him."

The doctor did not doubt it.

"You would do well to open a window." Pulling the curtains aside, he threw up the sash to admit some night air. Moving to the patient, he knelt at the daybed and reached into his bag. Drawing out a small case, he snapped it open to reveal a thermometer. "He has not eaten since?"

The housekeeper shook her head, "Nothing."

Pulling the blankets from the patient's face, Doctor Hayes gave an almost imperceptible look of alarm. He knew this man. Despite his pallid skin and red, quivering lips, he was clearly Aaron Thurlow, a marketeer at Covent Garden. Doctor Hayes had good cause to recognise him. Some months earlier, he had treated a fellow trader at the market for injuries sustained during a beating. The unfortunate victim had been reticent to go to the law as the perpetrator, one Aaron Thurlow, held great sway over the stallholders. He demanded regular payments with menaces and often threatened grievous repercussions if they were not made. A recent spate of fires at Covent Garden had proven him true to his word. The tiniest of smiles played about the doctor's lips.

"He is plainly near death, Mrs Fenwick," he lied. "Could I trouble you for a little hot water?"

The fat housekeeper gave a little sob and crossed herself. Bobbing in a ludicrous curtsey that amused Doctor Hayes more than it should, she left the parlour for the kitchen, mouthing a silent prayer under her breath as she went.

Doctor Hayes looked again at his patient. He was all but certain he was suffering from nothing more than food poisoning. Given time he would be back on his feet and back at work, but that was an eventuality to be denied him. The doctor reached beneath the man's head to retrieve his pillow. It was wet with sweat and stained with Thurlow's saliva. As his head rolled back, the poor man's mouth gaped open to emit a reeking stench. His breathing came in fits and starts. As the doctor lifted the pillow high above the man's head, his patient's eyes snapped open. Thurlow took a moment to focus on the doctor's face as it hovered before him. He gasped and tried to call for help, but no sound came. He lifted his hands to claw at the doctor. The last thing Thurlow saw was his assailant's terrible grin, and then he felt the pillow on his face. The doctor leaned against it hard. Even in his delirium, Thurlow put up quite a struggle, his arms and legs thrashing under the blankets as he fought for breath.

"Shhh," the doctor soothed as he put his whole weight against the pillow. Slowly, the struggle subsided. Thurlow's chest ceased its rise and fall and, after a final spasm, all was quiet.

The doctor sat back, pleased with his night's work. Wiping his face with a sleeve, he snapped his bag shut and stood to await the return of the housekeeper. He would deliver the sad news with a practised, solemn expression. He would then offer her his invoice, exit the house with a tip of his hat and send word to the Kaiser that as Aaron Thurlow was dead, Covent Garden Market was theirs.

St. Saviour's Dock was between shipments. The Thames limped past at its lowest tide. The chophouses and inns had long since discharged their last customers. Some complained loudly as they staggered through the streets to their beds. The wharves loomed over the narrow alleys in the darkness. Stray dogs took the opportunity to scavenge amongst the piles of filth ejected from the tanneries and mills.

Rats ran for cover as the old nag limped down Shad Thames, pulling Finnegan's cart behind it. Finnegan was a sour-faced man, his mouth perpetually drawn down in a look of disdain. He had reason to look so embittered. A life lived on the fringes of crime had left him shouldering much of the responsibility but receiving little of the profit. The meagre hand-outs he had received from those he served through the years had brought him little more than enough to feed his horse every week. He supposed, he reasoned soberly, he should count himself lucky to have lasted so long. As he rounded the corner with his cart, clicking his tongue to coax his horse across the cobbles, Finnegan saw Ichabod Sallow standing by the door to Corder's Wharf. A half spent cheroot dangled from his lips. At a signal, Finnegan pulled his cart to a stop, his horse flicking her tail in a show of lazy indifference.

Ichabod's men worked quietly, opening up the doors to the wharf in near silence. As he lounged on the road smoking, they loaded sacks of tainted turmeric onto the wagon.

"Where's this lot headed?" one man asked of the driver.

"Bristol," came the reply. Finnegan leaned over and handled a parcel to Sallow.

"Out of sight, out of mind," said Sallow with a chuckle, counting through the bundle of notes.

The sacks loaded onto the cart, he gave the horse a smack across the rump for its pains. With a whinny, the old nag started on its weary journey to Paddington. There, the load would be transferred onto the morning train to the West Country. Sallow had made less than the market price for the spice, but half of it was flour. By any reckoning, it had been a good sale.

And so it was throughout the metropolis. All through the night, and every night, crimes were committed in the name of the Kaiser. Threats were made and money was collected. Stolen goods were passed on, those in authority were compromised. The whole of London lived in thrall to the devil in the dock. The city had become a chessboard. The pawns, bishops and knights were all in play, and soon the final move would be made.

XXIV

An Appointment

Sergeant Graves looked a troubled man. He cut a forlorn figure as he sat in Bowman's office, the morning light streaming through the window. Bowman could see he had taken Kitty's death hard. His eyes were cast down to the floor and his whole demeanour spoke of a man in conflict with himself.

"I have spent the morning with a Mr Thomas Baldwin of Ladbroke Grove, consoling him on the death of his niece." Graves sunk even lower into the leather wing-backed chair.

"She lived with her uncle?" Bowman sat on the opposite side of the desk, eyeing his sergeant carefully. His usually cheery countenance had been replaced with a look of consternation.

"She had no family but him," Graves continued. "A stonemason by trade, much in demand. He took the news very ill."

"I hope you assured him we will do all we can to catch her killer?"

"I did, sir, and he showed great confidence in us."

"Then, Sergeant Graves, we must not let him down." Bowman was suddenly aware that his hand was shaking. He moved it below the desk so as to be out of Graves' sight.

"What do you propose, sir?" Graves looked up.

"Sergeant Graves, I would have you go to the Home Office on Whitehall and ask to see the transportation and prison records for New South Wales. Do you have your notebook with you?"

Graves reached inside his coat to pull out his tattered notebook and the stub of a pencil. Bowman scratched some details on the page.

"Tracing your family tree, sir?" the sergeant winked, determined to lighten the mood in the office.

"Report back to me this afternoon," said the inspector plainly, as he passed the notepad back, "Then we might formulate a plan." He walked to the map on his wall, his fingers tracing the route of the Thames through the city. "I mean to shed a little light in the darkness."

"How's that, sir?"

Before Bowman could answer, there came a knock at the door. It was a knock of such force and impact that it could mean the arrival of only one man.

"Come!" Bowman turned back into the room. The door was flung open on its hinges and there stood Ignatius Hicks. He was dressed in a full-length coat that brushed the floor as he walked. His waistcoat was a garish yellow and an ostentatious cravat struggled to escape from beneath his huge beard.

"Ah, Bowman," he boomed, clearly unaware of the noxious fumes that rose from the bowl of his ever-present pipe. Bowman coughed pointedly, but to no avail. "I see you've started the day late."

In truth, Bowman had been here since the small hours. Unable to sleep, he had caught a cab to the river and walked to the Victoria Embankment from Lambeth Bridge. The few people that were abroad at so late an hour gave him a wide berth, and so he had wandered unmolested, deep in thought. Occasionally his hand would go to his pocket to close around the note he had discovered in his waistcoat. The message it contained and the visions he had had precluded any sleep despite the Madeira, and so he had set out upon the streets to clear his mind. The note could have been pressed into his pocket at any time during the previous day, but most likely when he had discovered Kitty's body at St. Saviour's Dock. There had been such a press of men and women that it could easily have been planted in the throng.

"What do you bring us, Hicks?" Bowman asked. "Aside from the smell of your favourite tobacco?"

Hicks waved a paw in the air to disperse the fug that had accompanied him and pulled a sheaf of papers from the folds of his coat. "Reports from the provinces, Bowman." He slammed the papers down on Bowman's desk, upsetting a bottle of ink in the process. "It seems your gang of kidnappers have been busy."

Bowman moved to the desk to leaf through the documents. It was a collection of telegraphed communications from various police stations around London, from Gravesend in the east to Isleworth in the west.

"Those reports contain the details of almost twenty disappearances that could be ascribed to the same perpetrators," Hicks drew on his pipe.

"Twenty?" Bowman's moustache twitched.

"These reports stretch back over a year." Hicks blew smoke from his nostrils. If Bowman looked carefully, he could see the inspector's moustaches had become discoloured by the practice. "They each concern the vanishing of healthy young men," Hicks continued, oblivious to Bowman's gaze. "And they each coincide with the sighting of a black brougham in the vicinity."

Bowman raised his eyebrows.

"Hardly a strange sight on the streets of London," exclaimed Graves from his chair. "One may see twenty such carriages in a day."

"But," rounded Hicks, triumphantly, "these kidnappings took place at night, when such a thing is more conspicuous."

Hicks strode to the map at the wall, a fat hand reaching up before him. "A labourer taken in King's Cross last June." He indicated a narrow street near the station. "A black brougham was seen nearby in Cheney Street at two in the morning." His arm swung through the air to land at a point just north of the Thames. "A Spanish rat catcher from Fulham." He tapped a street on the map. "Taken on Hestercombe Avenue in September. A black brougham spotted at three in the morning."

"Thank you, Inspector Hicks." Bowman's voice was thick with emotion. The very thought of the black brougham called back his visions of the night before. He walked to the window to gaze out across the river, his hand closing around the note in his trouser pocket.

"And what news from The Sisters Of Mercy?" Bowman grumbled.

"Very little news." Hicks shrugged his great shoulders.

Bowman turned his gaze upon him. "Inspector Hicks, Sister Vincent came to me with news of a violent murder in her infirmary. I had hoped you would return with more than very little news." The tone in Bowman's voice was enough to still the room. Graves and Hicks shared a look that brought Bowman up sharp. Would this meeting appear in their reports to the commissioner? Bowman remembered Graves' expression of concern at his demeanour the previous day. With a start, he realised he had omitted to shave again. Was every innocent gesture to be examined and interpreted?

Hicks cleared his throat awkwardly. "There is very little news because barely anyone would say a word."

"You spoke to the patients?" Bowman was speaking softly, deliberately.

"They all swore they had seen nothing, despite Jonas Cook so obviously having been strangled in their midst."

Bowman nodded. "Fear is a powerful tool." He looked up to see his two companions regarding him closely. "Inspector Hicks," he continued, "I should like you to join Sergeant Graves back here this afternoon. I have a matter to attend to first, which may shed more light on proceedings."

"Care to elucidate?" Hicks held his arms wide, expectantly. Sergeant Graves leaned forward on his chair.

With a dramatic flourish, Bowman produced the note from his trouser pocket and pressed it flat against the desk. Graves rose from his seat as the inspector continued.

"This was hidden about my person at St. Saviour's Dock."

Graves' eyes widened as he read the message. Hicks puffed his cheeks out almost comically. The paper was torn from a large book, its left and bottom edges ragged. In a rushed, spidery hand, could be read the words; 'COME ALONE TO THE SUBWAY AT NOON AND THE KAISER SHALL BE KNOWN.'

Bowman looked from Graves to Hicks, nodding slowly at their silent enquiries.

"It is an appointment I intend to keep."

A glass or two of brandy had served to quell the tremor in his hand. Alone in his office, Bowman took the revolver from his gun cabinet beneath the bureau where his decanter stood. The Kaiser had said come alone, he thought grimly. He had not said come unarmed. Shrugging on his coat and jamming his hat on his head, Bowman hailed a cab from Scotland Yard's front gate. The streets were full of weekend traffic and those simply out to take the air by the Thames. The great embankments that ran the length of the river were something of a draw to tourists and Londoners alike, and the spring sun had roused many to walk their wide esplanades and spend time in their gardens. The cabbie drove at quite some pace. They were soon rattling under the great bridges of London; Hungerford, Waterloo and Blackfriars, before turning away from the river to traverse Upper Thames Street to the east. The wharves and tightly packed slums of All Hallows The Less and St. Magnus The Martyr soon gave way to more impressive buildings. The traders at Billingsgate Market were packing away their wares for the day, whilst lines of businessmen queued to gain access to Custom House, an august building of Palladian pillars, porticos and Portland stone.

Soon, the carriage was ejected onto Great Tower Hill. A wide promenade opened up as it slowed near Trinity Square and the cabbie joined a rank of traps awaiting their next fare. Paying his driver, Bowman slipped from the hansom and stood to gather his resolve. The Tower Of London stood, imperious and impregnable before of him. Crowds of tourists fought for space and the opportunity to buy some roasted peanuts from a street seller, or have their portrait sketched in charcoal by a bohemian-looking man at an easel. Rough-looking children ran between the legs of hapless tourists as they stopped to marvel at the crenellations and towers above them. The stronghold at the heart of the palace precincts stood proud against a clear blue sky. Its clean, white stone glinted in the sun.

Bowman swallowed hard and reached instinctively to feel the gun in his pocket for reassurance. There before him, squat and unassuming, stood the entrance to the Tower Subway. It was an innocuous brick building, broad and cylindrical, with the appearance of a truncated tower some twelve feet high. Improbably, a perfectly ordinary looking door stood ajar to admit entry, framed by heavy stone pilasters and a lintel.

Bowman pulled a fob watch from his waistcoat pocket to check the time and joined the short queue at the door. It was fifteen minutes until noon. The note had not specified a location beyond mentioning the subway. It would be impossible to discern which entrance was meant, reasoned Bowman, either on the north or south bank, so it was a logical assumption that he should head beneath the Thames into the subway itself. The inspector's eyes flitted between his fellow pedestrians as he passed through the door into the gloom beyond, flipping his ha'penny toll to the attendant. Any one of them, he thought, could be the Kaiser.

As he trod carefully down the spiral steps, Bowman started to feel hot. There seemed very little room in the stairwell, and he shuffled along nervously by the outside wall as he felt his fellow adventurers jostling around him. With no natural light, gas lamps were suspended from the roof at intervals, casting shadows on the people's faces. Their eyes were quite lost in the darkness whilst the harsh light of the lamp bounced off foreheads, noses and chins. It was an eerie effect that served only to amplify Bowman's discomfort. He felt as if he were descending into the pit of Hell with only demons for company. He tried to slow his breathing. His palms were beginning to sweat. He felt a lurch in the pit of his stomach as he descended.

There were those around him who were in thrall to the whole experience, particularly a young couple with a child whose little legs were much too small for the steps. They whispered in the small boy's ear as they passed and shook him by the shoulder in an effort to impart their excitement. After them, however, came a small knot of individuals for whom this couldn't be less exciting. To them, it was simply a means of traversing the river, perhaps undertaken every day as they went about their business. Bowman clung to the iron railing as he emerged from the steps into the tunnel. It was so long, he couldn't see the end. He had the unnerving feeling of being in the guts of some great beast such as one might see at The Natural History Museum. He was sure, as he cast his gaze along its preposterous length, that it was moving. Bowman caught his breath. Sweat pricked at his eyes. Focusing on his fob watch for comfort, he saw that he had just ten minutes before his allotted time with the Kaiser. Just time enough, he reasoned, to make it to the centre of the tunnel, which seemed as good a place as any to make himself plain. With an effort, the inspector started the painful journey through the tunnel. The iron walls seemed to press in around him, and it was all Bowman could do to avert his mind from the River Thames above. That thousands upon thousands of gallons of water should at this moment be coursing above him, seemed hardly worthy of belief. The inspector fancied he could feel the weight of the mud and water upon his shoulders. He focussed his gaze before him. All around, people were coming and going through the tunnel. Most seemed quite nonplussed at the experience. He could see the young couple ahead with their child. They each had a hold of one of his hands, and were swinging him playfully between them as they walked. Bowman could hear them singing a fanciful tune that echoed back and forth off the tunnel's walls.

At last he found himself at a recess in the wall that he reasoned might well mark the midpoint. He stopped and leaned against the wall, looking back along the tunnel where he had walked. People were streaming past. Some were alone, others with companions. Bowman's eyes narrowed, looking for signs that any of them could be the subject of his mysterious assignation. A tall man in a heavy cape and hood looked as if he were slowing, only to stop and pick up a handkerchief dropped by a lady ahead of him. A stocky man with mean features seemed to look at Bowman for longer than might have been reasonable, only to tip his hat in greeting as he passed. Bowman turned towards the tunnel ahead of him. Two nuns were gliding towards him, their faces animated in gossip. Behind them, a young man with a hair lip was swinging a bag over his shoulder as he walked. Bowman pulled the fob watch from his waistcoat pocket. It was now precisely midday.

Looking up, he saw a taller head bobbing up and down amongst the crowd. Bowman swallowed hard. His breathing quickened. He recognised the face. The man had a fine head of hair styled fashionably with pomade and his face was adorned with an impressive set of muttonchops. Bowman's fingers closed tight around the handle of the revolver in his pocket and he tensed his body in readiness for the confrontation. Pressing himself into the recess, he kept half an eye on the figure striding purposefully along the tunnel. The man had met his eyes now and slowed his pace. Bowman saw him reach into his pocket and so the inspector drew his revolver.

"Halt!" he cried, his voice echoing up the tunnel before him. Heads turned and a woman screamed. "Everybody stand back!"

Those ahead quickened their step towards the end of the tunnel in alarm, calling for help or crying in fear. The young couple swung their boy up into his father's arms and they ran into the darkness.

"I am from Scotland Yard!" Bowman shouted. "Keep back!"

Behind him, a man's voice implored with others to walk no further, entreating them to turn about and flee to the north bank. He heard their footsteps retreat back up the subway. Soon he was alone with the man, his revolver drawn. He was gazing into the steely, grey eyes of Chief Inspector Callaghan.

"Fire that thing in here," Callaghan said calmly, "and there's no telling where the bullet might end up."

Bowman's mind was racing. He kept his grip on the gun.

"What in God's name are you doing here?" Callaghan asked, his arms wide in submission. "Have you gone quite mad?"

Bowman blinked. "Reach slowly into your pocket," he said carefully. "Take out your gun."

"I could have you disciplined for this, Detective Inspector Bowman." Callaghan kept his eyes locked on the inspector's. "Drawing your weapon on a senior officer?" He shook his head, sadly. "Perhaps you should think carefully about how such a thing will look."

"Take out your gun!" Bowman repeated, sharply.

Callaghan leaned in closer. "I don't have a gun," he hissed.

Bowman blinked. "Why are you here?"

"I was sent a note," Callaghan snapped back. "To meet with my man from St. Saviour's Dock."

Bowman thought quickly. "You expected to meet with Ichabod Sallow?"

Callaghan nodded. "He was to pass some information concerning the Fenian plot."

"There is no Fenian plot!" Bowman's voice echoed off the walls. "Only the Kaiser."

The chief inspector's eyebrows rose on his forehead. "Have you taken leave of your senses?"

"He calls himself the Kaiser," Bowman stuttered. "He holds the whole of the south bank in his thrall and perhaps the whole of London." He was quite aware of the ridiculous nature of his assertion.

"Is this the result of your investigations, Inspector Bowman?" Callaghan gave the inspector a condescending look. It was the same look Bowman remembered from their meeting at the Trafalgar Club. "A bogeyman? You might as well have told me of Spring Heeled Jack."

"I too received a note." Bowman was reaching into his pocket with his free hand, keeping his gun trained on the chief inspector all the while. "I was to meet with the Kaiser here at midday." Shaking the paper open, he thrust it towards Callaghan's face.

"Ah," Callaghan nodded as if all had suddenly become clear. "And so it follows that I must be your Kaiser."

Bowman stuffed the note back into his pocket and tightened his grip on his revolver. "Are you?"

Improbably, Callaghan threw back his head and laughed. "What should I say to satisfy you?" He threw his arms wide as he posed the question. "If I answer yes, you have your man, but further investigation will lead you nowhere. If I say no, you will arrest me or shoot me. If you arrest me, your investigations will lead you nowhere. If you shoot me, you will have killed a superior officer."

Bowman blinked the sweat from his eyes. His neck burned beneath the collar of his shirt. "What were you reaching for, if not a gun?" he asked.

Callaghan lowered his voice. "If you will permit me?"

Bowman gave a curt nod.

Slowly, the chief inspector reached into his coat pocket. He kept his eyes locked on Bowman's, careful not to make any sudden movement. He knew the inspector to be unstable and did not wish to provoke him.

Gingerly, he pulled a piece of paper from his pocket and presented it before the inspector. "I had intended to show you this," he explained.

Bowman let his eyes drop to the paper. There, in a spidery hand he recognised, were the words; 'COME TO THE SUBWAY AT NOON AND THE PLOT SHALL BE FOILED.' It was undoubtedly the same handwriting.

"It was delivered by runner to my office this morning," Callaghan was saying. "I did not think to come with my revolver." He raised his eyebrows pointedly at Bowman's weapon and waited.

Slowly, Bowman lowered his revolver, uncocked it and placed it in his pocket. "Then it seems," he began slowly, "we have both been played."

"That much is clear," agreed Callaghan, reluctantly. "But to what end? Who would want us both here at the same time, and why?"

"To solve a problem?" Bowman asked, his eyes suddenly wide in understanding. Pulling his watch from his pocket, he noted the time. "It is now three minutes past midday."

"And what of it?" Callaghan spat, exasperated. "Why bring us both here now?"

Bowman cast his eyes feverishly around the tunnel. "With no

other indication given in the note, I chose the midpoint for our assignation," he mumbled as much to himself as to the chief inspector.

"Likewise," agreed Callaghan.

"But how did the Kaiser know we were to meet here? Chief inspector, what would you have done if you had not met me at this point?"

Callaghan shrugged. "Walked on, I suppose. Until I found Sallow."

"Then it did not matter where in the subway we met, just that the meeting took place."

Callaghan threw his arms up with impatience, "Again I ask, to what end?"

Bowman was suddenly alive with activity. "As I waited for you here, I saw several people pass."

"Of course."

"But one man stopped. A tall man in a heavy overcoat, and hooded too." Bowman was moving a few feet back up the tunnel, his eyes scanning the ground beneath his feet. "I saw him retrieve a handkerchief from the ground, dropped by another pedestrian." He was replaying the event in his mind. "And then he moved on."

"Then chivalry is not dead," the chief inspector harrumphed, at a loss as to where Bowman's train of thought was leading them.

"What if he not only retrieved something, but left something?" Bowman was on his haunches, lifting a pile of discarded rags from the floor. As he rose, he turned to the chief inspector with a look of horror on his face. In his hand he held a bag. Reaching gingerly inside, he withdrew a bundle of several tubular sticks tied together. A clock face and a timing mechanism were attached via copper wires that protruded from their ends. A look of panic passed between the two men. Callaghan thought quickly and spoke even quicker.

"Can you disarm it?"

Bowman looked down. "I may not have the time."

"We were instructed to meet here at noon, why has the thing not gone off?" Callaghan was backing away from Bowman as he spoke, clearly readying himself to break into a run.

Bowman felt rooted to the spot in fear. That he held such destructive power in his hands seemed impossible. That it might explode at any moment and bring about his end and that of the Tower Subway was too horrific a thought to contemplate. His mind retreated from it. "Self preservation," he said, his voice affecting a note of eerie calm. "To give the Kaiser the time to escape the subway."

Callaghan was breathing hard. "Then, Inspector Bowman, if he has the time, then so do I." With a look of apology that Bowman found disconcerting, the chief inspector turned on his heels and ran onward through the tunnel to the north side, tripping in his haste to escape. Bowman heard the sound of his footsteps decreasing with every stride.

The inspector was alone and suddenly alive to the situation. Looking down to the device in his hands, he could see clearly the timing mechanism was set to detonate at ten minutes past the hour. Plenty of time for the Kaiser to get clear, but was it time enough for him? A thousand thoughts collided in his brain. He could not leave the bomb behind, it would destroy the tunnel and with it those unfortunate souls who had not made it to the end. But did he have time to reach the south side? And what would he do if he did? There was bound to be a crowd of people waiting to gain access to the subway. He would need a way to dispose of the bomb. Taking a breath, Bowman gripped the device hard in his hands, held it before him and broke into a run.

A small group had gathered at the entrance to the subway on Vine Street to the south of the Thames. They had been denied access by a young man and his wife.

"He had a gun," the man explained as his wife cradled their crying boy in her arms. "He said he was with Scotland Yard."

"How can you be sure?" asked a large woman with a basket of flowers. "I say call for a constable."

A young man with a dog on a length of twine pushed his way into the crowd to offer his opinion. "What's the point if he's Scotland Yard?"

"I must cross the Thames or I shall be late," grumbled an elderly man in a smart coat and top hat. Still more joined the throng, all eager to cross the river and be about their business.

Amongst the melee, some were still exiting the subway in a state of distress and breathing hard. Their faces were flushed from

159

having run half the subway at some pace, and all told the story of the mad man with the gun. As they each confirmed the tale told by the man and his wife, those around them grew more excited.

"Together we could overcome him!" proclaimed a brawny young man with a dirty face and missing teeth.

"I should like to see you overcome a revolver," chimed the lady with the flowers to general hilarity. As they chatted and laughed amongst themselves, no one noticed the figure in the long, hooded cloak emerge from the shadows of the subway. Skirting the crowd, it melted into the streets on the south bank, passing from Vine Street towards Tooley Street and the alleys of Bermondsey.

"If he misses, there's no telling where the bullet would end up." The young man with the dirty face was shaking his head.

"How could he miss?" asked the man with the child. "He was facing the man point blank."

"When do you think we can go down?" The smart businessman was practically hopping from one foot to the other in his haste to cross the river.

"I'm going to fetch a constable." The large lady with the flowers turned away from the subway's entrance, lifting at her skirts.

"A constable's no good," cried the young girl. "There's a dangerous man down there. We need an officer with a gun."

"He *is* an officer with a gun!" exclaimed the businessman in exasperation.

There came a sudden shout from the entrance to the tunnel, and the man with the child was pushed violently aside. His wife screamed as she saw a man standing at the subway door, his eyes wild. There was a collective gasp as the crowd beheld the scene.

"That's him!" she cried, "He's the one with the gun!"

"What's he got in his hands?"

"Lord save us, he's got a bomb!" There was a scream and the crowd stepped back, unsure of what collective action should be taken.

Bowman was a blur. Doubling back past the entrance to the subway, he ran down Vine Street to the river. He knew the bomb could explode at any moment. Surely enough time had elapsed to allow the Kaiser to escape to a safe distance. If that were the case, he might have just seconds. His legs ached from taking the steps from the subway two at a time and he was unsteady on his feet.

The blood rushed to his head, making the wharves around him seem to sway and loom towards him. At last he was at Pickle Herring Stairs. The Thames was in full spate before him. With the tide so high, there were fewer ships on the open water. Bowman knew a great many of them would be unloading their goods at the docks. He ran to the very edge of the steps, his boots and trouser legs submerged in the murky water that lapped at the southern shore. With an effort, he swung his arm back and heaved the bomb as far as he could over the water, the momentum pitching him forward and face down into the Thames. Scrabbling back to the shore, Bowman heard a thump behind him. He turned his head in time to see a hump of water rise in the river, erupting into a shower of debris that rained down harmlessly around him. Feeling the spray hit his face, Bowman shielded his head with his forearm, grateful for the good fortune that had given him time to dispose of the bomb safely in the waters of the Thames.

XXV

Brought To Book

"Did you intend to discharge your firearm?" The commissioner's tone was firm. He stood at the window to his office with his one arm behind his back. As ever, the empty sleeve of his jacket was pinned to his chest. He shook his head as if in despair. "You understand the consequences had you fired?"

Bowman shuffled in his seat. "I should have thought the consequences would be less than those following an explosion of a bomb in the Tower Subway."

He felt Detective Chief Inspector Callaghan bristle in the chair next to him. They both knew, following such a serious incident, that a report would have to be made. Callaghan had decided time was of the essence and demanded that they both face the commissioner in person. Bowman sensed he was being plotted against.

"You pulled a revolver on a superior officer!" The commissioner flushed, his usually calm demeanour replaced with a raging fury.

Bowman swallowed. He would have to choose his words carefully. "I will admit to being under some misapprehensions," he said.

Callaghan guffawed beside him and shared a look with the commissioner. "I should say that would be the least of it."

Bowman turned to face him. "As were you." Callaghan scowled.

"Chief Inspector Callaghan?" The commissioner turned to him, his eyebrows raised expectantly.

Callaghan cleared his throat and shot a look of exasperation to Bowman. "I had expected to meet an agent with regard to Operation Vanguard." Bowman frowned at the term. This seemed more specific than Callaghan's interest in a Fenian plot. "But I was compromised."

"Someone wanted to get us both together at the same time, that an end might be made of us," Bowman explained. "We were both compromised." The inspector felt the air in the room grow thick. The commissioner and Callaghan were sharing a look, as if uncertain how to continue. It was clear that Callaghan had strayed further than he should into delicate territory.

With a sigh, the commissioner turned to gaze out the window. The afternoon sun glinted off the white Portland stone of the government buildings around him. He had spent all his adult life in the service of his country. Indeed, he mused, he bore more scars than most because of it. He picked absently at his empty sleeve with his remaining hand. Following his military career, he had sought ways to continue to serve and had accepted the post of Metropolitan Police Commissioner gladly. Now, as he stared into the streets beneath him, he had his doubts. As a military man, only one thing had concerned him; the pursuit and destruction of the enemy at all costs. He had laboured under the luxury of having a clearly defined adversary. Often, even their location was known. In his position at The Force, however, he was denied such comforts. Looking out across the roofs of London, Sir Edward Bradford knew the enemy could be anyone and anywhere. Fighting crime in this city was like trying to hold water in his one remaining hand.

"You will know," the commissioner began, 'that Chief Inspector Callaghan, in his position at the Special Irish Branch, has been investigating the possibility of a Fenian cell in operation at St. Saviour's Dock." Bowman could sense Sir Edward picking his way carefully through the matter. "He has a man implanted among them whose duty has been one of careful cooperation, that he might gain their trust."

"Yes," Bowman nodded. "One Ichabod Sallow. I have had dealings with him and believe him guilty of murder."

Callaghan threw his hands up in despair. "For God's sake, man! He is a detective sergeant with the Special Irish Branch!"

Bowman turned calmly to meet Callaghan's gaze. "Does that fact alone preclude him from investigation?"

The commissioner had turned back into the room. "Inspector Bowman, you were placed at St. Saviour's to provide security. It seems you have strayed from your remit."

Bowman sat forward in his seat, eager to explain. He was suddenly aware that a tiny muscle was twitching beneath his left eye. "It was in the pursuit of those duties that I came across Sallow. I believe he is implicated in the injury and subsequent murder of a fellow dockworker, Jonas Cook."

Callaghan puffed out his cheeks at the accusation. "Why would Sallow do such a thing?"

Bowman took a breath. "He either is, or serves the Kaiser."

There was a silence in the room. Bowman's words seemed to hang in the air. Suddenly, the commissioner threw back his head and laughed. "The Kaiser?" he boomed. "Preposterous! What should the Kaiser want with meddling on the south bank? I should imagine he would have enough on his plate with Bismarck at his back." Even Callaghan allowed himself a smirk.

"He calls himself the Kaiser and he holds much of London in his thrall. I have evidence he might even have influence over the local constabulary."

"Tread carefully, Detective Inspector Bowman," the commissioner breathed. "You have been brought here to give an account of yourself following an incident that could have led to the loss of one of my most prominent men," Callaghan looked smug at the description, "Not to cast unfounded aspersions and innuendo at those who would serve in the Metropolitan Police Force."

Bowman swallowed hard, his neck beginning to itch beneath his collar. "It was Ichabod Sallow who wrote the note to you, was it not, chief inspector?"

"Of course," nodded Callaghan. "It was he whom I was due to meet."

Bowman reached into his pocket and took out the note he had received the day before at St. Saviour's Dock. "My note was written in the same hand." He placed it, unfolded, on the desk before him. "A note suggesting I might meet the Kaiser at noon today in the Tower Subway."

The commissioner slid the note to his side of the desk. Balancing a monocle at one eye, he read its contents, carefully. "Chief Inspector Callaghan," he began, slowly, "can you confirm this to be Sallow's hand?"

Callaghan gave the note a cursory glance. He already knew his answer. "I cannot," he said, quietly.

"How useful has Sallow been to you, chief inspector?" Bowman asked in all innocence.

"Detective Sergeant Sallow has been instrumental in the instigation of Operation Vanguard. He has my total confidence and authority to proceed as he sees fit in the case." Callaghan sat back, his arms folded resolutely across his chest.

"Including murder?" asked Bowman simply.

"Inspector Bowman, just what evidence do you have to implicate Sallow in this man's death?" The commissioner was clearly losing his patience.

Bowman responded daringly. "I would ask Chief Inspector Callaghan just what proof Sallow has provided in connection with a Fenian plot?" He looked at the chief inspector, his eyebrows raised in the expectation of an answer.

"Sallow has provided several papers from the dock master at St. Katharine Docks. They appear to place him at the centre of their financial systems."

"And why would he place a bomb at his own dock?"

Callaghan cleared his throat. "I believe the explosion was the result of an accident."

The commissioner turned to the chief inspector. "An accident?"

"Explosives are notoriously unstable," Callaghan continued. "Clearly the blast was as a result of careless handling. He might even have lost some men of value in the blast."

"Tremont tells me the papers were planted."

"You have spoken with Tremont?" Callaghan's tone of voice betrayed his incredulity.

"Such a thing would be wholly irregular," warned the commissioner, sternly.

Bowman shifted his weight under the commissioner's gaze. "I have visited Tremont in the cells at Bow Street." He could sense Callaghan shaking his head in wonder. "He is certain the papers were placed in his safe to implicate him."

"And the explosion?" The commissioner sat heavily on his chair, his remaining hand rubbing his chin in thought.

"Set by the Kaiser as a warning." There was an audible sigh in the room. Callaghan was pinching the bridge of his nose. Bowman continued. "Tremont told me of regular payments he had been forced to make. The blast was in response to his recent refusal to continue."

"Tremont is lying!" Unable to contain himself any longer, Callaghan stood to address the commissioner. "Just how long must we suffer this litany of half-baked theories and questionable untruths?"

The question remained unanswered. Bowman resisted the urge to tell more. He reasoned he had nothing to gain from pressing the matter further. Graves' stories of Sallow's meddling with the turmeric at Corder's Wharf would remain unspoken.

"It was Sallow who told you of Tremont's papers?"

Callaghan nodded. "And Bracewell organised some men to retrieve them."

Bowman rose from his chair to look the chief inspector in the eye. "I believe Sallow has gone native."

Callaghan puffed his cheeks out in despair. "I have known the man for five years," he implored, turning to appeal to the commissioner, "I have the utmost confidence in his conduct in this matter."

"Then how do you account for his behaviour?"

"Operation Vanguard is a delicate matter, Inspector Bowman," Callaghan hissed, his grey eyes blazing. He turned to the commissioner. "Sir Edward," he began, "I believe the evidence we have obtained is enough to continue with Operation Vanguard." He threw his arms wide in exasperation. "Can we afford not to?"

A silence followed. Bowman was aware of a tremor in his right hand, his index finger twitching against his palm. Folding his arms to hide it and fixing the chief inspector in his gaze, the inspector summoned the strength to pose a question.

"Just what," he asked simply, "is Operation Vanguard?"

Callaghan met Bowman's gaze. He was breathing through gritted teeth. A vein pulsed on his forehead. With a growl of anguish, he shook his head and collapsed heavily into his chair, clearly unwilling to speak any further in the matter.

"Her Majesty The Queen has been on a sojourn to the continent." Bowman turned. The commissioner was tracing the gold leaf inlay at his desk with a finger as he spoke. "From April," he continued, 'she has been painting in Hyeres in the south of France and, for the last week, visiting friends in Darmstadt. She is due to return tonight."

Callaghan was breathing heavily where he sat, clearly angry that such sensitive information should be divulged.

"Chief Inspector Callaghan's investigations have led him to believe an attack upon Her Majesty by the Fenians is likely. He has been coordinating a response. Operation Vanguard."

Bowman's mind reeled at the news. Clearly, Sallow and Bracewell had been leading Callaghan in the wrong direction. But to what end?

"She is due to cross the channel tonight, then travel by train to Dartford. From there she is to sail up the Thames aboard the Victoria And Albert to Custom House. Having been away, she is keen to see the progress of Tower Bridge for herself."

Bowman had often seen pictures of the craft in the London press. Her Majesty's Yacht Victoria And Albert was a twin-paddled steamer of impressive proportions and luxurious design. He nodded slowly in understanding. In truth, an attack would not be unlikely. Since the beginning of her exalted reign, Her Majesty had been subject to half a dozen assassination attempts. What better way to promote one's cause than to attempt the death of the sovereign? It had been more by luck than judgement that, so far, all attempts had failed. But if Ichabod Sallow was no Fenian, what would be his cause? If he was the Kaiser, as Bowman believed, what could be gained from so audacious a plan?

"Then I may have some pertinent information with regard to your operation," Bowman offered. Callaghan sat up in his seat. "What are the specifics of the plot against Her Majesty?"

The commissioner turned to Callaghan. "Well, chief inspector?"

Callaghan cleared his throat. "Only that an attack will be made at Dartford train station as Her Majesty's train arrives. That will be at seven of the clock this evening."

"And that is where you are to concentrate your resources?" Bowman was thinking fast.

"My men have been there since first light."

Bowman sat, smoothing his moustache between thumb and forefinger. "And just who gave you that intelligence?"

Callaghan paused. A small smile flickered across his lips. He knew just what Bowman was implying. "Ichabod Sallow," he said slowly.

"Commissioner Bradford," began Bowman, his expression severe, "I am not convinced."

"It does not matter if you are convinced," growled Callaghan. "You were sent to St. Saviour's to check the locks on the doors."

Bowman let the jibe go. Swallowing hard, he addressed the commissioner. "Yesterday, I sent Sergeant Graves undercover at

St. Saviour's."

"You did what?" Callaghan was on his feet again, this time with his fists clenched. If the commissioner had not been present, Bowman was sure the Chief Inspector would have swung for him.

"Such a thing is most irregular, Inspector Bowman," the commissioner barked, holding up his hand to soothe the fractious chief inspector. "You had no authority for such an action."

"I believe that Sergeant Graves' investigation into the body discovered at Vinegar Yard and my investigations at the dock are linked."

"This is not your investigation!" Callaghan was at the window now, running his fingers through his hair and breathing deeply in an attempt to keep calm.

"That is shaky ground indeed, inspector." The commissioner shot him a warning look. "And what did Sergeant Graves find there? I should hope such a foolhardy enterprise at least bore fruit?"

"It did," Bowman ploughed on. "In the course of the day, Graves became party to certain information concerning a delivery at the dock."

"A delivery? What sort of delivery?" The commissioner placed his elbow on the desk, leaning forward to rest his chin upon his hand. Even Callaghan turned from the window.

"That, I do not know," Bowman admitted. "But it may be connected with recent efforts by the Kaiser to raise funds."

"How so?"

"Graves witnessed a bare-knuckle fight at Butler's Wharf. Funds were raised as people placed their bets. The fight was fixed, of course."

"A fight between whom?" The commissioner was intent on hearing the details.

"Two men that I believe were kidnapped by the Kaiser for just such a purpose. They were put to work at the dock and made to fight for money. They both bore the same mark as the body in Vinegar Yard. A brand to the chest in the shape of the Devil."

Callaghan harrumphed.

"There is a legend that tells of the Devil collecting the dead from a gibbet at St. Saviour's Dock," Bowman explained. "The Kaiser has adopted the symbol as one of ownership."

"This is all supposition!" roared Callaghan.

"Nevertheless," interjected the commissioner reasonably, 'this business with the delivery might well benefit from further investigation."

"You would take the word of a madman?" Callaghan stood by the window, his eyes burning with accusation.

Suddenly lost for words, Bowman felt his face flush. "Sergeant Graves is more than reliable," he stammered. "If my word is not enough then perhaps his might be." Bowman swallowed. "It is his evidence that points to the delivery," he continued, quietly. "Not mine."

The commissioner rose from his seat to defuse the situation. "Chief Inspector Callaghan, I wish you to accompany Detective Inspector Bowman to St. Saviour's Dock for the next high tide this evening." Bowman could tell Callaghan was fighting the urge to speak. "You are to offer him all assistance in searching the shipment for any signs of nefarious activity."

"But Vanguard – " began the chief inspector.

"Vanguard will continue," rounded the commissioner. "I shall personally take charge of proceedings at Dartford." Callaghan gave a curt nod, holding Bowman in his gaze across the room. The commissioner continued. "As far as this delivery goes, your investigations will put an end to the matter, one way or the other. Isn't that what you want?" The commissioner raised his eyebrows.

There was silence.

"Will that be all, sir?" Callaghan hissed through gritted teeth at last.

"Thank you, Chief Inspector Callaghan."

With a last look at Bowman, Callaghan gathered as much dignity about him as he could, and strode from the room.

The commissioner turned to Bowman as the door swung shut behind the retreating chief inspector. "I am a reasonable man, detective inspector, and I can see when a man has a scent of something."

"Thank you, sir," Bowman mumbled, standing to leave.

"You will still have to answer for your unauthorised investigations at St. Saviour's Dock," Sir Edward continued. "And your sending Sergeant Graves to do your dirty work." Bowman nodded in understanding. "Now, inspector, you have six hours before high tide. Get yourself home, have a shave and get some sleep."

XXVI

Transported

The Silver Cross seemed infinitely more appealing. Even Harris the landlord was surprised at the usually more abstemious Inspector Bowman ordering both a glass of porter and a brandy at this time of day. "Night off, Bowman?" he leered, his dank hair hanging over his eyes.

"Quite the reverse, Harris," said Bowman enigmatically as he threw his change onto the bar. He downed the brandy in one draft and wiped his lips on the back of his sleeve. Looking around the inn, he could see it was emptier than the last time he had visited. London was at work. The labourers would be busy transforming the skyline. His eye landed on the chair by the fireplace and, picking up his hat from the bar, he made his way over to take his place. Hanging his coat on a hook on the chimneybreast, Bowman slipped into the chair with a sigh and sipped at his porter. Looking out the window, he saw people coming and going about their business, their silhouettes warping through the glass. He imagined each one of them going about their daily lives. The businessmen and the vagrants, the housekeepers and the stallholders, the craftsmen and the labourers. Each with secrets of their own. With such a propensity for darkness at the heart of every man, Bowman visualised a tide of crime sweeping the city. Like the Dutch boy with his thumb in the dyke, the Metropolitan Police Force stood between a civil society and the deluge. Sometimes, it felt a hopeless task.

Just how far did the Kaiser's influence reach, Bowman wondered as he settled back with his glass. He was troubled by the implication of Hicks' report in his office. The Kaiser had been kidnapping men to work at the dock using a black brougham. There was something about that detail that troubled him. As he sipped from his porter, his mind drifted back to the events on Hanbury Street, almost a year ago.

Sergeant Williams had uncovered an operation to kidnap vulnerable children from the streets to send north for labour in the mills and factories. He had requested that Graves and Bowman accompany him as he was sure force would be needed to detain the perpetrators. And he had been right.

Williams, Bowman and Graves had lain in wait in a doorway across the road. A line of young children was waiting in the cold to be admitted to the workhouse. Wrapping their rags around them, they hopped on their bare feet in a vain attempt to keep warm. Some were even singing to keep their spirits up; a plaintive tune in the face of their adversity.

"Here they come," Williams had hissed as a black brougham carriage hove into view from Deal Street. "Be ready now."

Bowman could hear the hooves thundering towards him. He could see the dirt kicked up behind them. Williams held his hand high to ready his men as the brougham edged closer to the kerb by the workhouse. As Bowman watched, his hand tight around his revolver handle, he saw the door to the carriage swing open. As the brougham approached the kerb, an arm reached out and plucked a small boy from the waiting line. Kicking and screaming, he was held aloft for a moment, then pulled into the carriage. Bowman shifted his weight forward to peer closer at the figure in the brougham. There was something about the slope of its shoulder and the briefest glimpse of its profile that seemed familiar. He reached for it in his mind, straining to conjure the image of the man in the carriage. And suddenly it was gone.

"Sir?"

Bowman woke with a start. Sergeant Graves had joined him in The Silver Cross, an expression of concern on his face. "I was told I'd find you here."

Bowman cleared his throat self-consciously. "I needed time to think," he mumbled. Graves' eyes flicked almost imperceptibly to the half-empty glass at the inspector's table. "Will you join me in a drink?"

Graves shook his head. "You asked me to report to your office, sir," said the young sergeant, testily.

Bowman rubbed his eyes with the palms of his hands, "Did I?" He smoothed his moustache between his thumb and finger. "I'm sorry Graves," he said. "I've had quite the afternoon."

"How was your assignation in the subway?" Had the subject not been so serious, and Graves not so concerned to find his superior asleep over a glass of porter, Bowman was sure the sergeant would have allowed himself a wink and a smile.

"Eventful," Bowman replied with masterful understatement.

Graves slid onto the opposite chair and listened, focussed and attentive. Bowman recounted the events in Tower Subway and the details of his subsequent meeting in the commissioner's office.

"The commissioner has instructed Chief Inspector Callaghan to accompany us on a further investigation at St. Saviour's Dock this evening."

"I'm sure the chief inspector was delighted to hear it," Graves smiled.

"We are to intercept the shipment on this evening's tide."

The sergeant nodded. "As the man in the chophouse told me."

"With Hicks with us, that'll make us four. Both Callaghan and I will be armed."

Graves looked serious. "What do you expect we'll find?"

"Trouble, Graves." Bowman sipped at his porter, suddenly deep in thought. Sunk into his chair, his shoulders slumped and his chin unshaved, Graves thought he looked a diminished man. His eyes were bloodshot and his hair dishevelled. He was turning his glass slowly in his hand.

"Sergeant Graves," the inspector said slowly, "I need to speak with you about Hanbury Street." Bowman saw Graves flinch visibly.

"Yes, sir?"

The inspector looked pained. He was unsure how to proceed. "Was the brougham recovered?"

Graves looked thoughtful. "No, sir," he said quietly. "It never was. The horses were evidently halted several streets away and, amid the confusion, the occupant of the carriage took the reins."

Bowman nodded thoughtfully.

"If it's a consolation, sir, the urchin was recovered in good health."

"That is consolation, indeed," said Bowman as he stared into his glass. There was a silence. Graves shifted uncomfortably where he sat.

"I have news from the Home Office, sir."

Bowman started in his chair, as if drawn from some deep contemplation. "Of course." He sat forward. "What progress did you make?"

Graves slipped his notepad from his pocket and, licking his fingers, flipped through its pages until he found his place. "I looked into the records of the penal colony in New South Wales, as you requested, sir." Graves lowered his voice as he leaned over the table. "The regime was strict, with many convicts dying during their sentence. That's if they made it there in the first place. Many died on the voyage." Graves cleared his throat and lowered his voice. "They were treated in the most appalling ways, worked into the ground and lashed for trivial offences."

"Let's not forget these men were convicts, Graves," Bowman cautioned. "They were merely answering for their crimes." Graves nodded. "Did you find anything more about the governor?" the inspector asked.

Graves sat for a moment, aware of the import of his discoveries. "Sir, look as I might, there was no sign of the name you gave me in the list of governors," he said, enigmatically.

"What?" Bowman let his glass drop to the table.

Graves continued. "I then looked through the convict records. With such a distinctive name, I knew the search would be relatively easy. And there, in the list of prisoners transported to New South Wales aboard The Blenheim, I found him. Beaurepaire. Robert Beaurepaire."

"He was a convict?" Bowman's frown cut deep into his forehead.

"Charged and found guilty of several crimes including night poaching, battery and one of murder. He was sentenced to transportation and penal servitude in Eighteen Forty Nine."

Bowman reeled at the news. "Are you sure there was no Governor Beaurepaire?"

"I am certain of it."

The inspector sat back in his chair, perplexed. He had had Graves investigate the matter on a hunch. There was something about Alma Beaurepaire's story that had struck Bowman as inconsistent. The daughter of an Australian governor would not have been simply thrown upon the fates as she had described. There would have been procedures to protect her and bring her home. As a servant of Her Majesty's Government, a governor would have been eligible for certain privileges and protections. It was unlikely his bereaved daughter would find herself on the filth-strewn streets of Bermondsey, even with her mother dead, too.

"He must have been one of the last," Bowman mused.

"He was, sir," Graves confirmed. "Transportation to New South Wales was abolished on October the first, Eighteen Fifty. Beaurepaire served his seven years and was then granted his Certificate of Freedom. His records show he was not the most compliant of prisoners."

"Oh?" Bowman's eyebrows rose as Graves traced down the page of his notebook with a finger.

"He was frequently engaged in acts of violence with his fellow inmates. He received regular floggings for subordination. He attempted escape three times and was sentenced to solitary confinement."

"He was lucky not to hang," Bowman observed.

"He was, however, branded."

A silence hung between the two men as Graves allowed his words to find their mark.

"Branded?" Bowman's mouth hung open.

"The governor felt Beaurepaire's three attempts at escape should be punished with a branding. That would ensure his identification if discovered beyond the prison limits again. It was not unusual."

"But it's a rather telling detail," Bowman mused.

"There's more, sir." Graves was plainly enjoying the opportunity to be the bearer of so much information. "There are records of Beaurepaire's activities after his release."

"In New South Wales?"

Graves nodded. "Convicts were granted the opportunity to have passage home or stay to make a life in Australia. Beaurepaire opted for the latter." He had reached into his pocket and drawn out a large piece of paper folded in half. Bowman was enrapt. "This is a marriage licence," Graves continued, "issued by the authorities in New South Wales to a Robert Beaurepaire, giving permission for him to marry a fellow convict released at the same time."

"He married?" Bowman was enthralled by Beaurepaire's story.

"She had been transported for several charges of theft and breaking and entering. I think she just wore the judge down." Graves allowed himself a smirk. "She was sentenced to three years and was released the same time as our man."

"Would Robert have been allowed to fraternise with her during his sentence?"

Graves had to suppress a laugh at the euphemism. "I think the governor was alive to the benefits of such fraternisation. And alive to the fact that, following the cessation of transportation, a settlement would have to be established. Families would have to be reared." Bowman noticed the sergeant's eyes were twinkling gently.

"Is anything more known of their fortunes?"

"Only that they had a daughter before they both died."

Bowman sat stock still at the news. "A daughter?"

"She was left on her own aged just five and was taken in by the erstwhile governor."

"Graves." Bowman was searching for meaning in the news. "What was the woman called? The woman whom Robert married?"

"Ah," teased Graves. "Now, this tops everything, sir. On April the fourth, Eighteen Hundred and Fifty Seven, Robert Beaurepaire married a petty thief and fellow inmate." He held up the marriage licence for effect. "She is named on the licence as Frances De Keyser."

XXVII

High Tide

The evening chill had set in. Low clouds roiled across the sky as the light faded. Across the south bank, lanterns were lit in windows and lamplighters carried their poles from post to post. Once again, an exodus was in progress. With the rising tide, the populace disgorged themselves from their lodgings onto the streets, kicking the filth before them. Those who had not been chosen for the morning ritual had slept the day away. A man asleep does not need money and he does not need food. Others yet, those more lucky in their search for employment that morning, had wasted the intervening hours in the inns and taverns, spending what little money they had earned at St. Saviour's on the morning tide. The younger among them ran to the dock, their shoeless feet treading heedlessly in the detritus on the road. One or two older men shuffled as best they could. Life as a docker was thankless. Life as an old docker was worse. Many had not worked for days. Some begged by the roadside, others sat on the kerb in a fug of cheap gin.

This time, Graves had foregone his disguise. He walked with a purposeful stride behind Inspector Bowman down Willow Walk towards Bermondsey police station. Looking to his side, he caught a glance from one or two of the dockworkers, a faint and momentary gleam of recognition in their eyes. If they remembered him from his work at Corder's Wharf, they said nothing. To his other side, Inspector Hicks was in a serious mood. His eyes were narrowed and his teeth clamped hard on the bit of his pipe. He swung his arms in an almost military fashion as he walked, his great beard jutting before him and his coat tails flapping around his ankles. Ahead, with Inspector Bowman, walked Chief Inspector Callaghan. He looked ridiculously out of place in his smart frock coat and top hat, like a diamond in the rough. His smart spats were already spattered with mud and the hems of his trousers were trimmed with dust. Bowman was in an introspective mood. Even from behind, Graves could tell by his demeanour that he was deep in thought. He walked with his head down, his hands deep in his coat pockets. When he did look up, it was to scan the crowds for any sign of trouble. To Graves' relief, the dockers were more intent on their passage to St. Saviour's than questioning any strangers in their midst. He knew the two inspectors ahead of him were armed, but to lose that advantage so early on would be disastrous.

Turning onto Upper Grange Road, Bowman quickened his step.

"This is madness, Bowman," opined Callaghan, as the crowds thinned around them.

"We are operating under the commissioner's orders, chief inspector."

"Our orders were to intercept the delivery at the dock, you are taking us in the wrong direction entirely." Callaghan was clearly at the end of his tether. He resented being placed with Bowman and would much rather have been spearheading an investigation of his own at Dartford. He trusted the men under him at the Special Irish Branch. He knew The Royal Yacht would be made safe and the station secured, but still he felt anxious to join them. Operation Vanguard was a matter of the highest import, with the life of Her Majesty herself at risk. This business with St. Saviour's was a potentially dangerous distraction.

Bowman bounded up the steps to the police station two at a time, a hand securing his hat to his head. A closed, wooden door greeted him and Bowman made a fist to rap against it, demanding entry.

"Scotland Yard!" he bellowed. "Open up!"

Graves looked around them. The crowd had thinned and it seemed their activities were going largely unheeded. Callaghan stood at the bottom of the steps, hands on hips, a surly look upon his face.

"Face it, Bowman," he drawled. "They've locked up for the night."

Bowman gestured to his two colleagues and Graves and Hicks joined him on the top step.

"Inspector Hicks, Sergeant Graves," began the inspector, "put your shoulders to the door."

Hicks gave a snort. "I'll have you know, Inspector Bowman, this coat was specially made for me in Jermyn Street."

"Then you can bill the commissioner for any damage," hissed Bowman. Graves suppressed a chuckle at the exchange.

A look passed between them and the two men braced themselves against the door. Bowman closed his hand around the revolver in his pocket. At a signal, the two men rocked back then slammed their shoulders into the door. It seemed Hicks' weight alone would have sufficed. The door gave way easily and the two policemen scrambled for purchase against the frame. Hicks stood brushing himself down pointedly as Bowman stepped into the room. Graves looked around. The desk stood deserted in the middle of the room, a great ledger lying closed upon it.

"There's no one here, sir," the young sergeant said, his eyes darting to the corners of the room.

With a curt nod, Bowman walked briskly to the back of the room. Chief Inspector Callaghan stepped through the shattered door.

"Empty," he pronounced, simply.

Motioning that Callaghan should join Sergeant Graves in checking the upper floors, Bowman nodded that Hicks should accompany him to the basement. The portly inspector, already out of breath with his exertions, gathered himself to follow.

Quietly, the two men crept down the steps, Bowman in the lead. Pulling his revolver from his pocket, he stood at the bottom of the stairwell. Cautioning that Hicks should stay behind him, he pivoted into the room. It, too, was empty. Bowman threw open the wooden lockers that stood along the far wall. Reaching up, he pulled down a bundle of clothing. Thackeray's police uniform.

"Hardly a surprise to find such a thing in a police station, Bowman," scoffed Hicks, his chest puffed out before him.

"I'm guessing," concluded Bowman, "he has no intention of wearing it again."

"All clear upstairs, sir." Sergeant Graves bounded down the stairs like an excitable schoolboy.

"You've led us on a wild goose chase, Bowman, just as I said." Callaghan had pocketed his revolver and now stood impatiently by the shattered door. "We should be at the dock investigating your precious delivery."

"We'll be in good time," Bowman retorted, walking to the heavy wooden desk that sat in the centre of the room. From behind, he could see it was comprised of deep shelves, each of which held wooden filing boxes and loose sheaves of paper. A large, well-thumbed ledger lay discarded on the desktop, slammed shut with a pen and ink well standing to one side. "It is this I have come to see."

He fingered the leading edge of the cover, then flipped it open to reveal the pages within. It was a large book, some ten or even twelve inches high by eight wide. The paper inside was lined and margined, with the first two thirds or so filled in with a variety of inks and hands.

"Do you have your instruction to meet at the subway about you?" Bowman asked, turning to Callaghan at the door.

"I do not," the chief inspector replied with a surly look.

Bowman lifted the pages and turned to the back of the book. Leaning in closer, he called Graves to join him.

"Sergeant Graves, what are we to make of this?"

His hands on the desk to support himself, Graves peered at the volume before him. Where the last page should have been, he could see a ragged margin where it had been torn out.

"There's a page missing, sir," Graves said. Callaghan rolled his eyes.

"Nothing unusual in that, surely?" boomed Hicks, his hands on his hips.

Bowman had drawn his note from his coat pocket. "It is not the fact that a page is missing that is of interest," he began, unfolding the paper in his hand. "It is the fact that *this* page is missing."

He laid his piece of paper flat against the inside back cover of the ledger. It was clearly the same as the rest of the book. The faint blue lines were of the same width and the margin the same red. Bowman's paper was almost exactly half the height of the book.

"I would wager, Chief Inspector Callaghan," Bowman said calmly, 'that your note would constitute the other half of the page."

Callaghan's expression betrayed his sudden interest.

"And look, sir." Graves was flipping back through the pages to the beginning of the book. "That's the same handwriting."

Graves was pointing at some entries on the page. In truth, there were many hands there but, amongst them, Graves had identified the same spidery scrawl.

Bowman nodded. "Indeed so."

Callaghan and Hicks drew closer to the desk.

"So someone in this police station," Hicks began, tapping the bit of his pipe against his chin in thought, "wrote those notes?"

Bowman turned to his fellow inspector. "It certainly narrows it down."

"Would Sallow have been among them?" Callaghan was looking askance at Bowman, careful not to show any signs of doubt in his man.

Bowman's eyes narrowed. "I would think it unusual for an undercover Special Irish Branch officer to attend to his correspondence in the local police station."

"Then he did not write my note?"

"No more than he wrote mine." Bowman slammed the ledger shut and made for the door. "Come on Sergeant Graves," he called over his shoulder. "Time and tide wait for no man."

With an apologetic look to Callaghan, Graves strode after the inspector, glad to see him so invigorated.

Bowman often marvelled how well he had got to know certain streets in the course of his duties. He had rarely found himself in Bermondsey in all his previous thirty-seven years. Now, he knew these streets as well as those around his own rooms in Hampstead. Passing down Upper Grange Road, he led his companions onto Alscot Road and across the tramway that ran the length of Southwark Park Road to Rotherhithe. Striding down Neckinger, they could already hear the hurly burly of activity from St. Saviour's Dock. The ship's funnel was just about visible from Dockhead as the party squeezed their way through the usual throng. Bowman could see a barge being towed into the dock. Several sacks of produce were already being thrown into the waiting arms of the dockworkers. Ropes were tied to pilings. Ramps were lowered to allow the men on board. All around, there was mayhem. The foremen were directing the dockers to their respective wharves, making a note of their names as they answered. Bowman saw the gibbet had been removed overnight. From the corner of his eye, he noticed Graves looking moodily at the hole in the dirt where it had been erected.

"We need to stop that shipment," rasped Bowman. There was much riding on his investigation.

Callaghan was at his side, his eyes agog at the swarm of activity before him. "And how do you propose we do that?"

The words were barely out of his mouth when he heard a loud blast by his left ear. His heart racing, he ducked to the floor, covering his head with his hands. Once the ringing in his ears had subsided, he looked up to see Bowman on the wall that separated the road from the dock. He held his revolver in one hand, and his papers in another.

"Detective Inspector Bowman, Scotland Yard!" he was shouting. "Hold that cargo!"

Peering over the wall, Chief Inspector Callaghan could see the maelstrom of activity had come to a halt. He was relieved to see that many others had also ducked to the floor in response to the shot. Some stood frozen where they were, a sack or pallet balanced dangerously on their heads. All eyes were upon Bowman. Sergeant Graves leaned into the chief inspector. "Well," he breathed excitedly, 'that got their attention."

"Stand back from the water!" Bowman yelled.

"We've a boat to unload!" The inspector saw a young, brawny man at a barrow. There was a chorus of agreement. "Got to get this spice off or we don't get paid!"

"We're impounding this ship! Where's the captain?"

"I'm the captain!"

Bowman saw a tall, wiry-looking man with a bandana on his head. "Then you must talk to Inspector Hicks."

Hicks' eyebrows rose high on his head at the mention of his name. Bowman leapt from the wall, his coat tails billowing behind him.

"Seize his papers, Hicks," hissed Bowman. "And his log. We need to know just what he's picked up and where." Hicks nodded sharply. Bowman turned to Callaghan and Graves. "You two," he breathed, "stay with me."

The inspectors strode into Shad Thames and through the open doors of the wharves to the dock front. With a gleam of determination in his eye, Bowman shouldered through the throng of wharfingers who stood awaiting their employment at the dockside. Burly men blocked their way at every turn. Eager to earn their pay, they were aware that time was of the essence.

"The tide won't wait," bellowed one into Bowman's face.

"Nor will my investigation," shouted the inspector as he strode to the water's edge. "Stand aside."

The boat in front of him was a converted Scottish steam barge. More used to ferrying fish from the Scottish ports, the Thistledown had been fitted with additional sails and had her hull reinforced for ocean voyages. Steam belched from her cast iron funnel to the aft as her engines idled. The captain stood aloft, leaning against the wheelhouse.

"Captain," bellowed Bowman. "I must have access to the hold."

"You'll have it just as soon as I talk to the loading officer." The captain eyed Bowman cautiously. "I'll have everything done by the book."

"Where is Bracewell?" Bowman asked the nearest foreman.

"He's not been seen this evening," the man said, with a shrug.

"Reckon he's workshy!" jeered a stocky man in a tatty felt jacket, to murmurs of approval.

"Then," continued Bowman, "I'm commandeering this ship on behalf of Her Majesty."

There was laughter from the captain. "Comin' to search it herself, is she?"

"Can you do that, sir?" whispered Sergeant Graves from the inspector's shoulder.

"I have the authority as a police officer," shouted Bowman to the captain. "You may question it in court when you are charged with the obstruction of an investigation." He turned to Graves. "No, I don't Graves," he said quietly. "But I'm hoping he won't risk a day in court." Graves only just suppressed a smile at the inspector's gall.

The captain was still for a while, chewing on his lip in thought. He was clearly weighing up his options. Then, throwing his arms up in submission, he strode from the deck and across the gangplank to the dockside. Squaring up to Bowman, he jutted his chin into the inspector's face.

"If my cargo is not despatched before the tide turns, then Scotland Yard will know about it."

Bowman could smell tobacco on his breath.

"Inspector Hicks," Bowman began calmly, determined not to blink in the face of the man's threats, "would you take the captain to a quieter place and question him as to his boat's cargo?"

The captain cleared his throat and spat the resultant spume to the floor, narrowly missing Bowman's shoes. "Albert!" he called. A young boy poked his head from a hatch on the boat's deck. "Bring our cargo manifest and landing papers, would you, lad?" Through all this, the captain held Bowman in his gaze. "You'll find nothing out of the ordinary, inspector."

"Then you have nothing to fear," Bowman returned, slowly. He turned sharply and nodded to Hicks.

"This way, captain," said Hicks, gesturing with his great hand that he should follow him. "Let's find a quiet corner, shall we?"

The look in Hicks' eye gave Bowman the suspicion that he might well have meant a quiet corner in a public house. No matter, thought the inspector, so long as he got the job done.

With a grunt, the captain gave way and followed the inspector, but not without a last look of contempt at Bowman.

"Chief Inspector Callaghan, would you be so good as to accompany Sergeant Graves into the hold?" Callaghan murmured his assent as Bowman turned to one of the dockworkers, a swarthy looking man with a crooked face. "You," he commanded. "Follow them down and render such assistance as may be necessary."

The man looked at his colleagues. Finding no support among them, he rolled his eyes and strode on board the Thistledown. Lifting the hatches along the length of the deck, he stood with a surly look, awaiting his orders.

"Off you go, Graves," Bowman said to his companion, quietly. "Don't miss a thing."

"Righto, sir." Graves was beaming with excitement. "And what will you do?"

"I need to look for Bracewell." Bowman's eyes narrowed as he thought. "Is it mere coincidence that he's disappeared just when we had most need to talk with him?"

Graves clicked his tongue in response and, with a look to Callaghan, tripped carefully over the gangplank to the Thistledown's polished, wooden deck.

As Callaghan passed in front of Bowman, he swung the top hat from his head and threw the inspector a look of exasperation. Bad enough, he was clearly thinking, to be subordinate to a mere detective inspector. Worse still to be wasting time with such trifles. Bowman returned his gaze, his moustache twitching slightly on his upper lip.

With his two companions descending the ladders to the hold, Bowman turned to the men on the quay. "No one leaves this dock. I charge the foremen to be sure of it."

"How long will you be?" shouted a younger man from the opposite side of the dock.

"We'll take all the time we need, but you will not leave."

With a collective groan, the men sauntered back from the water's edge to sit and bemoan their fate.

Inspector Bowman walked the length of Shad Thames to the steps down to the river. His eyes scanned the open wharf doors for anything that looked improper or out of place. The wharfingers sat on barrels and carts, cursing at the inspector's intervention and the passing of time. Every minute that was wasted was a threat to their wages.

Reaching the bottom of the steps, Bowman turned the corner to face Tower Bridge. The sun was setting behind it, imbuing the stonework with a fiery red. It looked like it sat in some great furnace, its ironwork glowing like embers. The labourers were gone for the night and all was still on the towers and gantries. Bowman saw the bascules had been left in their raised position in anticipation of the arrival of the Royal Yacht. Turning to his right, Bowman found himself in the very same spot where he had first met Cornelius Bracewell just two days before. He had felt uneasy in the man's presence, he remembered. The bead of sweat that had rolled from his hairline seemed to signify a man not to be trusted. There before him was a dilapidated door marked 'loading officer'. It seemed to be made from various bits of planking nailed together. A small, dirty window enabled Bowman to peer in before knocking loudly at the jamb. The lack of response from within only served to confirm Bowman's suspicion that the office was empty. He wrapped a fist in the tails of his coat and held it some inches from the glass. Bracing himself, he punched at the window and shattered the glass. Grimacing at the impact, he pulled his fist back, rubbing at his knuckles to ease the pain. Peering through the frame, Bowman was able to get a good enough look around at the loading officer's lair.

There was no sign of a hurried exit. The books, charts and ledgers that lay on the tables and shelves had been placed in their particular places according to alphabetical order. Bowman could see a chart of tide times on the wall. A pile of papers was laid carefully in a tray marked 'manifests', whilst others were labelled 'customs', 'fines' and 'permissions'. All was in order. Bracewell was clearly keeping an appointment somewhere, and one for which he had had good notice. There was no sign of any business left unfinished in his office. Rather, he had clearly had the time to finish his daily duties and set them aside before he left. But where was he? If the Thistledown was carrying the delivery he and Sallow had been expecting, why were they not at St. Saviour's Dock? Unless the Thistledown was not carrying the delivery. Bowman turned with a sigh to stare across the seething Thames. Through the various masts and funnels that crowded the river waiting for a berth, he could see St. Katharine Docks. There was little activity there following the explosion, but Bowman could see three or four men at work to clear the debris.

His eyes traced the course of the river downstream and away from Tower Bridge. A two-man skiff manoeuvred skilfully between a tea clipper and the north bank, its occupants perhaps minded to spend their evening in the seedier parts of the city. A pair of squabbling gulls fought over possession of a wooden post that protruded from the water. And there, tethered to a pier some half a mile from where the inspector stood on the south bank, a tug bobbed lazily on the swell. Bowman squinted against the glare of the evening sun on the water, his forehead creasing into his habitual frown. The Thistledown was a distraction. The delivery wasn't at St. Saviour's Dock, at all. That was just what Sallow had led his men to believe, sure in the knowledge that someone would talk. Bowman allowed himself a smirk. Sallow had got to know his fellow dockworkers well. He had exploited their predilection to gossip and led the inspectors to precisely the wrong place at precisely the wrong time.

Turning sharply, Bowman saw Sergeant Graves appear from the door to Corder's Wharf, a sack of tea on his shoulder. He beckoned the sergeant to join him down the steps, and Graves loped down the road, rubbing the dust from his hands.

"Graves, we're in the wrong place," said Bowman breathlessly. "Look."

Graves followed Bowman's gaze up the Thames to the tug on the pier.

"How do you know, sir?"

"Your informant told you there would be a delivery." Bowman had him by the shoulders now, his face set in concentration. "We assumed it would be here at St. Saviour's. It was the perfect diversion."

"Diversion from what, sir?" Graves was rubbing dust from his hands.

"The real delivery, of course. Come on Graves!" Bowman was already striding back up the steps to Shad Thames, his coat flapping behind him.

"You can't leave," complained a grey-haired man with tattoos on his neck. "We need to get this boat unloaded."

"Chief Inspector Callaghan is my direct superior," Bowman called over his shoulder as he passed the wharf to Tooley Street. "It is to him you should address your complaints." Graves allowed himself a smile as he fell into step behind the inspector, his blond curls dancing about his head as he picked up the pace.

The streets were quieter now with so many men at the dock. Those who had been unlucky in their search for work had wandered back home to bed, or were propping up bars in the local public houses. Soon the pair were passing beyond the dock to Mill Street and Bermondsey Wall that ran parallel to the river bank. Even at this hour, the sound of a mechanical saw sang into the air from the slate works. With time of the essence, the two men sprinted past Duffield Sluice and Fountain Dock. Graves just had time to glance at the dry dock as they ran, its steep brick walls curving down to a deep floor as if some great beast had taken a scoop out of the riverbank.

On they ran past Fountain Stairs and the great granaries that reared up at the corner with Cherry Garden Street. Once the site of formal gardens and orchards for the citizens of London to enjoy, the area was now home to great soaring wharves, rice mills and tanneries that smudged the skyline with their smoke and steam. Even in the fading light, Graves could see where furnaces and chimneys had scorched the brick. Graves saw the inspector gasping for breath as they rounded the corner to Cherry Garden Pier and even the sergeant, young as he was, could feel a stitch in his side.

Cherry Garden Pier had once been the loading place for crates of fruit destined for the north bank and the markets beyond. It was soon to serve a more prosaic purpose. With the many bends in the River Thames, it had been discovered that the operators of Tower Bridge may not have a clear enough view of approaching vessels to lift the bascules in time. It had been the city authority's intent that no vessel should have to await the lifting of the bridge, so a full time guard was to be stationed at the pier, his purpose being to give notice to raise the bridge as vessels rounded the bend at Limehouse. The pier reached some fifty feet into the Thames; a floating pontoon connected to the shore by a jointed walkway. Its boards were suspended on wooden piles rising from the riverbed. The final stretch of the walkway was attached by a series of movable joints to the pontoon, allowing it to rise and fall with the ebb of the tide. The pontoon itself, tethered to the riverbed by anchored cables, was populated by a motley collection of dilapidated huts and cabins, several of which had had their windows broken and their doors forced. Hitched to the moorings on the far side, was the steam tug that Bowman had seen from St. Saviour's Dock.

Bowman broke his stride and grabbed at Graves' coat, pulling him against a dirty wall out of sight of the pier.

"What is it, sir?"

Bowman peered slowly round the corner. "Take a look, Graves. It seems someone would deny us access."

Leaning past the inspector to look across to the pier, Graves could see that the entrance was guarded. A bull terrier, tethered by a piece of rope to the guardrail, was clearly taking his responsibilities very seriously. Picking up their scent, the dog sprang to its feet and ran towards the two detectives, only stopping when he was jolted back by the rope at its neck. Graves heard a low, guttural snarl escape the dog's throat, its eyes blazing with menace.

"What do we do?" Graves pressed himself back against the wall, his heart pounding.

Bowman's eyes searched the darkening street for inspiration. "Wait here," he said. With that, he crossed the road into an open yard by a boat maker's workshop. Searching through the piles of debris by the gate, he pulled out a heavy length of wood and a canvas tarpaulin.

"Here," he breathed as he returned to his companion. "Take this." He handed Graves the tarpaulin as he spoke. "Someone is very keen that we don't see inside that tug. Which is all the more reason to try." He held the piece of wood aloft, feeling the weight in his hand. "He's a fighting dog. His instinct will be to jump and to bite." He turned to Graves with a look of serious intent. "Stay close," he cautioned.

Slowly, the two men advanced towards the pier and its grisly guard. Graves could see saliva dripping from the dog's mouth to the floor in great strings. It bared its teeth as they approached, its claws scratching at the wooden planks beneath as it strained against the rope. Its tether was just long enough to stretch across the full width of the gangway, leaving them no room to go around the beast. As Bowman raised a hand to gesture that Graves should come level with him, the dog let forth a cacophony of barking that echoed down the narrow streets behind them. Each was punctuated by a menacing growl.

"Steady, Graves," whispered Bowman, the wood balanced before him. "Steady." He waved the post before him in an effort to distract the dog. Sure enough, the beast followed it first with his eyes, then his whole body, jumping to snap at the wood with its ferocious jaws. Bowman swung his arm left and right as Graves lifted the tarpaulin high. Bowman saw the rope go slack and knew the time had come to strike. The dog crouched low as the inspector swung the beam to the ground. Sensing Bowman moving to lift the wood into the air again, it prepared to jump, the muscles rippling across its flank as they tensed in anticipation.

"Now, Graves!" boomed the inspector as the dog jumped up. Jamming the wood into the dog's gaping jaws, Bowman forced it to the ground and onto its back. The dog gave a yelp of surprise as it hit the deck, the force of the impact driving the breath from its body. Graves pounced, throwing his whole weight onto the dog and struggling to wrap the beast in the tarpaulin.

"I've got him, sir, but I'm not sure I can hold him."

The terrier struggled furiously in an effort to be free but the more it squirmed, the more it became entangled in the material. Bowman had thrown the beam to one side now and joined Graves in trying to subdue the dog.

"Come on, Graves," he panted. "Let's get him out of harm's way." Unhitching the rope from the guardrail, he helped the sergeant carry his restless burden across the bridge to the pontoon. Twice the tarpaulin threatened to fall from the dog, but Graves was quick enough to pull the canvas tight around its body.

Finally, they reached the collection of ramshackle cabins. By now, Graves was struggling to contain the beast in his arms, his face taut with the effort. Bowman had run ahead to try the cabin doors. Finally, he found one that would be secure enough to hold the beast. The padlock had been ripped from the handle and thrown to the ground in signs of a previous forced entry. Bowman guessed the hut had recently provided shelter to some vagrant. Foregoing any niceties, the inspector drew back the bolt and threw open the door with scant regard to any potential occupants. The hut, he saw, was empty. Trestle tables that had once stood around the perimeter of the room had collapsed under their own weight. Debris littered the floor. Bowman saw iron jemmies, pulleys and hooks. Coils of rope had been piled into corners or thrown carelessly across the floor to unravel.

"Graves!" he pointed. "In here!"

The sergeant struggled through the door, the dog writhing and snapping in his arms. Bowman stretched across him to keep the canvas taut about the dog's head. On a count of three, they lowered him to the ground. Bowman wrapped the beast even tighter in the tarpaulin, but not so tight that he wouldn't escape in time.

"Get ready at the door, Graves," Bowman panted, and the young sergeant sprang across the room. When Bowman saw his companion was ready, he reached for a heavy crate and slid it across the floor towards him. Lifting one side, he lowered it to anchor the canvas to the floor for the precious moments he needed to get to the door.

"Ready when you are, sir," said Graves from across the room. With a look at his companion, Bowman gave a nod and raced for the outside, his shoes scuffing at the mess on the floor. The moment he was through, Graves slammed the door shut and lowered the latch, sliding the bolt across in an almost simultaneous movement.

The two men leaned with their backs against the wood, both breathing hard. Barely a moment had passed before they heard the dog barking from within. A moment later and he was at the door, clawing at its dilapidated planks.

"It'll hold him, Graves."

Graves had turned to the tug. "Seems empty, sir. Looks like we're too late."

Bowman followed his gaze to the boat that lay bobbing silently at the pontoon's edge. Aside from the wheelhouse and the single, gently steaming funnel that rose amidships, there was little to see. The workhorse of the fleet, it had clearly been built for utility rather than speed. There were no graceful lines, rather a snub-nosed design that gave it a solid, obstinate look. The lack of a cargo deck meant that any delivery would have been lashed to the stern. Squinting into the half-light, Bowman could see discarded ropes and a length of oiled canvas that suggested just that. The inspector was thinking.

"Who would set a dog to guard an empty boat, Graves?"

The sergeant answered Bowman's question with a tilt of his head. "Shall we take a look, sir?"

Checking one last time that the bolt was secure, the two men picked their way carefully across the gangplank to the tug. The engine was idling beneath the hatches, ticking and banging at intervals like some impatient animal. Occasional puffs of steam escaped from the safety valves and pipes that led to the drive shafts and flywheels beneath the deck. The boat was strewn with chains, tools and chests of equipment. Graves kicked at the canvas. "Reckon this is where they carried the delivery?" he called, resting on his haunches to examine the deck.

"Almost certainly." Bowman was approaching the wheelhouse, a small, cabin-like construction towards the bow of the tug. A dark shape was resolving itself beneath the wheel in the gloom.

"What were they delivering?" Graves was musing from the stern. "Drugs? Equipment? Arms?"

"Graves!"

The note in Bowman's voice brought the sergeant up sharp. He rose to his feet, suddenly alert. Moving swiftly to the wheelhouse he could just make out Bowman's silhouette against the sunset, bending to something beneath the wheel. As Graves approached, he saw it was a body. It was slumped with its head on the deck as if in prayer. Bowman lifted the man's head. Even in the failing light, Graves could see a milky, white eye staring blankly ahead, as if into oblivion itself.

"Ichabod Sallow," Bowman muttered in confirmation.

"That's why they set a dog to guard the pier." Graves ran his fingers through his curls as he spoke.

"Indeed." Bowman was examining the dead man. A slick of blood emanating from a thin wound at his neck left no doubt as to the cause of his death. "To prevent the discovery of Sallow's body, for the time being at least."

"Why would the Kaiser want Sallow dead?" Graves asked. "From what you've told me, he's proven invaluable to their cause."

"So far, yes," Bowman smoothed his moustache between his thumb and finger, deep in thought, "But just how far would you trust a man you knew to be a Special Irish Branch detective? Sallow might've been trustworthy so far, but he's clearly disposable now." A worried look passed across Bowman's lean face. "The Kaiser must be on the verge of executing their plan."

"But where have they gone, and with what?" Graves stood again and looked around the deck for any clue, but Bowman's attention was suddenly upstream.

As the sun set lower over the Thames, the shadow of Tower Bridge lengthened across the water towards them. The horizon seemed ablaze with an angry glow, the river a sea of boiling metal. Against this dramatic panorama, the bridge seemed all the more strange and unearthly. It was an apocalyptic image, thought Bowman as he faced the sunset, as though the End of Days had come to the heart of the Empire. The clouds above him were aflame. The air was suddenly thick with heat and Bowman breathed hard to quell a sense of panic. Loosening his collar about his neck, his eye was drawn to the south bank where the approach to the bridge met the shore. If he moved his head slightly to the right of the wheelhouse and fooled his eye by focusing beyond the bridge, he could just see a single light blinking, as if being carried. He knew the bridge labourers would have ceased their work as the light faded. Perhaps the last of them was leaving.

"Sir!"

Graves was suddenly at his side, his hand cupped before him. Bowman realised with a sense of embarrassment that he had been muttering to himself. He rubbed at his eyes to clear his head. "What is it, Graves?"

"Take a look at these." Graves opened his hand to reveal what appeared to be half a dozen or so splinters, each three or four inches in length. "Cordite," he said at last. "They were taking delivery of explosives."

Bowman thought quickly. "Graves, if you wanted to inflict a wound on the Empire itself, what would you do?"

"I don't follow, sir." Graves was blinking into the sunset.

"If you felt hard done by, deserted by your queen and country, and you were of a mind to exact revenge upon them, what form would that revenge take?" Bowman turned to face upstream again. "What would be your target?" Graves' eyes widened in alarm as Bowman nodded. "The Kaiser is going to blow up Tower Bridge."

XXVIII

Operation Vanguard

Cornelius Bracewell wiped the sweat from his face with a sleeve. Even in the cool evening air, he felt hot from his exertions. His leg ached. Rubbing his shin where Big Tam had kicked him just three nights before, he cursed the Scotsman and his damned foot. Still, he had fetched a pretty penny in the ring. The Kaiser had been pleased. Looking out across the Thames from his vantage point, Bracewell allowed himself a chuckle. He was about to rock the whole of the Empire to its very core, and he was about to make himself rich in the process. In exchange for his services, the Kaiser had promised him wealth beyond compare. It had been easy enough to mislead Callaghan. The chief inspector had been so desperate for answers and even more desperate for advancement through the ranks, that he had jumped at anything that might present itself as truth. Fenian plot indeed, chuckled Bracewell as he bent at his work, his great, wide face aglow in the sunset. A little judicious planting of evidence at St. Katharine Docks had been enough to place Tremont in the frame and throw Callaghan off the scent. There was indeed a plot afoot at St. Saviour's, but it was not and never had been Fenian. Ichabod Sallow had been the one wild card. He had overstepped the mark with Jonas Cook. Sending him to hospital had risked the entire operation. Sallow had feared exposure if the man talked, but had chosen the wrong moment to act. To injure Cook in sight of a Scotland Yarder had been bad timing indeed, and had necessitated the Kaiser taking matters into their own hands. Cook had been despatched easily enough, he understood, and the witnesses scared into silence, but Sallow had sealed his fate with that one act at St. Saviour's. Now, his usefulness expired, he had paid the price. Bracewell's mind turned to the events on the tug. With the delivery made, the Kaiser had acted swiftly. Bracewell doubted Sallow had even felt the wire at his throat. He chuckled again. With Sallow gone, there would be more money to go round. Perhaps he could plead with the Kaiser for the dead man's share. Bracewell looked up at the hooded figure working on the approach to the bridge. He knew they had made good time. The labourers had long gone and the sole guard on duty rewarded handsomely for his indifference. The bridge had been theirs for the best part of an hour, and the work was almost done.

"Everything in position?"

Bracewell turned to see Thackery had dropped from a gantry above. He was dressed in a loose docker's jacket and felt trousers. Bracewell nodded. "It is that," he said.

"Good," replied Thackery. "I've laid more in the tower and run the fuse off the bridge."

Bracewell nodded and stood to face his accomplice. "Where will you go, Thackeray?"

Thackeray weighed his response before answering. "South," he lied. He didn't trust Bracewell any more than he had trusted Sallow. "Some sleepy Cornish fishing village would do me fine."

Bracewell smiled. Part of him wanted to stay to watch. To be part of the most audacious plot against the Crown and yet not be present at its culmination seemed a cruel deprivation. To be present at the scene, however, was to risk capture. With their work almost done, he knew the Kaiser would dismiss them both and it would be up to them to make good their escape.

Moving the barrel a foot further to his left to where a steel joist met the support beneath the tower, Bracewell bent to pick up a bundle of copper wires. Handing them to Thackeray, he stopped for breath again. Blowing a bead of sweat from his nose, he allowed his eyes to roam across the skyline. How still the city slept, he mused. How peaceful and serene. How unaware of the tiger in its midst.

Callaghan had had enough. He had upturned just about every sack and crate within the boat's hold and found nothing beneath. Sergeant Graves, he noticed, had deserted him. He was no doubt swinging the lead on the dockside, letting his superior do the donkeywork. Wiping his hands on his trousers, the chief inspector cursed beneath his breath. He had let himself be compromised again. Bowman had led him, and the commissioner, on a merry dance. Heaving himself up the ladder, he stood on the deck of the Thistledown, looking about him. A crowd of dockers stood on the quayside. Some had their arms folded across their chests, others flexed their fists at their side. All had a belligerent gleam in their eye. Time was clearly up and they had a wage to earn. As they advanced upon the ship, Callaghan looked from man to man.

"Where is Inspector Bowman?" he demanded, a rising note of panic in his voice. "And Sergeant Graves?" He held his arms wide, imploring.

"Left you high and dry, I reckon!" rasped one of the men, beating his fist into an open palm. There was laughter all around.

"The rats have left the sinking ship!" screeched another to yet more amusement.

Callaghan saw several of the men pointing out to the Thames. Turning to face the river, he saw a small, snub-nosed tug steaming past the mouth of the dock. At its helm, stood a tall, lean figure in a long coat and bowler hat.

"Bowman," he muttered beneath his breath.

"Where will you land?" Graves shouted above the noise.

Bowman looked ahead. A battered two-man coracle was pulling away from some steps by the south bank. "There!" he replied, pointing to the vacated mooring. The inspector leaned heavily on the throttle. In their haste to effect their plan, the Kaiser's men had left the fire burning in the coal box, and there was water enough in the boiler. It was a simple matter of opening the valves to allow the passage of steam. Bowman heard the rise and fall of the pistons and felt the screw beneath his feet begin to turn. Soon they were underway and Cherry Garden Pier receded behind them. It had seemed a quicker option than attempting the mile or so to the bridge on foot.

"So Sallow didn't kill Jonas Cook?" Graves was asking as the wind whipped about his curls.

"I did not see it at the time, but there was one other perfectly placed to kill him." Bowman had a light hold of the wheel as they flitted past St. Saviour's Dock. "Sometimes the best place to hide is in plain sight."

Alma Beaurepaire turned to Bracewell and Thackeray. She felt powerful before them. They shuffled nervously as they waited, like children awaiting the judgement of a parent. "Is all set?" she asked.

Thackeray nodded. "All that's left is for you to light the fuse. I have run it down the stairwell to Shad Thames. That should give you distance and protection enough." He threw her a box of matches from his pocket. "It's a safety fuse, impervious to wind and rain. You could drop it in the Thames and still it would burn."

"Why would you not let Thackeray set a timer?" Bracewell asked. He was beginning to shiver now his exertions were over.

Alma Beaurepaire shook her head. "I want to see it all," she replied. "I want to see her pay."

Bracewell and Thackeray shared a look between themselves.

"And the money?" Bracewell asked bravely.

"There is a jeweller's in Covent Garden," Alma said. "He will have your instructions in his safe. They will lead you to your money."

Thackeray nodded in understanding. For the second time in twenty-four hours, he would have the pleasure of seeing Frank Jolly quake before him.

"And yes," Alma continued in response to Bracewell's unspoken question. "You will have Sallow's share between you."

Bracewell's eyes were glistening with tears. He held out a hand. "Thank you," he said, simply.

The Kaiser returned the gesture, holding Bracewell's hand as she spoke. "You have both given me so much." She was looking deep into Bracewell's eyes. "The future is before us. We will bring the Empire to its knees."

Thackeray took her hand next. He did not care for her talk of Empire. He had never shared her fervour for its destruction. Like Bracewell, his mind was on the money and the new life it would bring him. He shook her hand. It was a suitably business-like gesture, he thought. The deal concluded.

"Now, go!" Alma commanded. The two men paused for a moment on the bridge, the structure around them seemingly aflame in the sunset. The silence between them was palpable. And then they scuttled away, both of them walking to the south side of the bridge where a hansom cab was waiting to take them to Covent Garden. The driver, they knew, had been bought. What they could not know was that he had been furnished with a revolver and instructions to drive the two men to wasteland beyond the city, there to dispose of their bodies.

Alma lowered her hood and stopped to gaze down the Thames. History is made of turning points, she reflected as she turned from the rail and walked towards the south bank. Feeling the weight of time upon her, Alma strode purposefully down Tower Bridge Approach and towards Shad Thames where Thackeray had set the fuse. The streets, as she had planned, were deserted. Certain members of the local constabulary had been happy enough to see some extra money in their wages in return for closing the roads for three hours. Lifting her face to the end of the street, she could see two of their number. They did not know, of course, that by accepting the bribe, they had become complicit in the crime of the century. Smiling at the irony, Alma Beaurepaire descended the steps into Shad Thames and came face to face with the barrel of a gun.

Graves' curls danced in the wind as Bowman steered the tug to shore. The inspector had been briefing his sergeant on the matron at Bermondsey police station.

"So you believe her to be the daughter that Robert Beaurepaire had with Frances de Keyser?"

"She told me her father was the Governor of the colony in New South Wales. That he and her mother had died, leaving her alone at a young age and at the mercy of the authorities."

"But her father was a convict."

"And her mother, too. Subject to the harshest and most strict of regimes." Bowman was steering the tug to Horselydown Old Stairs, easing back on the regulator to slow their progress.

"But why blow up Tower Bridge?"

"The bridge isn't the target, Graves. We know the Queen is to return to London via her Royal Yacht this evening. The Victoria And Albert will pass along just this stretch of the Thames."

Graves' gaze rose towards the hulking shadow of Tower Bridge as it reared up before him against the sun. Its raised bascules reminded him of a giant maw, red with blood. An involuntary shiver passed down his spine as he contemplated the import of Bowman's words. "She's going to kill the Queen?"

"Any moment now," Bowman continued as he brought the tug to bear, "her yacht will round the bend at Limehouse. Just a few minutes more and she will be beneath the bridge. Who better represents the power and reach of the British Empire but the Queen herself?"

"But she can't hold the Queen responsible," said Graves, aghast.

"The Queen sits at the centre of her empire just as the Kaiser sits at the centre of hers." Bowman shifted the throttle and the engine idled as they steered to the steps. "She's going to do more than kill the Queen, Graves. She's going to inflict a mortal wound upon the Empire itself."

Graves stared at the bridge for a moment, his mind reeling at the thought. His reverie was interrupted by a bump. Seeing the river wall beside him, he lunged for a rope to tie the boat off at a mooring.

"Forget that," Bowman boomed as he leapt from the deck to the steps. "Time is of the essence!"

Graves let go the rope and followed the inspector, leaving the tug to drift behind them. Bowman sprinted towards the approach to Tower Bridge. Drawing his revolver as he ran, he called over his shoulder to his companion. "Keep back, Graves, we've no idea if they're armed!"

Graves slowed his pace in response. He noticed the tide was receding already, leaving a watery shadow on the wall as an imprint of its presence. Turning onto Shad Thames, Graves noticed Bowman suddenly slow. As he rounded the corner he saw the inspector had stopped, his revolver stretched out before him. Tracing his aim, Graves saw a woman at the bottom of the steps to the bridge, her eyes wide in surprise. She was wearing a long, hooded cloak over her clothes.

"Hello, George," she was saying. "What are you doing here?"

"Stay where you are," Bowman commanded.

"Sure, I will," Alma purred. "But please, could you put that thing away?"

Bowman swallowed hard. "Miss Beaurepaire," he began, blinking furiously, "you should know that you are under arrest."

Alma held her long arms wide, subtly shifting her weight forward onto her front foot. "For what?" Improbably, she was smiling.

"For the murder of Jonas Cook and for being an accessory to the murders of Harry Pope and Kitty Baldwin." Bowman fancied he heard Graves catch his breath at the mention of her name. "And for acting with intent to harm the Crown through use of an explosive device or devices."

"I would love to see your evidence for those charges, George." She looked him square in the face with that easy confidence he had got to know so well.

"I have evidence enough," Bowman gulped. "Both Chief Inspector Callaghan and I received notes written to the effect that we should meet in the Tower Subway at noon today."

"Well, how lovely," beamed Alma. "A tryst."

Bowman was unnerved at her calm demeanour. "Both notes were written in your hand on paper from your ledger at Bermondsey police station."

"Is that so? How extraordinary." Alma had her eyes locked on Bowman now, and he fought to read her intention. Was she going to give herself up?

"And you were with Jonas Cook at The Sisters Of Mercy," he continued. "You murdered him and threatened the other patients to keep their silence."

"Did I really?"

Bowman blinked. Was she toying with him?

"Sir!" Graves had taken a step towards Bowman's shoulder, hissing in his ear. "It's the Vic And Albert, sir. The Royal Yacht. It's just rounded the bend at Limehouse."

Quite involuntarily, Bowman whipped his head round to look downstream. There, indeed, he could see the twin funnels of the Royal Yacht steaming down the centre of the Thames, its long, sleek lines lying low against the water. He could see the Royal Standard fluttering from its forward mast.

"Pretty thing, ain't she?" There was a strident tone to Alma's voice that brought Bowman up short. Turning quickly to face her, he saw that she had drawn a small pistol and had it aimed squarely at his head. "We've got, what, five minutes before she's with us?" Alma was moving slowly towards the river wall as she spoke. "A lot can happen in five minutes."

Bowman fought to make sense of it all. "Why?" he asked, simply.

"I've built an Empire of my own, George!" Alma looked triumphant.

"And given yourself a new name," Bowman breathed. "A corruption of your mother's maiden name; De Keyser."

"The Kaiser suited me well. A signal of my opposition to the

Empire."

"The Empire gave you a home." Bowman's eyes narrowed. He had caught a glimpse of something on the bridge above and, as Alma spoke, he fought to focus in the fading light.

"The Empire forsook me, George," Alma spat. "My father was transported and left to rot. He fell prey to a harsh regime that branded him with a sign of ownership."

"Just as you branded your prize fighters." Bowman heard Graves speak up behind him, but his eyes were on the object above. There, parked close to the heavy balustrade that guarded the road from the steep drop to Shad Thames, was Bracewell's carriage. The carriage that had driven into his wife on Hanbury Street. He even recognised the horses from his journey to Greenwich, two handsome-looking dark chestnut mares. Bowman felt a lurch in his stomach.

"Your friend is very quick, George," Alma laughed. She trained her gun on Graves. "How would you like to join your little girl?"

Graves gritted his teeth, fighting the urge to swing for her. He took a breath. "The records show your father married and made a life for himself upon release."

"The governor was a monster and released him a broken man," Alma hissed. "And he was abandoned."

Bowman was breathing heavily now. It was the cruellest trick of fate that Bracewell's brougham should be here now. If he looked closely, he fancied he could even see the stitched fabric in the canopy where his bullet had penetrated not a year before.

"That coach - ," he began, but Alma was in full flow now.

"He was abandoned by his queen and country. And so was I."

Graves could see Alma moving almost imperceptibly to the river wall, but why? He had to find a moment to disarm her. His eyes flicked to Bowman. The inspector was standing stock-still.

"Both my parents were in the grave by the time I was five."

"That coach," repeated Bowman, his mind reeling back to Hanbury Street. He was standing again by the workhouse as the carriage sped towards him.

"I was left in the care of the prison governor." Graves heard a catch in Alma's voice. "You will never know how ill he used me as I grew, nor how I know he kept a portrait of Her Illustrious Majesty on his bedroom wall." She spat the words.

"Here they come," Bowman heard Williams whisper in his ear. "Be ready now."

The brougham's wheels kicked up the sludge as it rounded the corner. Bowman felt every muscle in his body tense as he watched it approach the kerb and slow just outside the workhouse. He saw the carriage door swing open and a man reach out. As the carriage passed the line of urchins waiting at the workhouse door, its occupant leaned further out into the road, the better to reach his quarry.

Bowman could see him now. The very angle of his shoulder was unmistakeable. As the inspector's eye rose up the man's neck to his face, he seemed frozen in an instant of time, his arm reaching out, his jaw clenched. A single bead of sweat rolled from his forehead. Bowman gave an involuntary gasp. He suppressed the urge to retch. Cornelius Bracewell had been the man in that coach, and he was operating under the command of the Kaiser.

"You!" he breathed.

Alma's eyebrows rose at the interruption. "Are you quite well, George?" Still she edged closer to the river wall.

Bowman was suddenly struck with a dreadful realisation. Only two days before, he had shaken the hand of the man who had been in that coach as his wife fell beneath its wheels. More than that, he was now holding a gun to the head of the woman who had overseen the entire operation. Bowman squinted down the barrel of his revolver.

"You killed my wife."

Alma blinked, innocently. "Really?" she gasped in mock surprise. Graves saw her reach into the pocket of her robes as she spoke.

"Sir," he cautioned.

"You killed my wife!" Bowman repeated fiercely. He advanced on the woman in front of him, gripping the handle of his revolver all the tighter. His finger squeezed against the trigger as he spoke, his voice thick with emotion.

"Your so-called Empire has led to many deaths," he was blinking furiously now. "My wife among them." The muzzle of Bowman's gun was just inches from Alma's forehead. Graves marked how eerily calm she remained in the face of Bowman's onslaught. She had even lowered her gun.

Bowman shook his head. As he blinked, his vision blurred. His hand was shaking uncontrollably now. He had no idea how the explosives had been primed. If with a timer, then he must get to the bridge to disarm it. He knew he had to shoot. Bowman felt suspended. The blood raced to his head.

There before him, stood Anna. Her eyes were smiling in their familiar greeting. Bowman realised with a start that he had his gun trained upon her.

"Sir!" Graves was calling, as if from far off. The whump of the Victoria And Albert's engines seemed to beat inside the inspector's chest, a heavy, rhythmic thump.

Bowman squeezed at the trigger again. He knew he had to fire. But, Anna. She took his breath away. Tears pricked at his eyes as he scanned her face. Her skin was flawless and seemed to glow in the half-light. Her eyes caught the sunset and burned a deep, passionate red. "I can't," he heard himself say and he let his gun fall to his side. As Bowman stood panting in defeat, he saw a flurry of movement from Alma's hand, and an improbable flash of light.

"Step back!"

Bowman felt Graves barge into him from behind. It was enough to send him reeling to the ground, and bring him to his senses. There was a sharp crack and Bowman saw Alma drop to the dirt, her hand reaching to contain the spurt of blood at her shoulder. Confused, Bowman looked to the flagstones by the river wall. There, he saw a length of fuse that ran up the stairwell to Tower Bridge above. A match lay just inches from the fuse, its flame guttering in the evening breeze. Lifting himself onto his elbows, Bowman looked around for his companion to see him lunging towards Alma where she lay, writhing in the mud. Beyond him, he could see the source of the bullet that had wounded her. With his back to the River Thames and the Royal Yacht as it steamed unhindered beneath the bascules of Tower Bridge, stood Chief Inspector Callaghan. His top hat was back on his head, his grey eyes blazed, and the smoke from his revolver twisted about him into the evening air.

XXIX

Coda

A church had stood on the site for almost a thousand years. The Parish of St John's in Hampstead sprawled away to the south, whilst to the east rose Parliament Hill. The church had room for over a thousand devout souls, but Bowman was ashamed that he had only twice stood beneath its vaulted roof; firstly at his wedding ten years before, then again at Anna's funeral. The two most important and defining moments in his life were intimately bound up in the church's tall copper spire and red brick buttresses. The brightest of blue skies greeted him as he walked solemnly along Church Row from Fitzjohns Avenue. It had been warm enough for Bowman to leave his coat at home. Even in the shade of the fine town houses that lined the wide boulevard, he felt the need to catch his breath. He stood for a while at a lamppost to contemplate the church in all its grandeur. Ivy clung to its lower reaches, tenacious and destructive, while the spire reached high into the cloudless sky.

Plot number Forty-One was marked with a simple enough stone. It stood in the shadow of Frognal Hall to the west and amongst the cheeriest collection of crocuses that Bowman had ever seen. He slowed his pace as he approached, his head bowed in apology. He had never before been to visit her grave. He felt suddenly ashamed. The grief consumed him as he raised his eyes to her gravestone, and he felt the surge of tears.

"To The Memory of Anna May Bowman," the inscription read, "Of Belsize Crescent, Hampstead, born 13th January 1860, died 19th May 1891, aged 31 years. In The Midst Of Life We Are In Death." It was one year to the day. For all he could see, there was no sign of there having been any other visitors. No remembrances or memento mori adorned her grave. Bowman sank to his knees.

Leaning to clear some weeds from the grave, he stopped to lay his hand upon the warm stone. For a moment she was alive again, his hand at her face. He imagined her reaching up to smooth the frown on his forehead. Hearing someone approach from behind, Bowman wiped his face of his tears and stood.

Graves found Bowman patting his wife's headstone in an oddly affecting gesture. For the longest time, the two men stood in an easy silence. An audacious magpie landed on an adjacent stone, its head cocked in interest. Bowman allowed himself a wry smile.

"One for sorrow?" he said as he turned to his silent companion. He was surprised to see that Graves too was weeping quietly. Bowman was filled with a sudden sense of guilt. In all these months, he had never once considered the burden that the young sergeant must carry.

"I'm sorry, Graves," he whispered. He placed a hand on the young man's shoulder.

"Callaghan's taking credit," Graves said when he had recovered himself.

Bowman looked up to the sky. "Of course he is," he said simply. "He is a driven man, Graves. He will rise through the ranks if it kills him, no matter who gets in his way."

"But there was no Fenian plot," Graves complained, recovering his usual tenacity.

"Not this time, no." Bending for a last touch of Anna's gravestone, Bowman turned his feet to the path and gestured that Graves should follow. "Callaghan was pursuing the only truth that made sense to him. Which of us has not been guilty of that?" He swung his jacket over his shoulder as he walked. "Where is Miss Beaurepaire?"

"In the cells at Bow Street for now," Graves answered as he ducked beneath the bough of a sprawling cedar. "She'll hang, for sure."

"Oh, no doubt," Bowman concurred. "But that does not mean we shouldn't feel a little sympathy for her plight."

Graves shook his curls in disbelief. "How so, sir? She's been operating as the Kaiser for years. We've evidence of her running rackets in the West End, and we know she wasn't above kidnapping, extortion and murder when the occasion demanded."

Bowman nodded sadly. "We're all the sum of our experiences, Graves," he replied, meaningfully. "She more so than others. To be so used at such a tender age is a terrible thing."

"Well, she'll pay the price, no doubt," said Graves, unconvinced. The two men walked in silence a while.

"Does the commissioner wish to see me?" asked Bowman at last.

"He does, sir," Graves nodded, sadly. "First thing tomorrow

morning."

Bowman rubbed at the beard on his chin. "Then perhaps I should go home and make myself a little more presentable."

Graves threw the inspector a cheery look and clapped him on the back. "Yes sir," he said with a smile, his blue eyes dancing in the morning sun. "Perhaps you should."

Bowman offered the sergeant a smile by way of reply. As they said their goodbyes, Graves hailed a cab back to Scotland Yard and Bowman turned towards his rooms on Belsize Crescent. He realised with a start that, for the first time in many months, he was happy to be going home.

End Note.

It could be argued that the British Empire owed its existence to trade. Spanning a quarter of the Globe, it had a voracious appetite. At its heart – or stomach – lay the Port of London. The docks here enabled goods and produce to be landed on the shores of the Thames from all around the world. Destined for the mills of the north or the markets in the home counties, this produce required ever larger vessels which, in turn, required ever larger basins in which to unload. The early docks at the Isle Of Dogs and Blackwall were soon superceded by the much deeper waters of the Royal Victoria and the Royal Albert docks. The larger workforce was soon make its muscle felt as dockers campaigned for fairer pay and conditions. The London dock strike of 1889 saw the Port of London capitulate entirely to the dockers' demands, including a fairer wage and better pay for overtime.

Although female police officers with the powers to arrest weren't sworn into the Force until the early twentieth century, the Metropolitan Police Force was already employing women in police stations as matrons. Their role was limited to the care of children and women who had been detained, and they had no real powers to investigate or arrest. It wasn't until Edith Smith was enrolled into the Grantham Police Force in 1915 that women began to play a far larger role in policing.

The Fenian threat to the UK was very real. Campaigning for an Ireland free from British rule, they instigated the Dynamite Campaign between 1881 and 1885. Targets included military barracks at Salford, Liverpool Town Hall and the Tradeston Gasworks in Glasgow. Two bombs were exploded in the London Underground at Praed Street in Paddington and on London Bridge. The latter explosion resulted in the deaths of three members of the Irish Republican Brotherhood.Queen Victoria herself was the subject of eight assassination attempts during her long reign. The perpetrators ranged from a disgruntled farmer, an unemployed bricklayer and an Irish dissenter. Following the last attempt upon her life – a failed attack at Eton Station thwarted by some schoolboys with umbrellas for weapons – Queen Victoria wrote; "It is worth being shot at to see how much one is loved."

Richard James, March, 2020.

SUBSCRIBE TO MY NEWSLETTER

If you enjoyed *The Devil In The Dock*, why not subscribe to my newsletter? You'll be the first to hear all the latest news about Bowman Of The Yard - and I'll send you some free short stories from Bowman's Casebook!

Just visit my website **bowmanoftheyard.co.uk** for more information. You can also search for and "like" Bowman Of The Yard on **Facebook** and join the conversation. I would love to hear your thoughts.

Finally, I would appreciate it if you could leave me a review on Amazon. Reviews mean a lot to writers, and they're a great way to reach new readers.

Thanks for reading *The Devil In The Dock*!

Richard